The Master of the Prado

Also by Javier Sierra

The Lost Angel
The Secret Supper
The Lady in Blue

The Master
of the Prado
A Novel

Javier Sierra

Translated by Jasper Reid

ATRIA BOOKS

New York   London   Toronto   Sydney   New Delhi

ATRIA BOOKS
An Imprint of Simon & Schuster, Inc.
1230 Avenue of the Americas
New York, NY 10020

First Atria Books hardcover edition November 2015

ATRIA BOOKS and colophon are trademarks of Simon & Schuster, Inc.

Photography: LARA, AP, AESA archive, © Oronoz/Album, © Eric Lessing/Album, Akg-images/Rabatti, Album/Universal ImagesPrisma, Album/© Franck Raux/ RMN-Grand Palais (Musée du Louvre), courtesy of the San Ambrosio basilica, Sterling & Francine Clark Art Institute, Williamstown, USA/The Bridgeman Art Library/Index, © Francisco Alcántara Benavent/Bellas Artes museum of Valencia, © M. C. Esteban/Iberfoto, IGDA/Image of *The Immaculate Conception* of Juan de Juanes courtesy of Sagrado Corazón de la Compañía de Jesús/ National Gallery of Art Samuel H. Kress Collection/ Interior files and images are courtesy of Editorial Planeta S.A.

For information about special discounts for bulk purchases,
please contact Simon & Schuster Special Sales at 1-866-506-1949
or business@simonandschuster.com.

The Simon & Schuster Speakers Bureau can bring authors to your
live event. For more information, or to book an event, contact the
Simon & Schuster Speakers Bureau at 1-866-248-3049
or visit our website at www.simonspeakers.com.

Manufactured in the United States of America

19   8   7   6   5   4   3   2   1

Library of Congress Cataloging-in-Publication Data has been applied for.

ISBN 978-1-4767-7696-5
ISBN 978-1-4767-7698-9 (ebook)

To the guards of the Prado Museum, who have witnessed the passage of so many anonymous masters,
And to Enrique de Vicente, for twenty-five years of friendship

What the reader learns from a text, the illiterate—
who perceive only visually—can learn from images,
since the unschooled see through images what
they otherwise would read. In this way, the illiterate
discover that they can, in a sense, read.

—POPE GREGORY I, sixth century [1]

Things of perfection must not be regarded in haste,
but rather with time, judgment, and discernment.
To judge them requires the same process as to
create them.

—NICOLAS POUSSIN, painter, 1642 [2]

Spain, land of spirits and angels, has left its mark
in the halls of the Prado, and on its ancient texts,
and also on its people, in particular its poets.

—JUAN ROF CARBALLO, doctor and academic, 1990 [3]

The Prado is a hermetic, secretive, monastic place
where the essence of what is Spanish steeps and
thickens, and hardens into monument.

—RAMÓN GAYA, painter, 1960 [4]

Contents

The Master of the Prado

This story begins with the first touches of cold in December of 1990. I have very seriously questioned the wisdom of publishing this, especially because of how personal it is for me. It is, essentially, the story of how an apprentice writer was taught to look at—and see—a painting.

As with so many great human adventures, mine began in a moment of crisis. At the beginning of that decade, I was a nineteen-year-old youth from the provinces who had just arrived in Madrid with dreams of making his way in a city full of possibilities.

Everything seemed to be teeming around me, and I got the impression that for our generation, the future was unrolling faster than we were capable of perceiving. The preparations for the 1992 Barcelona Olympics and the Expo in Seville, the building of Spain's first high-speed train, and the appearance not only of three new national newspapers but also the first non-government-run TV stations—these were just the most visible pieces of that frenzy. And though I was convinced that one of these changes was sure to affect me, in the end none of them did.

In my starry-eyed way, I believed myself to be on the threshold of carving out a role in the world of media—something I'd dreamed of since I was a kid. As soon as I got to Madrid, I did everything I could to visit radio stations, TV news sets, press club meetings, book signings, and media workshops, both to try to meet the journalists I admired and to get a sense of my chosen career.

Soon enough, however, Madrid was to become for me a place of much higher voltage.

On one hand, my instinct told me to be out in the streets of the city, drinking in its rich life. On the other, I needed to do well in my second year at the university and get the best grades I could so that I wouldn't lose the scholarship that had gotten me this far. How was I going to reconcile two such opposing needs? Whenever I looked up from my books, I saw time slipping through my fingers. Twenty-four hours in a day just wasn't enough, though in fairness, there were two other factors to blame for my hemorrhaging hours in this way. One was a part-time entry-level job that a friend had gotten for me at a start-up monthly magazine devoted to scientific discovery, and the other was my passion for spending what time I could lost in the galleries of the Prado Museum. It was there, in that latter setting, that the tale I'm about to relate was forged.

You could say that it all happened because the museum's galleries offered me what I most needed at that time: serenity.

The Prado—majestic, sober, eternal, oblivious to daily concerns—instantly impressed me as a setting rich in history. Both welcoming and filled with cultured people, it was a place where you could pass the hours without attracting attention for being from somewhere else. Moreover, admission was free—it was probably the one great attraction in Madrid where you didn't have to pay to enter. In those days, you could just present yourself at the door with a Spanish identity card and you'd have access to its treasures.

Now, with the perspective of time, I believe my fascination with the Prado was due in large part to its paintings being the one thing in Madrid familiar to me. The great museum had had a big impact on me when I first discovered it in the early eighties, holding onto my mother's hand. I was a child with a wild imagination, and that endless sequence of extraordinary images electrified me from the start. I can still remember how I felt on that first visit. The exquisite images of Velázquez, Goya, Rubens, and Titian—to name just the masters I knew from my schoolbooks—imprinted themselves on my mind and became living history for me. To see them was to have a window into scenes from a remote past that seemed to have been preserved in amber, as if by some magic.

For some reason, that childhood vision caused me to see each painting as a sort of magical machine, capable of sending me to forgotten times, situations and worlds which, years later, I'd be fortunate enough to understand thanks to the old books I purchased at the little stands on the nearby Cuesta de Moyano. I could never have imagined, however, that on one of those gray afternoons at the end of October 1990, something would happen to me that would far surpass those early imaginings.

It all began in the museum's Gallery A, where I stood facing the huge wall where the Holy Family paintings by Raphael are hung. I was absorbed in the painting that Philip IV used to call *The Pearl*, as it was the jewel of his collection, when a man who looked as if he'd just stepped out of a Goya appeared at my side, seeming to admire the same painting. I wouldn't really have noticed him were it not for the fact that at that moment we were the only two people in the entire gallery, and though we were surrounded by more than thirty large masterpieces, for some reason we had both decided to look at this one. We spent a good half hour in silent contemplation of the painting, and then, impressed by the fact that my companion had barely moved in all that time, I began to examine him with some curiosity.

At first, I watched his various small movements—the guarded stares, the slight hisses of breath—as if half expecting him suddenly to seize the painting and make off with it.

When that didn't happen, I tried to imagine what he might be hoping to find in *The Pearl,* and came up with increasingly outlandish theories. Was he playing a trick on me? Trying to latch on to me? Feigning great cultivation? Did he mean to scare me in some way, or even rob me? Or perhaps he was engaged in some surreal competition to see who could last the longest in front of one painting.

My companion carried no guidebook of any kind, not even the then–popular *Three Hours in the Prado Museum* by Eugenio d'Ors. Nor did he show any interest in the small card beside the painting which gave its history. or bother to adjust his position to avoid the annoying glare of the spotlights on the canvas, as I did.

He looked to be around sixty years old. Gaunt, with a full head of hair in the process of going gray, he wore no glasses and had a thick gold ring on his left hand. He was well dressed, with gleaming shoes, a cravat, and an elegant, black, three-quarter-length coat. He had a rather severe— even dark—gaze, that, even after all this time, I can still feel on my back when I find myself in that gallery.

The more I observed him, the more appealing I found him. There was something magnetic I couldn't define but was in some way connected to that power of concentration he had. I assumed he was French. His smooth, angular face gave him an erudite look, like some smart, cultivated Parisian, and this dispelled any possible suspicions I might have harbored about a perfect stranger. My imagination quickly took over. I wanted to believe I was standing next to a retired professor from some institute. A widower, with all the time in the world to devote to appreciating art. An aficionado of Europe's great museums, who no doubt ran in higher circles than I did. I was just a curious student with a headful of dreams and a love of journalism, history, and mystery books, who needed to make sure he got back to his residence hall in time for dinner.

It was at that moment, just as I was finally about to let him have *The Pearl* all to himself, that he decided to come down from his cloud and speak.

"Are you familiar with the saying, 'When the student is ready, the teacher appears'?"

It came on the quietest voice, as if he were afraid someone might overhear him. I hadn't been prepared to hear the question posed in perfect Spanish.

"Are you speaking to me?" I asked.

He nodded. "I am indeed asking you," he said. "Who else? Tell me," he persisted, "do you know the saying?"

Out of this simple exchange was born a relationship—I never quite dared think of it as a friendship—that would last just a couple of months. What came next, which I propose to relate here in detail, would bring me back to the museum over and over again, one afternoon after the other, through the last days of that year and the first days of the next.

Two long decades have passed since my encounter with the man in the black coat, and I still don't know if what I learned from him there within the great walls of the Prado, safe from the rigors of the Madrid climate and far from my everyday concerns, was all imagined, or if he really did teach me those things.

I was never sure about his real name or where he was from, much less his profession. He never gave me his card, for instance, or his phone number. I was much more trusting in those days.

He had only to extend an invitation to show me the hidden secrets of those galleries—"If you like; if you have the time"—for me to let myself be carried along by those conversations and to continue meeting there, each time with greater enthusiasm.

I decided, in the end, that I would call him "the Master."

For twenty-two years, I have kept silent about these events, never feeling there was enough of a reason to speak out publicly. Especially since, one day, without any warning, he stopped appearing for our meetings. He simply vanished. That disappearance—abrupt, complete, and incomprehensible—has only become more unbearable over time. Though we never exactly had a formal relationship, he became a kind of secret godfather for me, an ally during my first days in that big city. The embodiment of an enigma—*my* enigma.

Perhaps because of this, and out of a nostalgia about how I learned to see—not just to look at—some of the Prado's paintings at his side, this feels like the right moment to tell the story of how I was initiated into certain mysteries of art. I'd also like to believe that I'm not the only one to have gone through something like this, and that once my account is published others will emerge who were also illuminated in the same way by my evanescent Master, or perhaps some other.

However, before I begin, let me be clear: The reader should not think that what I experienced in my youth in any way blunted my critical assessment of what I learned in those sessions. On the contrary. In putting these lessons to paper, many of them strike me as extremely strange, almost as if lifted from a dream. Nonetheless, as I go over them I see that some of these lessons have also found their way—in small and considered doses—into my best novels. Their influence can be seen in *The Lady in Blue (La dama azul)*, *The Templar Gates (Las puertas templarias)*, and *The Secret Supper (La cena secreta)* to such an extent that any attentive reader will quickly pick up on it.

So it is only fitting then that to that opportune visitor to the Prado and others like him, to those masters, and to those books that arrive at the moment when we are best prepared to receive them, I dedicate this work with gratitude, affection, and the hope that we may one day meet again.

1

The Master

Let me start at the beginning—in the beginning was the doubt.

What if it had just been a ghost?

People who know me are aware of my penchant for stories where the supernatural ends up deciding the ending. I've already written about these a lot, and am not likely to stop now. Here in the West we live in an increasingly materialistic society that tends to scorn the transcendent, but I don't think it's anything to be embarrassed about: Poe, Dickens, Bécquer, Cunqueiro, Valle-Inclán—all these writers fell under the spell of this fascination for the unknown. They all wrote about ghosts and tortured souls and the beyond, in the vague hope of being able to explain the here and now.

In my case, as I grew up I left most of those stories behind, only holding onto the really important ones, the ones where the protagonists have actually played a role in shaping our civilization. When you consider these, the mysterious stops being just anecdote, and becomes vitally important. Which is why I've never hidden my interest in encounters between the great figures of history and these mysterious "visitors." Angels, spirits, guides, daemons, genies, *tulpas*—it doesn't matter what we call them. These are just various labels that we use to mask our ignorance of that "other side" that all cultures talk about.

One day I will set down in writing what really happened when George Washington came across one of "them" at Valley Forge in the winter of 1777, during the campaign against the British that led to America's independence. Or the account of Pope Pius XII, who was seen talking to an angel from another realm in the private gardens of the Vatican, according to more than one witness.

Following the trail of events like these can lead us to the very origins of our written culture, and can also often bring us warnings about the future. Tacitus gives us a good example. In the first century, the illustrious Roman historian and politician wrote of the encounter that none other than Brutus—Caesar's protégé and assassin—had with one of these intruders. The ghost foretold his ultimate defeat at Philippi, in Macedonia, and the warning drove him to such despair that he chose to throw himself on his sword rather than to live with his defeat.

In most of these stories the visitors take a human form but also give off something invisible and powerful that marks them as different. Exactly like those "messengers" I wrote about in *The Lost Angel.*

So who—or what—was the unexpected teacher who appeared to me in the Prado that day? Did I find him, or did he find me?

Could he have been one of *them?*

I can't be sure. I do know, however, that my apparition was flesh and blood, and that he uttered the ancient Eastern proverb, "When the student is ready, the teacher appears," then proceeded to introduce himself.

"Dr. Luis Fovel," he said, clasping my hand as if he didn't want to let it go. He had a grave tone of voice and spoke with authority, while at the same time managing to respect the hush of our surroundings.

"I'm Javier Sierra," I replied, surprised. "You're a doctor?"

He arched his eyebrows then, as if my question had amused him.

"In name only," he replied.

His tone revealed a hint of surprise, as if he hadn't expected this young man to respond with a question. Which is perhaps why he then took control of the conversation, leaving a deathly coldness in the palm of my hand as he turned his eyes to the painting by Raphael that I'd been gazing at.

"I couldn't help noticing how you look at that painting, young man, and I'd like to ask you something. If you have no objections, of course."

"Go ahead," I said, curious.

"Tell me," he went on, in a rather familiar tone, as if we'd met before, "why does it interest you so much? It's not exactly the most famous painting in the museum."

Following his gaze, I cast another glance at *The Pearl*. I didn't know much about the painting then, let alone how it had been esteemed by King Philip IV of Spain, the monarch with perhaps the most exquisite artistic taste in history.

There are only four paintings in the Prado that come directly from Raphael's hand, plus another few from his studio, and various copies from that era Out of all of them, this is without a doubt the best one. It shows the Virgin Mary and her cousin Elizabeth sitting in front of some ruins and tending two infants who, upon further examination, begin to look suspiciously similar—the same blond curls, the same chins and cheekbones. One of the infants, who has a subtle halo and is partly dressed in an animal skin, is John the Baptist. The other—the only figure in the painting without a halo—can only be the baby Jesus. St. Elizabeth, John the Baptist's aging mother—who could also boast an immaculate conception—regards the children with a pensive expression, while the little Savior's own attention appears to be caught by something or someone outside the frame of the painting. Not St. Joseph, Mary's husband, who is in the background engaged in some activity impossible to divine. Whatever it is that the young Messiah is looking at is beyond the edges of the scene.

"Why am I interested in this painting?" I exhaled loudly, taking a moment to weigh my reply. "Actually, Doctor, it's pretty simple—I want to know what it means."

"Aha!" He lit up at this. "Isn't it obvious? You're looking at a religious scene, a painting that is meant to be prayed to. The Bishop of Bayeux commissioned this from the great Raphael Sanzio after he was already famous and working for the pope himself in Rome. The French bishop would have heard plenty about Raphael and his paintings of babies and virgins, and would have wanted one for his own devotional purposes."

"That's it?"

The doctor wrinkled his nose, as if my incredulity amused him.

"No," he replied, his voice switching to a low, conspiratorial tone. "Of course that's not all. Usually in paintings from this period, nothing is what it seems. While you may at first think you are looking at a religious scene, in fact, there is something there that is decidedly unsettling."

"Yes, I can sort of feel it," I admitted, "but I can't put my finger on it."

"That's how real art works, my boy. Paul Klee once said that 'art doesn't reproduce what we see—it makes us see.' If art simply showed us what was there, it would be tedious, we'd tire of it, and in the end, we wouldn't value it."

He paused. "Tell me, do you have a few minutes? I can

Raphael and Giulio Romano, *The Holy Family*, or *The Pearl* (1518).
The Prado Museum, Madrid.

show you exactly what it is that this extraordinary painting is doing."

I nodded.

"Very well," he said. "Here's the first thing you should understand. Though we're not really conscious of it, we Europeans have for centuries learned about the world principally through myths, stories, and religious tales. These make up our common intellectual heritage. Because we've heard them countless times at Mass, or from the mouths of our parents, or in films, we all more or less know the stories of Noah and Moses and Abraham and Jesus. And even if we're not particularly religious, we know when Christmas and Easter are, and who the Three Wise Men are, and we're even familiar with the name of one particular Roman prefect: Pontius Pilate."

"What does all that have to do with this painting?" I interrupted.

"A great deal," he replied. "When someone like us, brought up in the Christian West, stands before a painting like this, we usually know the story that the painting is based on, or we can figure it out. But what if the painting is instead telling us a different story, one that doesn't fit with what we know, or that questions or contradicts what we know, even in a subtle way? Then—watch out! That sets off alarm bells in our cultural memory."

"Yes, but . . ." I wasn't sure what to say.

"The reason you're fascinated by this painting—which, remember, Raphael painted for a bishop—is that the story that it tells is not to be found anywhere in the Bible. Your brain is working, spending a long time searching its archives—consciously or unconsciously—for the story that fits that painting. That's why the painting holds your attention for so long. But even after searching, you can't recall the story. And if you think that's disconcerting for you, imagine just how upsetting it would have been for someone in Raphael's time!"

"But," I tried again, "the Virgin, the baby Jesus, St. Elizabeth, John the Baptist—these are all figures we know well from the Gospels. There's nothing strange about them."

"Such a blessed innocence, my boy! But you must always remember to be careful when you come across common or everyday images in a work of art. The masters often use these ordinary images to signal their most important secrets."

"That's what I really want to know!" I said.

"I could show you a few that are hidden right in this museum, if you're interested. If you have time."

"Of course I'm interested!" I assured him.

"Well, then, let's start with this one here," he said, sounding pleased with himself, as if we had just signed a contract that committed us to doing something magnificent together. "Let me tell you some more about what this painting is telling us."

"Great! Please continue."

"Out of all four of the Gospels that you know, only Luke tells of the mysterious pregnancy which is visited upon the old and sterile Elizabeth. Do you see which one she is? There—the one with the turban. Well, Luke reveals this rather unexpected event near the beginning of his Gospel. According to him, the angel Gabriel appears to Elizabeth, wife of the priest Zechariah, and announces to her that she is pregnant with the future John the Baptist. Imagine the husband's reaction! An angel appears at the door, giving them the child that nature had denied them in all those years of marriage."[1]

"Just a minute," I interrupted again. "Did you say Gabriel? The same angel who appeared to the Virgin Mary? The one that Fra Angelico painted in *The Annunciation* hanging in the gallery next door?"

"The same," he replied. "You know, Gabriel is quite an unusual angel. He is revered by Christians and Moslems alike. During the Renaissance, they referred to him as 'the Messenger' because although he is only mentioned four times in the Gospels, each time he is the bearer of a vital message."

Doctor Fovel cleared his throat, and continued in a low voice.

"But it's not angels I want to talk about. What I really want you to consider are the two women in *The Pearl*. Aside from the initial mention of Elizabeth's pregnancy, Luke only mentions her one other time: when she visits the Virgin Mary *while both of them are pregnant*. Raphael depicted that event in another famous painting hanging in this museum.[2] In that one, Elizabeth is shown wearing the same turban and with the same expression the master would use a year later in *The Pearl*. But what is really incredible is that Raphael would then dare to produce a painting of a meeting that occurs later, after both children have been born—about which not one single reference is made in the entire New Testament."

"Are you certain about that?" I asked.

"Absolutely, my boy," Fovel replied. "The only visit that Luke describes occurs while both women are pregnant, not later. Moreover, the evangelist supplies details that add color to the event, for instance, that while in his mother's womb, the future John the Baptist gave a small jump when he heard the voice of the Virgin Mary.[3] "Therefore—"

Fovel took a deep breath, pausing in a way that struck me as rather theatrical, "The fact that the two mothers got together after their children were born to watch them play

School of Raphael, *The Visitation* (1517). The Prado Museum, Madrid.

together, could only come from a source outside the Bible, either apocryphal, or actually from some other text that he would have respected."

"What if Raphael just made it up?" I asked.

"Making up stories the way you think of it simply didn't happen in those times, Javier," he corrected me. "In the time of Raphael, the closest thing to inventing a story was to discover one—everything was based on something real, something that had happened. That's why even the great Raphael would always work on commissioned projects and under supervision. He had a reputation for being a sophisticated painter, who took care to include context in every one of his paintings. In other words, he followed what was there, what existed. And being so well read, Raphael was knowledgeable about several disciplines, such as archeology, theology, and philosophy, and he liked to use a variety of texts as sources."

"Well, if I follow what you're saying, then this painting derives from a secret source. It has a hidden message that goes against the orthodoxy of the time."

"Exactly!" The Master replied enthusiastically, his exclamation momentarily breaking the silence of the gallery. One of the guards appeared, book in hand, to give us a disapproving look before disappearing into the depths of the next gallery, no doubt annoyed at having his reading interrupted.

Fovel went on, undeterred.

"Look—we live in a time when no one seems to care anymore about the messages that art offers us. We've been made to believe that the only things that are important about a painting are the technical ones: the aesthetics, the methods and pigments used, the facts and circumstances of the artist's life. And all before asking why the artist decided to create the work in the first place! When we take this materialistic view of art, trying to divine a painting's message can seem like something speculative, or ephemeral, but it's not. In truth, it's paying attention to the spiritual core of the painting, to its true essence. Nonetheless . . ."

He paused.

"Yes?" I said, turning to him.

"Nonetheless, to be able to get at that core, you have to bring a certain humility to the task. When all is said and done, really miraculous art—as this piece most certainly is—can only truly be appreciated by a person with a modest sensibility. Those who insist on filling their heads with impressive facts and figures are missing the point—which is that art like this only works when it astonishes you."

"That's easy enough to say," I countered, "but art is subjective. Not everyone is amazed by the same things."

"True," he replied. "But the great masters nonetheless made use of certain subtle codes in their paintings, which signal the presence of a hidden message."

"What kind of codes, Doctor?"

Fovel seemed to relish the question—straightening slightly before responding.

"Well, for example, what the figures in a painting are looking at. In *The Pearl*, have you noticed where the baby Jesus is looking?"

"Y-yes, of course . . ." It was as if he'd been reading my mind.

"When a genius like Raphael paints the Savior gazing out beyond the borders of the canvas, he's showing us that the painting incorporates the magic of the mystical world. He is leaving it to the viewer to imagine what it is that is capturing the infant's attention. Thus giving rise to reflection on the supernatural."

"Did many painters use that particular code?" I asked.

"Indeed they did, my boy," he replied. "This museum is full of examples; you don't have to go any farther. Take Francisco Ribalta's *St. Francis Comforted by an Angel*. Right away you can see that the saint's gaze is aimed *above* the apparition that the artist has portrayed. Here, the code is telling us that what has the friar so astonished is something supernatural, something that lies beyond the edge of the canvas.

"The same thing is true with Murillo's *St. Augustine between Christ and the Virgin*. If one day you look for it in these halls, notice how the divine figures who inspire the saint's visions are actually behind him, leaving St. Augustine with no obvious point on which to fix his gaze. In one sense, Murillo is telling us that St. Augustine is using the eyes of his soul,[4] as it were, to witness what is sacred, rather than his mortal eyes. Back in the time of these painters, everyone knew and respected this language of symbols, which is easy to understand, even for us, and which Raphael used so masterfully in *The Pearl*. You see?"

Before going on, my new and unexpected philosopher of art lifted his eyes from the painting and glanced quickly around the gallery. I had the impression that he wanted to make sure we were still alone.

"By the way, my boy," he began, "are you religious?"

I hesitated before responding.

"In a way, yes, I suppose . . ." I muttered, sounding embarrassed.

"There you go—just like Raphael! Or like the bishop of Bayeux. There's no need to be embarrassed by that! On the contrary. They were all also religious *in their own way*. Neither one of them was your usual orthodox, observant Catholic."

"What do you mean?" I asked.

"Well, I've spent my whole life studying the secrets of the paintings in this museum, and you can't understand most of them unless you also understand a number of other essential things, such as what their creators really believed in, and the context in which they painted these works. Many paintings, like this one here, were created specifically to transmit or to keep a record of certain ideas which, at that time, would have been too dangerous to write down."

"Dangerous?"

"Extremely so, Javier." Doctor Fovel gestured toward the card on the wall that explains the painting to museum visitors. The text was dispassionate, clinical, advising the reader that the painting was in part the product of one Giulio Romano, a disciple of the Raphael school, and that one could discern in the painting the influence of none other than Leonardo da Vinci.

Fovel turned to me.

"What are the essential facts here? Both *The Pearl* and *The Holy Family with an Oak Tree*, which is also in this museum, were painted in Raphael's studio in 1518. What that little card does not tell you is that at that time, all of Europe, and Rome in particular, thought that the Christian model of the world was on the verge of collapse. The church's influence seemed to be waning. As corruption and nepotism established themselves more firmly in the Vatican, Islam was rapidly gaining ground. The Curia—the Vatican court—was more than a little nervous about its future.

"Extraordinary things were happening everywhere: the discovery of America, new theories of astronomy that questioned the medieval geocentric view, the French invasion of Italy in 1494, Luther's revolt against the pope, even fear of the end of the world—a great conjunction of the planets in

1524 convinced many at the time that this was imminent. All of these things were very much on people's minds, including the painters'. Many people went around believing they were living through the end of days. And you see, if you don't know all that, it's impossible for you to get the deeper meaning of this painting."

"That's quite a task!" I exclaimed.

"It does seem enormous. But for the moment, all you really need to know is that, at the beginning of the sixteenth century, there wasn't a cleric, nobleman, or pope unaware of all the prophecies and portents going around. Raphael's case was especially notable. At the time he painted *The Pearl* and *The Holy Family with an Oak Tree*, he was thirty-five and at the peak of his career. His vast talents and knowledge of astrology were displayed on the ceilings of Pope Julius II's private apartments, where he had painted the glorious *School of Athens* frescoes, filled with exquisite details that revealed his great erudition.

"But you should also know that at the same time he was painting these," he said, gesturing toward the paintings in front of us, "this maestro of Urbino was working on one of his great masterpieces: a portrait of his mentor, Pope Leo X, with the cardinals Giulio de' Medici and Luigi de' Rossi. Are you familiar with it?"

I shook my head, embarrassed.

"No matter." He smiled affably. "You're going to want to see it with your own eyes. It's a fantastic example of what I call 'prophetic art.' A kind of art that in those days, only Raphael dared to practice openly, attracting the most distinguished clients to his studio. Wait until you see it—the painting I'm talking about is now in the Uffizi Gallery in Florence. It depicts the pope seated behind a table, his hand on an illuminated Bible, with a small bell and eyeglass beside it. It appears to be a simple group portrait, and a very sober one at that. However, when Raphael painted it, Pope Leo had just barely escaped an assassination attempt unharmed. Once you know that, you can understand why he has that mistrustful look, which again seems to be directed beyond the edge of the frame."

"Ah! So you think he is looking for his assassins, is that it?" I said in a low voice, hoping to impress him.

"Well, as it happens, Javier, his assassin's identity was no secret. A Cardinal Bandinello Sauli confessed. It seems he had intended to poison Leo X because his personal horoscope and several *Vaticinia Pontificum*—papal prophecies that were quite popular then—suggested that Sauli was to become the Holy Father who would regenerate the entire church. And of course Sauli wanted to be pope instead."

"But popes don't believe in horoscopes or prophecies!" I protested. "In fact, the church condemns astrology."

Doctor Fovel smiled in the face of such naïveté.

"You're not serious? Are you aware that the first stone block for St. Peter's Basilica was laid by Julius II on April 18, 1506, because his own personal astrologer had designated that as the most cosmically propitious date? Or that in the corner of the very same salon in which Raphael had painted his famous *School of Athens* frescoes, as a kind of permanent horoscope, he also painted a celestial globe showing the constellations exactly as they were on November 26, 1503, the date of Julius's coronation as pope?"

This display of memory bewildered me. Seeming satisfied with my reaction, the Master continued.

"I see—you don't know anything! Well then, let me explain why I say that this portrait of Leo X was intended to be prophetic. Just two years before Sauli tried to poison the pope, another notable painter, Sebastiano del Piombo, depicted the same would-be assassin in a painting that is very similar to Raphael's. It was painted in 1516, and in this version, Sauli is shown sitting in a very regal pose next to another illuminated Bible and another small bell. And just as in his intended victim's portrait, several of his close advisers surround him. Obviously, the cardinal was preparing to become pope,[5] and this portrait was part of his public relations campaign."

"So why wouldn't Sauli go to Raphael to have his portrait done, if he was the most valued painter of the time?" I asked.

"Well, my boy, that's an excellent question. It's possible that he did. The one painting in the world that can clear up that question is right here, in the Prado. It's called *Portrait of a Cardinal.* It's one of Raphael's undisputed masterpieces, perhaps one of the most important paintings in this museum. With extraordinary realism and in exquisite detail, it depicts a cardinal with a severe look who, amazing as this may sound, has never been identified, even by experts. And it's not the only great portrait in the Prado with an unidentified subject. For example, there is El Greco's *Nobleman with His Hand on His Chest.* While most people agree that it could be a portrait of Cervantes,[6] we don't actually know who it is for certain."

"Those are big-time art mysteries!" I was impressed.

"Absolutely. A portrait without a name is like a flower without its scent; it lacks something vital. That's why when scholars get their hands on an enigmatic subject like this, they go into a frenzy coming up with suggestions. For this cardinal alone, they have proposed an endless list of names: Innocenzo Cybo, Francesco Alidosi, Scaramuccia Trivulzio, Alessandro Farnese, Ippolito d'Este, Silvio Passerini, Luis de Aragón . . . But I think mine is the best bet." He gave a mischievous smile. "If you compare this anonymous cardinal

Sebastiano del Piombo, *Cardinal Bandinello Sauli, His Secretary, and Two Geographers* (1516). The National Gallery of Art (Samuel H. Kress Collection), Washington, DC.

from the Prado with the portrait of Sauli that Sebastiano del Piombo painted in 1516, you can see right away that the two paintings are of the same person. It's quite obvious. Both have the cleft chin, the same thin mouth, similarly shaped heads—like an inverted triangle. There's very little doubt— our unidentified cardinal is the spitting image of Leo X's failed assassin. Don't you agree that my candidate could solve one of this museum's small mysteries once and for all?"

"Perhaps . . ." I replied, but I was stuck on another point. "But wait—when was that portrait painted? Was it also around 1518?"

"Well," he cleared his throat. "Here we have another very interesting clue. It's quite likely that this anonymous portrait that the Prado houses was painted by Raphael between 1510 and 1511—a good five years before Sauli was positioning himself to be the new reforming pope. It's odd that Raphael's portrait would be so influenced by the *Mona Lisa*, which Leonardo was working on in his studio at about the same time. In fact, when you compare the two paintings, you see that the cardinal has been painted in the same pose and with the same bearing as the *Gioconda*. However—and this is the important thing—Raphael did not include a particular feature in his painting that would mark it as one of his prophetic works. That's why Sauli had to go in search of del Piombo to get himself a prophetic portrait."

"What kind of feature do you mean?"

"The little bells, young man," he replied. "Placed like that, next to the Bibles as in Raphael and Del Piombo's later paintings, they are clear visual symbols. They signal that the subjects of both of these paintings have been foretold by sacred texts."

"Would they really put a symbol like that out in the open?" I asked.

Raphael, *Portrait of a Cardinal* (1510–1511). The Prado Museum, Madrid.

"Undoubtedly they had their reasons," he said. "Back in 1516, while Sauli was posing for del Piombo as God's envoy, a series of prophecies were finally being published in Venice after centuries of being very effectively suppressed. They were written by a Cistercian monk from Calabria, Joachim of Fiore, and they spoke of a new spiritual era in the world, to be led by a man who would bring together both spiritual and political power under his reign. Joachim had died back in 1202 without seeing his vision realized. However, his writings inspired another prophecy which was all over Rome in 1516, and both Sauli and Leo X believed in it completely. Have you ever heard of the *Apocalipsis Nova—The New Apocalypse?*"

I shook my head but said nothing, afraid of seeming like a complete idiot again.

"Don't be embarrassed. Sadly, hardly anyone remembers that book today, not even art historians." Another flash of mischief crossed his face. "Because it was never published. But let me tell you—it is also critical for understanding Raphael and his painting."

"And what did this *New Apocalypse* foretell?" I asked him.

"Among other things, it announced the imminent arrival of a 'pastor angelicus,' a pope blessed by the Holy Spirit who would ally himself with the emperor to impose peace among Christians and prevent the further advance of Islam."

In a grave voice, he intoned, "*Surget rex magnus cum magno pastore,*" and for some reason I shivered in spite of myself. "According to this manuscript, this was all supposed to take place at the very beginning of the sixteenth century. Imagine the scene! Half the cardinals in Rome aspired to be that super-pope, not only Sauli. Leo X had every reason not to trust anyone."

"I'm surprised that a pope, who's supposed to be the

guardian of Roman Catholic orthodoxy, would let a prophecy have that much authority."

"Let's just say that it had exactly the authority it deserved—no less than the Archangel Gabriel!"

"Wait, Doctor, I—I don't understand . . ." Fovel's statement had been so surprising that it had made me stammer.

He went on. "Absolutely everyone then—from the pope to a prostitute—believed that *The New Apocalypse* came directly from the mouth of the Archangel Gabriel, 'the Messenger.'" Here Fovel smiled. "Which is what its real author—Amadeo of Portugal—claimed, and thus everyone believed."

"I've never heard of Amadeo of Portugal."

"Which is not a surprise, my boy," said Fovel, falling short of actually scolding me. "What I'm revealing here is the inside history of this art, and one of Raphael's most important sources of inspiration. Shall I go on?"

"Yes. Please." I said.

"Amadeo was a Franciscan monk who was close to the true circles of power in the Vatican. He had risen to become no less than personal secretary and confessor to Pope Sixtus IV. By the time Raphael came to paint Leo X's portrait, poor Amadeo had been dead for over forty years, but his name and work were more famous than ever. Starting in 1502, handwritten copies of his book were being made and distributed everywhere. Obviously, they had to be kept secret. Only a select few could read them. A few copies found their way to Madrid. One of the oldest copies in existence has been kept in the El Escorial monastery since the reign of Philip II."

Dying of curiosity, I asked, "What was in the book, Doctor?"

His forehead creased like the bellows of an old accordion and his pale eyes became suddenly moist, almost hesitant.

"Well, now, my boy. It seems that the Archangel Gabriel had actually appeared to Amadeo, and over the course of eight lengthy trances, or raptures, Gabriel revealed how God had created the angels, the world, and man."

Fovel remained quiet for a moment before continuing. "The book was a summa, a Book of Everything, do you understand? The Archangel Gabriel told the friar all about predestination, the names of the seven archangels who guard the entrance to paradise, even the Franciscan idea of the immaculate conception of the Virgin, which was not then accepted by the Church. But most of all, during the fourth visitation, Gabriel told of the arrival of a pastor angelicus—a divine shepherd, who would appear to save the world from the errant path it was on. Decades later, when Raphael came to paint Leo's portrait, the pope knew all about the text and was anxious to present himself as the Pastor Angelicus of the prophecy."

My head was swimming. "So you're saying that Leo believed in Amadeo's prophecy because it suited him to."

"And had himself painted by Raphael, making sure that the portrait gave a nod to the book." He turned to face me. "Sometime when you have a chance find yourself a good reproduction of this portrait, and take a close look at that great tome that the pope has in front of him on the table. The Bible is open to the Gospel According to Luke—the same passages that inspired this painting of the Holy Family," he said, indicating *The Pearl.* "You can tell from the miniatures reproduced in the text.[7] The interesting thing here is that the pope is shown lifting a page with his hand, thereby creating a space. Now, both Sauli and the pope believed that *The New Apocalypse* was the inspired continuation of the Gospel of Luke. That's why the painting has the pope revealing the space after the Book of Luke—that space is for the new Gospel. Presumably the one that predicts that he will become the long-awaited Pastor Angelicus."

"Do you mean that that same text is the mysterious source for *The Pearl*?"

"Precisely!" he confirmed. In his excitement, he cut off my exclamation. "In fact, Amadeo's book reveals many things that are omitted in the Gospels. It gives new details of the young Jesus's encounter with the doctors in the temple and tells the story of the Good Thief's origins.

"One of the things that Gabriel's revelations told of in particular was the relationship that Jesus and John the Baptist had had since their infancy. But this was not all that significant to the Vatican when compared with a prophecy predicting the coming of a pope who would unify spiritual and earthly power. However, to certain painters who read this it was. And one of them," he finished triumphantly, "was Raphael."

"One?" My curiosity was growing.

"Yes," he replied. "The other was Leonardo da Vinci. Finding that text and painting its lessons almost cost him his career!"

2

Deciphering Raphael

Suddenly, Doctor Fovel broke off our conversations. At first I couldn't tell why. Without warning, my talkative new companion had gone rigid, like one of the nearby bronze statues by Pompeo Leoni. I had the impression that something he had seen or heard had put him on guard, and sure enough, when a group of silent visitors appeared at the other end of the gallery, he paled.

There weren't very many of them, perhaps seven or eight well-behaved tourists led by a rather waiflike guide who forged a path for the group with her rolled-up umbrella. Neither her manner nor her wardrobe in any way suggested a threat—in fact, she was kind enough to wait for one man who trailed the rest of the group, dragging his left leg with some effort, as if it had lost all feeling, and giving it the occasional tug with his hands.

As innocent as this all appeared, I could sense Fovel's fear, and though I didn't share it, my body reacted, and for the second time that day I trembled.

"Be here on Tuesday, and I will tell you the rest," said Fovel in a low voice, avoiding looking at the group of intruders. "And spend some time with Leonardo's *Virgin of the Rocks* before you come."

"Is it here?" I asked him.

He gave me a stern look. "No, it's in the Louvre. There

are no Leonardos in the Prado. Or so they say," he added, ominously.

"How will I find you?" I asked him.

"Look for me in this gallery. I'm always here," he said. "And if for some reason you don't see me, try Gallery 13— it's my favorite."

And then, just like that, without another word or even a good-bye, he disappeared into the next gallery, leaving me with my mouth open, preparing to reply.

It was very strange. I was confused by what he'd said. He talked more or less as if he owned the museum, but his reaction to the appearance of a mere bunch of tourists contradicted that entirely.

I was late to Sunday dinner in my residence hall. I had left the Prado around eight in the evening, still affected by my encounter, and walked toward the Banco de España Metro stop, letting a brief downpour help to bring me back to reality. Guided by the captivating Christmas lights, I strolled up the Paseo del Prado, soaked to the skin, avoiding the puddles and trying to find shelter from the rain under the building façades of the Army Museum and the Central Post Office.

The walk did me a world of good, so much so that I didn't question the cold chicken and baguette that I got in the dining hall. On the contrary, I was grateful. I had no desire to sit and have dinner with my fellow students, but I was starving. Without thinking, I improvised a sandwich out of my dinner offerings and took it up to my room to devour. By the time I peeled off my sodden coat, took a shower, put on comfortable clothes, and ate it was getting late for a trip to the library. But luckily for me it was exam time, and they stayed open around the clock, so I made my way there.

After a quick scan of the shelves, I assembled an impres-

Raphael, *Pope Leo X with Cardinals Giulio de' Medici and Luigi de' Rossi* (1518).
Uffizi Gallery, Florence.

sive collection of art books on a table. Before I finally retired for the night I wanted to see with my own eyes if the things that my new teacher had told me had any significance, however small.

It took me no more than five minutes to hunt down Raphael's portrait of Leo X. Fovel's comments didn't do the painting justice; it was a wonder. The figures radiated tension and expectation. You could almost hear them muttering. The reproduction took up almost the whole page of the encyclopedia I had open in front of me, and just as the Master had said there was the pope revealing the symbolic space in the pages of a large Bible.

"*The New Apocalypse* sign!" I muttered, as if it was something I'd just discovered myself.

Excited now, I went through the indexes of each of the textbooks I'd collected. Frustratingly, after almost an hour of looking I had not hit upon a single reference to Amadeo of Portugal or his book. My rather tentative new discovery seemed to be dissolving in front of me like a specter.

"Just like Doctor Luis Fovel," I muttered grimly, but immediately banished the thought. I decided to continue my search taking a different approach. Before I knew it, it was two in the morning. I sat there surrounded by enormous art books containing reproductions of paintings by Raphael, Sebastiano del Piombo, and Leonardo, and by various books on medieval history. In just a few hours, I had amassed more questions than answers, but I had at least learned a few interesting facts about the man who had painted the portrait of Leo X at the same time as the Prado's *The Pearl*. I was impressed by the fact that all the historians without exception lauded the young Raphael's gift for painting. Some suggested that he had inherited the gift from his father, Giovanni Santi, a poet and painter of altarpieces from the

Umbria region, who passed on his various skills as early as he could.

Thanks to his father, Raphael was able to apprentice himself at a young age to Perugino, who paved the way for the young prodigy to go to Florence, the mecca for painters at the time. There, as an adolescent, Raphael became immersed in the great cultural and philosophical revolution that had been set in motion by Leo X's predecessor, Cosimo de' Medici. In his new city, he met his rivals, Michelangelo and Leonardo, and soon he was on the front lines of the artistic revolution that was blooming in the heart of the city. It was during this period that he started to paint various versions of the Holy Family, scenes that would later make him famous.

His Madonnas are among the loveliest ever painted—female figures that are young, delicate, fine featured—and very beautiful. They radiate lightness as well as sensuality. But against all church logic, Raphael insisted on depicting Mary almost always in the company of two babies.

I read one of the descriptions: "St. John and the baby Jesus are not shown here the way early artists depicted them—as pious idols, sheathed in their holiness. These are real children—happy and mischievous—and yet one can tell that something mysterious and transcendent passes between them."[1]

I took that description as a good sign, a clue that seemed to confirm what Fovel had been telling me hours before in the Prado—that in creating his masterworks, Raphael used information from mysterious sources. Was this an example of one of those mysteries—to show St. John and the baby Jesus as twins? I didn't think anything of it, though at the time, I had no idea of the oceans of ink that had been devoted to arguments over whether or not Jesus had had a twin brother.

As I saw it—with my rather rudimentary knowledge of biblical history—since both children had been conceived through the Holy Spirit by way of the same archangel, it made sense to me that there would be painters who would want to show them as brothers in their paintings. Or was there another reason? As if that weren't enough, Luke himself mentions that the mothers are cousins (*syggenís*), and, while the Gospel does not make clear how closely related they might be, in the Middle Ages it was generally understood that they were first cousins. If that were true, that would make John and Jesus second cousins, which could explain their physical likeness.

That same night I looked for a good reproduction of the *Virgin of the Rocks*, as Fovel had instructed, and I got another surprise—there was not one but at least two *Virgin of the Rocks* by Leonardo. He had painted the older one of these in 1483, having just arrived in Milan, to decorate the altar of the chapel at San Francesco Grande.

The painting is majestic and tranquil, and clearly has many similarities to Raphael's *The Pearl*—particularly in the arrangement of the figures—but there are notable differences as well. I couldn't help observing once again how much Jesus and John resemble each other. The two children regard each other with a look that appears beyond their years, while the Virgin shields them and an angel seems to fix his gaze firmly on the viewer and to point to one of the boys, as if to say, "*This* is what you should be looking at." And that boy is John the Baptist.

I was intrigued by the fact that in the second version of the painting, which now hangs in the National Gallery in London, the angel's hand is no longer there. In that version, Leonardo works to emphasize the differences between the two boys, painting them with markedly different features. In both of Leonardo's paintings, this encounter between the two boys takes place against a dark landscape, much as in Raphael's version. When one looks at the two paintings side by side—*The Virgin of the Rocks* and *The Pearl*—it's not hard to see the influence that Leonardo had on his most ardent admirer.[2]

Out of everything that I read that night in the university library, nothing impressed me quite so much as the description of Raphael and his arrival in Rome by Giorgio Vasari. A well-known painter and biographer of painters, Vasari was a contemporary of the great geniuses of the Renaissance. It was his description that finally convinced me that there really was a mystery surrounding Raphael.

Having dazzled all of Medici Florence with his talent, Raphael at the age of twenty-five was picked by his friend Bramante to be part of the enormous project to refurbish the Vatican. "There," writes Vasari, "he was much celebrated by Julius II, and in the Stanza della Segnatura of the papal apartments, he began painting a scene that shows the moment when theologians reconciled both philosophy and astrology with theology. In this scene, he depicts all the great sages of world history, and added certain symbols, as did the astrologers who would add characters from geomancy and astrology to tablets they would send to the Evangelists.' "[3]

The painting that the chronicler Vasari describes is of course the famous *School of Athens*, which Raphael completed in 1509, just as Michelangelo was bringing the ceiling of the Sistine Chapel to life. It is a work that is full of clues to hidden reading. The figure of Plato, situated at the center of the composition, is in fact a faithful rendering of his revered Leonardo da Vinci. But Raphael also places himself in the scene. He is the figure gazing directly at the viewer from the right-hand side of the painting, next to Zoroaster, Ptol-

Leonardo da Vinci, *The Virgin of the Rocks* (1483). Louvre Museum, Paris.

Leonardo da Vinci, *The Virgin of the Rocks* (1497). The National Gallery, London.

emy, and a group of astrologers. Raphael's presence in the scene was not a secret, and was achieved, according to Vasari, "with the help of a looking-glass."[4] But Raphael added one more small mystery.[5]

Very close to where Raphael appears as an astrologer, we see Euclid,[6] the great mathematician and father of geometry, though here Raphael gives him the face of his great mentor, Bramante. He is shown bent over a slate on which he demonstrates his theorems to a group of students. There, on the gold-edged neck of his tunic, incorporated within the design of the brocade, one can pick out four letters: RVSM.

Nowadays we know it to be the painter's signature, and while it may not seem remarkable to us, at the time it was quite an act of daring. Why? Because no painter in the service of the church in the sixteenth century was permitted to sign his work. Not one. The ecclesiastical authorities whose job it was to commission work enforced this rule with a great zeal, claiming that it was to ensure that the artist not fall prey to the sin of pride.

The curious signature RVSM turned out to be simply an acronym for *Raphaël Vrbinas Sua Manu* ([Made by] the hand of Raphael Urbino). This discovery left me wondering. What did all this tell us about the great Raphael?

Suddenly, it became clear. *The Pearl's* creator had an innate opposition to rules. He was a rebel. Someone who, for some reason that I now felt impelled to discover, liked to leave pathways to his ideas by the means he knew best—painting.

Raphael, *The School of Athens* (1509). Vatican Museums, Rome.

Raphael, *The School of Athens* (details), in which we see Leonardo da Vinci portrayed as Plato, a self-portrait of Raphael among the mathematicians, and the brocade of Euclid that hides the mysterious RVSM signature.

3
———

THE NEW APOCALYPSE

The next day, Monday, I woke later than usual. Forcing my bleary eyes open, I felt as if I'd spent the night wandering among endless old paintings. One particular thought hammered in my head—hadn't Fovel said that there was a copy of the book that had inspired some of Raphael's and Leonardo's masterpieces no farther away than El Escorial? I glanced at myself in the mirror and rubbed my face. Why not take a look? After all, it was less than thirty miles from Madrid. Whether I'd be allowed to see it, of course, was another matter, but it wouldn't hurt to try.

Or would it?

I dressed quickly, stuffed a notebook and my faithful camera into a backpack, and left my residence hall, descending the stairs two at a time. Things were looking up for the first time in a while.

My encounter with the mysterious Doctor Fovel, which had come completely out of the blue, had put me on the trail of something really fascinating. It was exactly the kind of story I loved to read in the magazine where I had been working part-time. On top of that, my first trimester exams were over, the Christmas holidays were coming up, and the thought of escaping to the mountains outside Madrid was a million times more appealing than going in for the last week of lectures and being completely distracted wondering what my Master of the Prado would have to tell me next time we met.

There was also another contributing factor. My snazzy, new, red SEAT Ibiza hatchback had been parked behind my residence hall for the past few weeks without a chance to go anywhere. It was almost a miracle that I had the car in Madrid just then, because after I'd gotten my license and the car the summer before it had made more sense to keep it at my parents' house. But for practical reasons I'd brought it up to Madrid that month so that I could pack up my clothes, books, and computer and take them back with me for the Christmas break, which was to start in a few days. The car would rumble like a locomotive every time I started it up after a frosty night, belching smoke like a power plant. A good run along country roads to San Lorenzo de El Escorial would do it good.

So on that Monday morning, everything was lined up for me to track down *The New Apocalypse*. The one thing I couldn't have predicted was that a certain someone would make sure she was included in the adventure.

Her name was Marina and frankly, I wasn't sure whether we were going out or not. I hoped we were. Marina was gorgeous—about twenty, with blond hair and green eyes, sweet, curious, and kind. She'd captured my heart the day I saw her moderate a roundtable on fashion in my department halfway through the previous year.

I was attending the discussion because I had to, but then I heard her talk enthusiastically about glamour, and how the word itself was Irish, used by fairies to describe spells that would make one see things in a different way, and I knew we'd have a lot to talk about. I wasn't wrong. She was smart, eloquent, and very flirtatious. I quickly learned that she had the largest jeans collection in the whole university, and that with a little luck, she would soon be joining the Olympic swimming team.

But what really entranced me was that she seemed to have an endless curiosity about everything I was interested in, from science fiction and space exploration to Egyptian history and the mysteries of the human mind. However, I was hardly her ideal of a man. Despite my occasional attempts to move our relationship forward, she always managed to keep an exquisite distance between us. There was affection for sure, but love? The jury was still out.

Still, I couldn't fault her for that.

As much as my exams and a few minor assignments from the paper earlier in the winter had caused me to neglect my new car, I'd neglected Marina more. She was a second-year pharmacy student, and her classes were just across from the Department of Information Sciences building where I studied. In spite of this, most of our conversations were by phone, as on that morning.

"You're off to El Escorial? Today?!" buzzed her voice on the earpiece. I realized then how much I'd missed hearing it. A little ashamed, I decided to propose an outing that I didn't think she'd be able to resist.

I'd called her right at eight-thirty, after breakfast, when I knew her parents had left for work and she was alone in the house. My bag packed and ready to go, I sprang my treat on her.

"That's right—El Escorial." I hesitated. "It would be great if you could come, though I know you probably—"

"That sounds great!" Her enthusiasm threw me off. "You know what? I'm coming with you!"

Until that moment, Marina had always been pretty good at disguising her emotions. I was never sure if her bursts of enthusiasm were for me or for what I was telling her. At that moment, I went with the first option. Perhaps I was overly optimistic, but after two weeks without seeing her, the idea of having her with me for this adventure was really appealing.

"It might not be that exciting," I warned her. "I have to look up a book in the monastery library for an article I'm doing, and—"

"What?" Her voice came back over the phone. "The El Escorial library? You're going to the monastery library and you didn't tell me?"

"Y-yes. Why?"

"Well, I've never been, and we're always talking about it in class!"

"Seriously?"

"Yes!" She was excited; I could hear her smiling over the phone. "My History of Pharmacology professor says that they have the most valuable collection of ancient Arab, Jewish, and Native American medical texts in the world. I'm dying to see it. This'll be better than *The Name of the Rose!*"

I picked her up at her house just before eleven. She looked fantastic and was wearing a cream-colored coat, high boots, a hat, and matching wool gloves. She was dressed up as if for a special occasion, and her perfume smelled of roses. *Perfect*, I thought.

Ten minutes later, under an overcast sky that threatened snow, we made for the A-6 highway leading out of Madrid to the northwest. As we drove, we made plans to have lunch at the Hotel Miranda and Suizo in San Lorenzo before heading for the monastery to see Amadeo of Portugal's book— and Marina's medical texts, too, of course.

Everything went perfectly. Marina was as charming as ever, and I took advantage of the time to explain exactly what it was that I was looking for at El Escorial. I was careful not to alarm her with some of the details of my encounter

48

with Fovel, and yet when I told her—half serious, half jok-ing—that my odd doctor might even be a ghost, she was in-trigued.

"Doesn't that scare you?" she asked.

"No, no." I smiled. "He's very smart for a ghost. And a great conversationalist."

Once again, luck was with me. Like the Prado, the mon-astery was closed to tourists on Mondays, but this did not apply to the college, the offices, or to the reference library, and so it was a different set of people crossing the huge granite quad toward the library that day from the usual visi-tors. Monday was a kind of day for professionals. Not that Marina and I were really professionals, at least not yet. None-theless, our university IDs and my magazine credentials helped a lot in speeding us through the formalities. While Marina entered her signature and particulars in the visitors' book, I scrawled down the reason for my visit on another form: "Consultation of *The New Apocalypse*."

The security guard looked us over. "Okay then—through that door over there, keep on going until you get to the end, and you'll see signs for the library. And please stay in the marked area," he said, without a trace of emotion.

We did exactly as he said. The entrance to the library was directly above the main entrance hall in the front of the building. Marina and I climbed a plain stone staircase to get to it, and I still remember the clicking of her heels going up those stairs. There was a counter at the top, decorated with Christmas cards and garlands, and behind it, a monk wearing a black habit and an austere expression who greeted us.

"Good morning." He was in his forties, with a shaved head and a rather smart goatee. He looked us over sternly. "How can I help you?"

Much to Marina's disappointment, we were not in the great library hall that you usually see in postcards of El Escorial. More than a hundred feet long with seven enormous windows and an intricately decorated ceiling, that library is filled with glass-fronted bookcases packed with volumes stacked on their sides and the occasional spherical astrolabe. Instead, the room we'd been directed to was modern and functional, containing the day's newspapers, modern encyclopedias, and a number of reading tables with lamps.

"The New Apocalypse?" Our goateed monk raised his eyebrows as he read the additional request form I filled out. "Is it a manuscript?"

"I think it's early sixteenth century . . ." I mumbled.

"I see. Pamphlets and manuscripts are kept in another area. You'll need to come with me and make your request to Father Juan Luis. He'll see what he can do for you."

Diligently, the librarian led us out of the reception area and down a seemingly endless corridor to a group of offices that overlooked the Patio de los Reyes. Several men and women were sharing computers, and everyone was dressed either in a habit or a lab coat, and wearing cotton gloves. The center office, which we entered, was occupied by a monk who had to be at least seventy, and who was bent over an enormous antique missal with a pencil and magnifying glass. His office lacked even the slightest trace of technology.

Father Juan Luis made a grunting sound, which I took to be a protest of sorts, since it was clear that our visit had interrupted his work. He held my form up to his face and peered at it. The monk who had brought us to him took his leave of us, smiling for the first time.

"Yes, yes, of course! I know this book well," said Father Juan Luis.

"Really?" I said, feeling encouraged.

"Naturally. And why do you want to see this book?" he asked, addressing the question to both of us.

"Uh . . . we're writing a report on rare books for class," I said, accidentally handing him my Chaminade Residence Hall ID, rather than my University department ID.

"Ah! You're from the Marianists," he exclaimed when he noticed that my dorm was named after their founder. A smile spread across his face before I had a chance to show him my other card.

"I also live in a student residence right next door," he said. "The life of the student is a wonderful one, wouldn't you say?"

"Are . . . are you a student?"

The old monk laughed.

"Everyone is, in this place. I'm an art history professor, and still among my books, with no end in sight."

"That's impressive," I said.

"Not really," he replied dismissively. "In this cold, you could do worse than to be engaged in the work of the mind in front of a good heater! But you know all that! If it's rare books you're looking for, you've come to the best place in the world, and the particular one you're seeking is definitely rare. Not to mention that it's part of Don Diego's collection."

"Who is Don Diego?" I replied.

"Don Diego Hurtado de Mendoza," he said, making a sign for us to follow him.

Though the old monk was stooped and scrawny, and looked as if he might collapse under the weight of his cassock, he was suddenly filled with an impressive energy.

"You don't know who he is? What kind of history do they teach you in that college of yours? As it happens, Don Diego was the oldest son of the commanding general who took Granada back from the Moors for the Spanish throne, and the owner of one of the most important libraries in Spain. He was raised in the Alhambra. You knew *that* at least, didn't you?" He glanced sideways at us. "Don Diego was a gentleman. When he died, in 1575, all of his books, manuscripts and codices went to King Philip II, who of course added them to his Librería Rica, right here."

Father Juan Luis led us to a door that he unlocked, waving us in while he found the light switches. There were no windows, and the room smelled strange and musty. When the fluorescents had finished blinking to life they revealed a large room over a hundred feet square, filled with banks of wooden shelves, all of which were packed with leather-bound volumes and tied bundles of manuscripts, everything labeled and numbered.

The monk cleared his throat. "The item you're looking for is one of the most interesting in this collection here, which is certainly saying a lot when you're talking about the Royal Library of El Escorial!"

"I bet!" breathed Marina, her mouth agape at the sight of so many ancient texts. She had never seen anything like it. Neither had I.

"I can't imagine Philip II reading all of this," I muttered.

"Indeed?" The old monk seemed to be enjoying our astonishment. "No doubt your idea of Philip comes from the famous portraits by Titian, which show a tormented man, dressed completely in black, weighed down by his shifting fortunes. In school I imagine you learned of this ardent Catholic's great trials in the wars against the Protestants and the Turks."

We both nodded.

"However, what rarely gets taught is that Philip was also a

great humanist. He was curious about everything, and ended up developing some quite interesting ideas about the world."

"How do you mean 'interesting'?" I asked.

"Oh dear!! What a distorted view we have of the history of our Spain!" he groaned, without looking at us. "When you leave, make sure you go and take a look at the commemorative medallions that hang in the entrance to the basilica. You will see the monarch referred to in them as 'King of all Spains, the two Sicilies, and *Jerusalem.*' Our sullen-looking King Philip was obsessed with this last title, which explains why he insisted in having this monastery built in the exact image of the Temple of Solomon. Or did you not know that, either?"

Marina and I both shook our heads.

"The thing is," he continued, "Philip built up his personal library with as many treatises and manuscripts on that biblical monarch as he could. Most of the books are extremely strange, like one that describes visions that the prophet Ezekiel had of the temple, or various manuals of such things as architecture, magic, alchemy and astrology, including books by Ramon Llull and Pope Leo III. They're all here. And as to the sciences associated with that wisest of kings—Philip studied them all! With a passion! Our Phillip wanted to be just like Solomon. He even named his favorite dog after him." The old monk gave a fleeting chuckle, adding, "So you must be looking in the right place for Solomonic knowledge."

"Is that why he was interested in *The New Apocalypse?*" I asked.

"Very good, young man; yes indeed. Most likely Don Diego Hurtado acquired that book in Italy when he was King Philip's ambassador to Rome. Hurtado ended up being just as cultured as his boss, more so even. Some say that he was the real author of the famous picaresque novel *Lazarillo de Tormes*, if you can imagine that, and that he was every bit as interested in mysterious prophecies as the king. Ah! Here it is."

Father Juan Luis reached up toward one of the shelves and pulled down a thick volume of parchment, handing it first to Marina. It was more or less the size of a modern-day hardcover novel, but weighed a lot more than it looked. The old volume was covered with something that felt a bit like suede when you first touched it—a dark, greenish fabric, without any markings or lettering whatsoever. "But how do you know that this is the book we're looking for?" objected Marina, hefting the thing in her hand.

"Well, that's the funny thing." the old monk replied. "After years in oblivion, someone else was here last Friday, looking at this same book. I presume you're working with him?"

Marina and I looked at each other, not knowing what to say.

"Never mind; it's not important," he said quickly, guiding us to a large table with several chairs in the middle of the room. "I know how it can be with historians—every man for himself."

"Uh . . . exactly," said Marina.

But I couldn't contain my curiosity.

"That's some coincidence." I said, brightly. "You don't by any chance remember his name, do you?"

"*Ay*, no! I'm afraid I don't remember anything lately," he replied, pointing a finger at his temple. "Unless a name is more than three hundred years old and I studied it as a young man, I don't have much of a chance of remembering it. I could look it up, if you like."

He then carefully took the volume and placed it gently

on the table and had us sit down. Handing us cloth gloves, he nodded to indicate we could open the book.

"Luckily for you," he said, "this book is no longer on the secret list. You can read it without any restrictions."

"Weren't people allowed to read it in the past, Father?" Marina asked him. The innocent tone of her question, without a shred of guile, seemed to soften the old monk.

"Certainly not." He smiled briefly and then explained. "This is a book of prophecies, young lady. At the time when this book was written, prophecies were a very sensitive business. *Politically* sensitive. Take a look at this page here—read that." His finger tapped at a grayish sheet of paper that had been glued into the inside of the front cover. "It's a note handwritten by a former prior of this monastery, sometime in the last two hundred years. Our good father wrote it after reading through *The New Apocalypse.*

Curious, Marina and I leaned forward and read:

The various propositions contained in this volume have the air more of rabbinical rantings than divine revelations. They resemble sophomoric and impertinent questions more than Catholic doctrine, which judgment is indeed the most benign that can be passed upon this work. In light of the above, I hereby order that this volume—entitled *Apocalipsis S. Amadei*—be removed from general circulation, and kept from sight, no longer to be classified even as a relic or item of merit, as no one is to be advised of its existence. / May 5, 1815 / Cifuentes Prior / Place among the library MSS.

"So it was hidden then?" asked Marina, her green eyes wide.

"Locked up and the key thrown away," confirmed the

old Augustinian monk. "Like so many other books from this very room. We were, in fact, the first library in Christendom with a closed reading room. And with good reason."

"So how long did the book go without being read by anyone, Father?" she asked.

"Oof, well, to give you a proper answer I'd have to consult the registers. I will tell you that in the twenty years that I've been assigned here no one has ever requested it."

"Really?" I felt a stab of worry in my stomach.

"In fact, even I myself hadn't seen it."

"Father, when you have a chance, could you please check the register and tell us who had requested the book on Friday?"

I handed him a piece of paper on which I'd quickly scrawled my name and number.

"Yes, all right," he agreed, puzzled by my insistence. "Don't worry."

"Can we take a look at this now?" interrupted Marina.

"Oh—yes, certainly. Go right ahead, you two. You do read Latin?"

"Latin?" I said in alarm.

"The only Spanish in all of *The New Apocalypse* is that prior's sheet you just read. The rest is in Latin. The fellow who was here before to see the book told me that there are only three copies of this book extant in all of Spain—two in the National Library, and this one here. All three were written in the language of Virgil. And ours," he added, smiling with undisguised pride, "is the oldest. Did you take a look at the title on the first page?"

Apocalipsis sancti Amadei propria manu scripta. The phrase was written in a meticulous script, and I read it over a couple of times as the librarian pointed to the words to make sure that I fully understood.

"Is this . . ." I hesitated. "The original?" I asked.

"No, I don't believe so," replied the monk, clicking his tongue and shaking his head. "Someone added that later to make the copy look more important. The title page doesn't even seem to be the same age as the rest of the text. With these manuscripts you often see a variety of writing styles, all from different times. Some of them can be very difficult to decipher."

"Would you be able to help us read this, Father?" I asked, tentatively.

Marina added her own entreaty, brushing aside a lock of hair away from her face and fixing her sweet gaze on the old man.

It seemed to do the trick. He busied himself finding chairs, and sat down next to us, placing his glasses on his nose before carefully starting to leaf through the old pages with the additional help of a magnifying glass.

Father Juan Luis turned out to be a real gift. He read Latin as well or perhaps even better than his native tongue, and seemed to know a few things about Amadeo of Portugal to boot. Thanks to him, on that afternoon in the dim light of the reading room of the Monastery of El Escorial, I began to develop an admiration for this Amadeo, who was born in Ceuta in 1420 and died in Milan at the age of sixty-two. He was from a Portuguese family, and in his life was known variously as Juan Meneses (or Mendes) da Silva, Amadeo Hispano, Amadeo of Portugal, Amadeo da Silva or Beato (Blessed) Amadeo.

According to what Father Juan Luis told us, Amadeo was a mystic, from a family of mystics. His sister was none other than Beatriz da Silva, the founder of the Conceptionists, the "Blue Ladies," who would later champion the defense of the Virgin Mary's Immaculate Conception and achieve its eventual inclusion in Catholic dogma. We learned that Amadeo began his religious career with the Hieronymites, in the Royal Monastery of Guadalupe in Cáceres, but inspired by the idea of dying a martyr, he left the monastery to settle in Muslim Granada with the aim of converting infidels. He was lucky, and escaped being killed. No doubt what saved him was the Muslim belief that the insane are also men of God.

Far from discouraging him, this experience only reaffirmed his commitment to the missionary life, and on his return to Christian Spain, he traded in his robes for those of the Franciscans of Úbeda. From there he traveled to Assisi, in Italy, launching a shining career, founding several monasteries of his own. He established a variant of the Franciscan order, the Amadeans, before finally becoming the personal secretary to Pope Sixtus IV, also a Franciscan, and of course the prophet par excellence of the Pastor Angelicus.

Father Juan Luis's background explanations were invaluable. He told us that Amadeo was obsessed with the idea of the imminence of Judgment Day, believing that it was only a matter of a few years, and admonished his followers to be on the alert for the signs. One of these signs in particular caught my attention. Amadeo believed that when the end was truly imminent, the Virgin Mary would manifest herself in all her splendor through various pictorial images, similar to the way in which Christ is made present through the Eucharist, and he wrote that those special images would bring about miracles everywhere.[1]

That reference to images, or paintings, provided me with my next question for Father Juan Luis.

"Tell me, Father," I said, turning in my chair impatiently after nearly an hour of conversation. "Do you think that this idea of the Virgin Mary appearing in various images could have inspired painters like Raphael and Leonardo to represent her so much in their own paintings?"

The old man's eyes, having lifted from the text, grew wide. "Raphael of Urbino and Leonardo da Vinci?"

I nodded.

"You know, the Italian Renaissance was my thesis topic," he said after a pause.

I could not believe my luck.

"Yes. And you know, there's another reason to think that these master painters could have read this book," he said mysteriously.

"What is that, Father?" Marina interjected, clearly intrigued.

"Well, take the example of *The Virgin of the Rocks* by Leonardo. There are some details in it which could suggest that the altarpiece was inspired by the teachings of this Amadeo." He pointed to *The New Apocalypse* for emphasis. "Do you know who commissioned this work? Or why? Go look in any art book and you'll see the same old song and dance: that Leonardo and the two de Predis brothers, Ambrogio and Evangelista, were commissioned to paint three altarpieces for the chapel of the Confraternity of the Immaculate Conception at Milan's San Francesco Grande.

"The usual story you read is that the contract specified that there should be a central panel depicting the Virgin and Child, surrounded by angels and two prophets,[2] and that the other two panels would show a small chorus of celestial figures singing and playing instruments. However, for reasons that those books can't explain, it seems that Leonardo failed to execute the commission as agreed, and instead delivered a work entirely of his own creation. I have to say that after having looked into this, I'm not so sure."

"Why do you say that, Father? Please don't leave us hanging!"

"Well, what no one tells you is that *The Virgin of the Rocks* was painted just a year after Amadeo died, and that not only did Amadeo die in Milan but that several years earlier[3] he had been writing about his apocalyptic visions while living just a stone's throw from that *very same church*. Moreover—as if that wasn't enough—his funeral services were held within those walls, in that very chapel.

"What I think," he said, regarding us closely, "is that Leonardo was actually charged with creating a painting that would honor the ideas of the newly deceased author of *The New Apocalypse*. The whole story of the painting of the Virgin and the two prophets that was never delivered is nothing more than idle art history gossip."

"Hold on, Father," I interrupted. "Which ideas in particular are you referring to?"

"Well now . . ." Father Juan Luis, well aware that he had our rapt attention, savored the moment, slowly removing his glasses and thoughtfully rubbing his chin before going on.

"There's one idea in particular that Amadeo had about John the Baptist, which was that he thought that Jesus was in effect inferior to John in standing, since it was John who baptized Jesus in the River Jordan, and not the other way around. It's like a kind of hidden language. A metaphor, if you like. A subtle or indirect way of criticizing the Roman Church, the church of Jesus and Peter, which at that time was going through an unfortunate period of corruption and intrigue. Both the Franciscans and Amadeo advocated a return to the simple poverty of John, the hermit, and the wisdom of his desert visions. This painting supports that view."

I remembered Fovel's words in the museum: *A dangerous idea.*

"All of that from a single painting, Father?" asked Marina, incredulous.

"The way Father Juan Luis explains it all, it's pretty

clear!" I cried. "There's an angel in Leonardo's painting who looks out at you, the viewer, and points out who you should be looking at in the painting. And that figure is John; there's no doubt about it!"

"Not only that," interrupted the old monk. "When Leonardo used to explain the meaning of the painting, he would say that it represented the meeting of the two infants who'd been announced by the Angel Gabriel. A meeting that took place during the Holy Family's flight from Egypt, which absolutely none of the evangelists describe, but which Amadeo does, and which you can also find in the Gospel of Pseudo-Matthew, in the New Testament Apocrypha."[4]

"So Leonardo must have had access to *The New Apocalypse*." I murmured.

"Exactly," confirmed Father Juan Luis. "And the proof of that, oddly enough, is in Madrid." He rose slowly with the old book under his arm, and then returned it to its shelf.

Marina and I stared at him incredulously.

"It can be found in one of the only two Leonardo codices housed at the National Library. No one would have thought that we could have such an important manuscript here in Spain, but back in 1965, two original notebooks of Leonardo's turned up in the depths of our National Library after having been lost for decades. Interestingly, the notebooks contain a list of all the books that Leonardo had in his studio. The inventory was in his own hand, and clearly mentions a certain *libro dell'Amadio*,[5] which is undoubtedly the Amadeo book, though it doesn't mention a location."

"It could even be that book," said Marina, half-jokingly, pointing toward the manuscript he had just put away.

"Do you think so?" The monk's eyes twinkled. "That would be quite incredible. We might have been touching an actual book from the library of the great Leonardo!"

I interrupted his reverie. "What about Raphael? Do you know if he also had access to *The New Apocalypse?*"

"Raphael? I have no idea. However, those famous paintings of his in Madrid, which in their time were the glory of the Prado, used to be kept here, in this monastery. I will say this: It would not surprise me if the *divino* of Urbino had also known about the prophecies of our Blessed Amadeo."

"Well, if we had to guess, who knows—maybe Raphael created his Holy Family paintings to make sure that the Virgin would appear in the Last Days."

The monk and I laughed at Marina's new theory, not knowing quite how to respond. Perhaps this was the key I needed to understand the paintings that the Master of the Prado had been explaining to me.

I would soon find out.

4

———

Making the Invisible Visible

The Tuesday before vacation turned out to be a strange day. I was so excited with what I'd learned about *The New Apocalypse* at El Escorial that I could barely wait until I could return to the Prado and show my new guide what a worthy student I was. I'd even worked out a plan to get through the day's activities as quickly as possible: I would go to my class, have lunch with Marina at her department, and then finally, at 4:30, I would go back to the Prado and find Fovel. All I needed was a plausible excuse for my editor at the magazine, Enrique de Vicente, so that I could avoid my afternoon's writing duties at the building on the Fuencarral road.

I didn't allow for the possibility of my plans being upset by the unexpected, and of course the unexpected occurred. It wasn't a particularly notable incident, barely worth telling, but it started to make me wonder if everything in my life then wasn't part of something bigger.

As potential reporters, my fellow students and I were expected at all times to be up-to-date on current events. It had been a particularly tense time on the international scene. In August, Iraq had invaded Kuwait. The UN had spent months trying to get Saddam Hussein to withdraw his troops from the Gulf oil wells, to no avail. As if all that weren't enough, it had been only two weeks since the Security Council had authorized the use of force against the regime in Baghdad if he didn't comply by the deadline of January 15. In an alarming development, the papers had just reported that three American aircraft carriers were en route to the Gulf, to join a general deployment which could now only mean war. And for the kind of journalism we were being taught, war is the most powerful aphrodisiac.

It was as if everyone had gone crazy. The halls and classrooms were seized with feverish activity. Out in the courtyard, some students were organizing an antiwar march, while others were organizing a kind of peace conference with any faculty and students they could find who had any kind of Kuwaiti connection. The rest seemed to be engaged in churning out whatever placards and pamphlets would help to raise the political temperature of the campus.

And to heat things up even more, there was the news that Mikhail Gorbachev had decided not to go to Stockholm to receive his Nobel Peace Prize, citing "pressures of work." Everyone believed that a large allied attack on Baghdad was imminent, and even worse, that Saddam's reprisals against Israel would spiral out of control into a third world war.

In truth, I could not have felt more distant from all of this because everything I was concerned with was at least five hundred years old, and had little to do with geopolitics.

My contemporary history professor approached me that day and asked me to do something that would bring my thoughts back to earth.

"Weren't you the one who said in class a while ago that this war had been the subject of some European prophecies?" Now I understood why Don Manuel had had his eye on me for the past hour. "Can you put together a quick presentation on that theme for tomorrow, and be prepared to discuss it with the group? It should make for a lively debate."

The assignment threw me. Since Sunday, I'd been thinking of nothing *but* prophecies. The comment my professor
referred to was something I'd let slip at the beginning of the
course, right after the invasion of Kuwait. What had caused
him to remember just then? I was embarrassed to admit it,
but I was hanging on rather precariously in that course. I
had a choice: I could take on his challenge as a chance to
improve my grade or I could continue my own private edu-
cation among my Renaissance prophets.

I gritted my teeth and accepted.

For the rest of the afternoon, against all my will, I forgot
all about *The New Apocalypse*, *The Virgin of the Rocks*, El Escorial, and even Marina. Instead, my head was filled with seers,
verses from Nostradamus, messages from the Virgin Mary,
and a slew of modern prophets of various kinds. Little did I
know then that I would actually learn something useful from
my assignment.

By five that afternoon I had figured out what I would say
in class the following day. It had occurred to me that the
prophecies about a war in the Gulf were not as different as I
first thought from the prophetic fever that ruled over Raphael's Europe. In a matter of just a few hours I'd managed
to pull together a pile of predictions that could all apply
equally well to the current situation as to the era when the
Ottoman sultans threatened the nations of Mediterranean
Christianity. Everything that I got was from the newspaper
reading room in the library. In those days, there was no In-
ternet, or Google, and the few computer terminals you saw
on campus were mainly for show.

Among the most noteworthy of these prophecies, the
ones that really stood out were those of Pope John XXIII—
the "Good Pope"—the only pontiff in history who seemed
to have a prophetic gift. According to some articles pub-

lished in the mid-1970s by an Italian journalist named Pier Carpi—which I found *by chance* in the depths of my department library—in about 1935, Angelo Roncalli, who was then a bishop and the apostolic delegate to Greece and Turkey, had a series of seven dreams that were to convert him into a modest visionary.

In these dreams, he spoke with an old man "with the whitest hair, sharp features, a dark complexion, and a tender and penetrating gaze,"[1] who showed him two books containing revelations about the future of our species. Several days later, the old man surprised Roncalli in his small apartment on the Thracian coast, convincing him to take part in a type of Rosicrucian ritual. It was there, according to Carpi, that Roncalli transcribed the old man's prophecies. He wrote them out in French, onto sheets of blue paper. Years later, the same mysterious old man appeared to Carpi and submitted him to certain tests, aimed at establishing that he was a suitable recipient for these revelations, whereupon a portion of Roncalli's manuscript ended up in Carpi's hands.

It was a bizarre, elaborate story—baroque even—but enticing, and perfect for a group of future reporters. It had everything—exclusives, sources, and how to orchestrate an effective leak. And the more I studied the Roncalli case, the more similarities I saw between it and Amadeo's raptures. The two stories had almost the identical overall structure: Gabriel or some old man who appears from who knows where—that was the least of it—to involve some man of the cloth in prophecies. For Amadeo, through eight ecstasies; for Roncalli—who would become the future Pope John XXIII—in seven dreams.

Out of curiosity, I wrote down a few of these predictions in the notebook I'd brought with me to El Escorial. One of them read: "The half moon, the star and the cross will align.

Someone will hold high the black cross. The blind horse-men will come from the Valley of the Prince."[2]

And another: "The great army will burst out of the Ori-ent, inflicting eternal wounds, and its dreadful scars will never be erased from the flesh of the world."[3]

It was now late in the afternoon, and the dwindling light was slipping away behind the silhouetted campus buildings of the university. My work done, I left the department. I felt extremely strange. What kind of coincidence was it that everything that had happened to me in the past seventy-two hours had something to do with popes, paintings, and prophecies? What would my Doctor Fovel have to say about it all? Was he somehow responsible for all of this? Every time I thought about him now I couldn't help being reminded of Pier Carpi.

I arrived at the museum at ten to seven with an uncom-fortable feeling that had nothing to do with the cold. I was tortured by the thought that I had lost the bulk of the day working on my unexpected assignment. It left me with barely an hour to spend with Fovel. On my way there, rat-tling along on the Metro, I had imagined the worst, think-ing that perhaps this was a test of Fovel's, like the one Pier Carpi had been put through by Roncalli's old man. Perhaps if I was too late, I would miss my chance to gain access to all of Fovel's great secrets. If I failed to find him today, would I ever see him again?

I ran into the museum through the Velázquez entrance, ignoring the flashing Christmas lights. Arriving at the build-ing's central lobby, I took a rapid left, looking for the gallery of Italian art, where Fovel and I had last met, in front of *The Pearl*. I couldn't find him anywhere. Pulse racing, my eyes searched in every direction to see if I could pick out his black coat among the day's last visitors. Then I went through the adjoining galleries, in case the Master had decided to amuse himself among the Botticellis and Dürers, but to no avail. There was one other option—he could be in Gallery 13. I couldn't think of any other possibilities. That was where he'd sent me when we'd parted on Sunday. "It's my favorite," he'd said. Determined, I approached one of the museum information boards to figure out where it was. The Prado had a fairly simple layout, with seventy-four galleries divided between two floors, but where the devil was Gallery 13?

I approached a custodian guard. "Gallery 13?" I said, with some urgency.

She looked me up and down as if I'd asked her directions to Mars.

"I'm meeting a friend there," I added, by way of explanation.

She stared at me for another instant, and then let out a little laugh.

"Why is that funny?" I asked, perplexed.

"Someone's playing a joke on you! There isn't a Gallery 13 in the museum. You know"—she winked—"it's unlucky."

For a moment I couldn't believe what I was hearing. The Prado Museum, Spain's premier cultural institution, had decided not to number one of its galleries with that ominous number, just as some airlines omit row thirteen on their planes, or some hotels go straight from the twelfth floor to the fourteenth floor. I was stunned.

She tried again, "Don't try to find it—really. We've never had one."

At that moment, I felt like I knew nothing. I was suddenly at a dead end, an impassable wall.

Was I the victim of some elaborate joke of Fovel's? Or perhaps, as I preferred to view it, this was all part of a test.

When I had first seen him, for whatever reason, Fovel had

reminded me of another master, encountered by the very young Egyptologist, Christian Jacq, in front of Metz Cathedral, near Luxemburg in the early seventies, an incident that had had a great impact on me. Long before he was to become a world-renowned author, Jacq was admiring the cathedral reliefs when he was approached by a man "of average height, with silvery hair and broad shoulders"[4]—another figure like Pier Carpi's!—who offered to be his guide. He called himself Pierre Deloeuvre, a name with strong Masonic echoes, which can be translated literally as "stone of the work" or "mason's stone."

Whatever his true identity, the figure initiated Jacq into the secret meaning of cathedral iconography, providing him with a universal understanding of Christian temples, which, from then on, Jacq in effect saw as machines for accessing the divine. However, Deloeuvre's teachings came at a price. Jacq would have to pass some tests to prove that he was actually worthy of the knowledge he was to receive, and to vow that he would use the knowledge to spread light, and not more confusion.

Was Fovel doing something similar with me?

Or maybe it was just me! Perhaps, overwhelmed by all this information, I was seeing ghosts where there weren't any. Perhaps Fovel was just a nice, normal guy who enjoyed spending a couple of hours talking to a young fellow art enthusiast.

The first thing I needed to do was to calm down, rein in my imagination, and simply be patient. When the Master was ready to appear, he would do so. Maybe it was just a question of coming back the next day, and the next, with a little more time. Or maybe I should just forget the whole mess entirely, because finally the idea of being the subject of some sort of test was all in my head. Nothing more.

Somehow comforted by this idea, I retraced my steps toward the gallery where I'd seen *The Pearl.* Whether or not the Master was to arrive that day, I would calm myself down by admiring a few paintings that I now knew something about. A while spent meditating on these would do me no harm, and furthermore, I was now aware that one of the principal aims of the artists in painting these works was to induce a spiritual state in the viewer.

I chose Raphael's *Holy Family with an Oak Tree.* Or then again, perhaps it chose me.

The painting was a size similar to the one I'd examined on Sunday with Fovel, with the Virgin Mary and the two boys as principal points of the composition. Only, unlike the other painting, there was no St. Elizabeth, and this was a serious enough absence to cause me some considerable discomfort the moment I noticed it.

Unsure in the face of this mystery, and resigned now to my failed search, I tried to let instinct take over.

At first, I ignored the feeling of unease. But after five entire minutes without my eyes leaving the painting, that initial discomfort—which I had first attributed to nerves— had grown into an inexplicable anguish.

Hold on, I thought, rubbing my eyes. *Why is this happening?*

In an attempt to explain that first feeling, I tried to attribute it to the scene's geometry. The figures in both *The Pearl* and Leonardo's *Virgin of the Rocks* form a triangle. In this painting, the figures lined up along a diagonal, which gave the feeling of scattering them. Was it this disorder that was causing my anxiety? No, I decided, that couldn't be it. After all, this was a very bucolic scene. There was no trace of menace anywhere. Moreover, St. Joseph, who in the *Holy Family* painting was mostly in darkness, was clearly shown here gazing at the infants with a calm, thoughtful expression, com-

Raphael, *The Holy Family with an Oak Tree* (1518). The Prado Museum, Madrid.

pletely untroubled by what the future held for them. And in the distance was a dawn similar to *The Pearl*'s—a foretaste of the dawn that the children would bring to humanity.

In short, the painting was serene. A little melancholy, perhaps, but soothing.

So why did it disturb me so?

"You find it unsettling, don't you, my boy?"

"God!" I jumped upon hearing Doctor Fovel's grave voice behind me, as if he'd materialized there out of nowhere.

"It's good to see you again," he added, pleasantly.

I looked at his feet. I know it sounds strange, but I'd once read that ghosts have no feet. Of course Fovel's feet were just where they were supposed to be. In fact, he had on a pair of substantial English shoes with buckles, which I was certain I'd have heard approaching across the gallery floor. He stood there looking as impeccable as he had at our last meeting.

As if he knew exactly what I was feeling, he said, "It's not surprising that this painting makes you uneasy."

I forced a smile, trying to disguise my shock. Fovel had appeared in exactly the same spot as the first time, just as he had promised. Perhaps he'd been waiting for the museum to empty, for now that he was here, an almost absolute silence surrounded us.

He went on. "It's because the message here is just as contradictory as the one in the *Virgin of the Rocks* that we left off discussing on Sunday. Do you remember?"

I nodded.

"You know where that contradiction comes from? Look closely."

I looked, but said nothing.

"Do you see it? Imagine for a moment that you know nothing about Christianity. If you're not considering any religious meaning, this looks just like a portrait of a family with two children. But as you and millions of others know very well, Jesus was an only child."

"Of course!" I blurted out. "How could I miss that?"

"Another thing—take a look at the boys, and at the wicker crib. It's the same crib you see in *The Pearl*, but the difference here is that both boys have one of their feet resting in it, on the sheets. You don't have to be a genius to understand the meaning of that, do you? Raphael is telling us that they both come from the same place, the same crib— they both have the same genealogical origin . . ."

"The Angel Gabriel," I blurted out, not without a certain irony.

Fovel put a hand on my shoulder. A shiver went through me.

"This is no joke, my boy. At the beginning of the twentieth century, a philosopher from the Austrian empire named Rudolf Steiner believed that he finally understood why so many Renaissance painters insisted on always painting the Virgin Mary with two boys who looked almost identical. It wasn't just Raphael and Leonardo who did this, but Tiepolo, Yáñez de la Almedina, Juan de Juanes, Luini, Cranach, Berruguete—dozens! It actually became a kind of artistic fashion to paint a mother with two virtually identical boys. It was as if artists as a group had all suddenly come to understand something. As if they'd all suddenly gotten access to something that had been hidden until then, and had decided to share it with their patrons, albeit indirectly.

I scrawled the name down in my notebook—"Rudolf Steiner."

"Are you talking about something other than *The New Apocalypse?*" I asked Fovel.

"Yes indeed," he replied. "To Steiner, what these paintings showed was that there were actually two baby Jesuses, two messiahs born almost simultaneously in Galilee to two different families, not far from one another, and he decided to keep this extraordinary revelation secret. As Steiner would explain at his conferences, the first Christian communities agreed among themselves not to let this fact out, for fear that it could create needless divisions among them in the future. Centuries later, those who came to know the truth would hint at it in various ways in their iconography, typically disguising the second Jesus as John the Baptist so as to avoid scandal—or worse."

"Two baby Jesuses?! I've heard about speculation that St. Thomas was Jesus's brother because his name in Aramaic means "twin,"[5] but what you're saying is incredible! It's crazy!"

"Slow down, my boy," he admonished solemnly. "Keep your eyes open. Look at the world without prejudice, pay attention to your sources, and decide for yourself where the truth lies. That is the greatness of the path I'm offering you."

At that moment, I had no idea of how far his counsel would take me. I knew little of Steiner then, other than that he was a noted philosopher, follower of Goethe, writer, and painter, and above all the founder of biodynamic agriculture, as well as of clinics that regarded illnesses as having both a physical and spiritual component, and of course of the Waldorf schools. Steiner was a kind of early twentieth-century Leonardo—he painted, sculpted, wrote, and even came up with new architectural structures. In addition, he had developed a new system of learning that not only supported traditional study, but also intuitive learning and an emotionally-based approach to the arts. Hearing Fovel talk about him seemed very promising. I underlined his name in my notebook, and next to it I wrote down the name of someone who could tell me more about him—Lucia.

I kept that, however, to myself, and then blurted out what I'd been waiting a whole day to tell him.

"You know, Doctor, I'm glad you bring up the need to pay attention to your sources, because that's exactly what I did."

"Is that so?"

"Absolutely. Since I last saw you I've been to the library at El Escorial and actually held *The New Apocalypse* in my own hands. I now know how it was the inspiration for Leonardo and Raphael. Not only that—I can show that Leonardo had the book in his personal library!"

My revelation hit the old man like a bomb. I could see it in his eyes—his pupils dilated and his whole expression changed.

"Really?" his voice faltered. "That's quite a surprise."

"Isn't it?" I said, pressing home my advantage. "Were you by any chance consulting Amadeo's book at the monastery last week?"

I saw a hint of something behind the dark expression.

"No," he replied simply. "Why do you ask?"

"Nothing." I had a flash of doubt. "No reason."

"What about Raphael?" He went on. "Did you unearth his connection to *The New Apocalypse?*"

I shook my head, a little disappointed. "No one could tell me that."

"Well," he began, "it's really quite simple. Let's see—who is it that runs the El Escorial library?"

"The Augustinians," I replied readily.

"And they didn't tell you?"

"What should they have told me, Doctor?"

"That one of Raphael Sanzio's principal mentors in Rome was the prior general of the Order of St. Augustine, Egidio da Viterbo."

"I've never heard the name."

"How about Tommaso Inghirami, Pope Julius II's personal librarian?"

"No."

"They were the two who introduced Raphael to Pope Julius II's court at the urging of Raphael's countryman, Donato Bramante. They were also the ones who essentially directed the plan for the *School of Athens* frescoes. Both were followers of Marsilio Ficino, that erudite Florentine who, as you may know, translated the works of Plato and Hermes Trismegistus, sparking off a seemingly limitless enthusiasm at the time for the lost teachings of antiquity, or at least those which conformed to Christian doctrine.

"Ficino was in effect the man who invented the Renaissance from his academy in Careggi during the time of Cosimo de' Medici.[6] It was he who introduced the notion that philosophers ought to ground themselves in science first, and observe the rule of 'physics before metaphysics,' as it were. His followers believed that the material and the visible world contained the hidden door through which one gained access to the spiritual and the invisible. Indeed, to God.[7] And Raphael learned to paint alongside them, under that supreme proposition."

"So you're saying that Raphael's paintings are gateways to the spiritual world?"

"Exactly. In the same way as the great Gothic cathedrals erected by the master builders of the twelfth century are."[8]

"But then this is an idea that goes way back," I objected.

He nodded. "Actually, even back to prehistoric times. If you go back forty thousand years ago, to when people were living in caves, they were already painting images on the cave walls as a way to gain access to other worlds. They valued what little art there was for its practical use more than for its aesthetic merit, as it was able to create scenes and symbols that could often conjure up the supernatural. They had to learn to look with the soul rather than just the eyes."

"And Raphael? Did he succeed in opening those . . . gateways?"

Fovel lifted his hand and slowly smoothed back his hair, looking as if he were thinking of the best way to explain the next idea to me.

"Back in the Middle Ages and the Renaissance, everyone accepted that only the artists and intellectuals of the time— as well as the insane—were occasionally able to achieve mystical heights. They were, in a sense, viewed as the keepers of the keys to the beyond, who could unite the terrestrial and divine worlds."

"Like a medium," I suggested.

"This is an area where it behooves us to choose our words carefully, my boy," said Fovel. "But, yes, they were something like that. It was assumed then that any sublime human creation must involve or be directed by the higher spheres. It was from these that all order and harmony came. Ficino wrote a great deal about this, and we know that he himself received supernatural communications.[9] This mystery was studied by the great wise men of the church, like Thomas Aquinas. And you can be sure that Raphael's new Roman sponsors made sure he knew of the connection and how to use it."

"It all sounds pretty convincing," I said.

"It is, and I can prove it to you. I mentioned the librarian, Tommaso Inghirami."

I nodded, curious to see where this was going.

"Well, in 1509, while Raphael was in the middle of painting the *School of Athens* frescoes, he took a few days off to paint Inghirami's portrait. In this painting, Raphael's Neoplatonist friend is depicted with markedly crossed eyes. Now, this is the very same defect that we see years later, in the possessed child in Raphael's *The Transfiguration*. According to the symbolic code of the time, that particular characteristic represented the access that both child and sage—both with this *special gaze*—had to supernatural sources of knowledge. Both of these figures attained the spiritual realm—one through study, resorting occasionally to divination and various other sources of hidden knowledge, and the other through raptures."

"That's outrageous," I exclaimed. "If I accept what you're saying, then I have to believe that half of all the great men of the time were basically mystics, illuminati: Blessed Amadeo, the pope's librarian—and of course Raphael."

He shook his head. "Not half—all of them! And not just the great men, my boy. According to this Neoplatonist doctrine of Ficino's that was drummed into Raphael by his mentors Inghirami and da Viterbo, man is 'a rational soul that participates in the divine mind, but employs a physical body.'[10] His mission in descending to earth is no less than to be the 'the bond that unites God and the world.'[11] And as far as Amadeo—" Here Fovel relaxed his tone somewhat. "There's something that I have not told you that connects Raphael indisputably to *The New Apocalypse* . . ."

"What's that?" I was intrigued.

Raphael, *Portrait of Tommaso Inghirami* (1509). Palatine Gallery, Florence.

"The painting of *The Transfiguration*. The original is hanging in the Vatican. You ought to go and see it."

"I'm afraid that's a bit far, Doctor," I said with a sigh.

"No matter. You're in luck—there's an excellent copy of it painted by his disciple Giovanni Francesco Penni right here in this museum, as it happens. Vasari said that it was Raphael's 'great work,' his 'most divine and most beautiful.' I tend to agree. Actually, no other painting in history does a better job of showing how the visible and invisible worlds are connected."

"But there are plenty of paintings that show the celestial world above and the physical world below it," I objected.

"True. But *The Transfiguration* contains secret knowledge that you don't see anywhere else. This philosophy explains how the two worlds can interact using man as the connector, just as Ficino and his academy postulated."

I listened to this with a measure of incredulity. "Are you saying that *The Transfiguration* is a kind of treatise on how to communicate with the divine?"

"Why not give it a try? Stand in front of the painting and follow my pointers and you'll see. All right—in the lower half, you see the apostles in discussion about a boy who looks to be about twelve years old and who appears possessed. He has the *special gaze*. Above all, pay attention to how the boy is raising one arm to the heavens, while he points the other hand to the ground, in what is a clear expression of his function as an intermediary between the two worlds. Once again, you won't find this scene in the Bible. Nowhere does it describe a scene where a possessed boy was with the apostles at the foot of Mount Tabor.

"Nonetheless, there's Matthew sitting with a book open next to him and with his feet not touching the ground, which is telling us that our traditional ways of thinking are not going

Giovanni Francesco Penni, *The Transfiguration* (a copy of the original by
Raphael) (1520). The Prado Museum, Madrid.

to help us here in understanding the transcendent. Matthew is looking at a woman, who herself provides an important clue. The woman, who is kneeling in the foreground with her back to us, is an allegory for *sophia,* 'wisdom,' from the ancient Greeks. She points to the one bedeviled, or possessed. The painting seems to be telling us that wisdom—the woman—directs us to the key that enables us to move between the two worlds. The boy is the key. Of course, not everyone sees it the same way. Judas regards the boy with suspicion. As does Simon the Zealot, and James, and Thomas. Only Bartholomew is pointing at Jesus, who is ascending to heaven, though it's clear that the poor apostle does not see him. But take note: The fingers that point to the boy and to Jesus as he is resurrected are in effect screaming out the message that only through these special figures, like the possessed boy—or like Inghirami!—can we attain the supernatural realm. And we need to heed *sophia* to be able to recognize these special figures. You're quite right—it is almost a treatise on being a medium. One in which an epileptic and the Son of God are closely intertwined. What a lesson that is!"

I frowned. "Where is *The New Apocalypse* in all this, Doctor?"

"Ah, yes. I may not have mentioned it, but *The Transfiguration* was the last painting that Raphael painted before his death. The '*divino,*' as he was called, was only thirty-seven when he died, and he left the painting unfinished. It had been commissioned by Giulio de' Medici, one of the cardinals who appears with Pope Leo X in that earlier portrait we talked about, and it was to be the altarpiece at Narbonne Cathedral before Raphael's death brought everything to a halt. In any event, his studio finished the painting. Some say that it was finished in time for it to be brought to his deathbed. Others claim that it was finished later, only in time to be displayed in front of his casket at his funeral, which took place at the Pantheon. What surprises me most is that Giulio de' Medici ended up deciding to keep the painting in Rome, and to send it instead to the church of San Pietro in Montorio!"

Again I was lost. "I don't follow . . ."

"You'll see in a moment. In 1502, with a Spanish pope—Alexander VI—in the Vatican, a cardinal and fellow-countryman from Cáceres first revealed the manuscript of *The New Apocalypse* to the world. His name was Bernardino López de Carvajal, and he believed that he was destined to succeed Alexander and become the 'Angelic Pope.' He was responsible for the passion surrounding *The New Apocalypse* that spread among the elite of the time. And do you know why he chose this particular church out of all the parishes in Rome? Because it was where the Blessed Amadeo ended up in Rome. It was his church!"

"Excuse me, young man. The museum's about to close."

The voice of a museum attendant broke in on my reverie. The circle of connections that Master Fovel was building in front me suddenly required all my attention. Raphael, Blessed Amadeo, Leonardo. Paintings as a means of communicating with the spiritual world. As a repository for the safekeeping of the secrets of Christian history.

"Did you hear me? We're closing."

"Okay, okay; we're almost finished!" I said irritably, feeling pressed.

"Please be quick."

Fovel shrugged. "Tempus fugit, my young friend. It's better this way. It seems to me that you have plenty to think about, so take your time, digest what you've learned, and return when you're ready. I'll be here."

"In Gallery 13?" I asked.

Fovel broke into a broad grin. "In a sense, yes."

Then once again, without saying good-bye, this Master of the Prado with the French name just walked off, without a sound, and disappeared into the museum's depths, away from any exit.

"We're closing now!"

"I'm coming!"

5
———

THE TWO BABY JESUSES

It would take me a few days to take in everything that had happened in that fleeting visit with Fovel. That night I felt as if our second encounter had drained me of all my mental energy, leaving me so exhausted that I went straight to bed without even eating dinner or watching any TV.

Luckily, my presentation the following morning on prophecies and the war in the Gulf went much better than I had expected.[1] That one little spark of lucidity raised both my grade and my self-esteem. Unfortunately, when I tried just a little later to write down what had happened during my encounter with Fovel, or to relate it all to Marina, I found it impossible. All I could process were sensations, flashes of memory. Fleeting glimpses of images that proved difficult to make sense of. Overall I had the sense that I'd fallen into the grip of an unhealthy obsession, a kind of icon overdose that would only subside with time. I held out the hope that the Christmas holiday break would help calm things down. For ten days I could forget about the Prado and its strange Master.

I would have had my calm were it not for a lightning trip that I had to make first to the heart of Castile—to Turégano—which came up more or less out of the blue. I was never so happy to have a car as I was in those days. In Turégano, in the shadow of that spectacular Segovian castle in which King Philip II's all-powerful secretary, Antonio Pérez, was held prisoner, the actress Lucia Bosè had acquired an old flour mill with the intention of turning it into the world's foremost museum of art about angels. And right there, in the middle of that old ruin, among sacks of cement, ceiling tiles, scaffolding and plans tacked up on the walls, with an old radio pumping out Christmas carols, Lucia Bosè had made an appointment with me for coffee.

It was really my doing. Some time back, I'd been intrigued by some comments she'd made in a prominent Madrid newspaper about being an avid reader of Rudolf Steiner. My intrigue grew exponentially when Fovel brought Steiner's name up, and right after our Tuesday encounter I called her on a whim, leaving a long message on her machine. Not expecting her to respond so quickly, I was surprised to come back to my dorm and find a note waiting for me at the front switchboard: "*Venite presto*. Lucia." So of course I went.

My hostess turned out to be the living embodiment of the illusion—Miss Italy 1947, international film star, married at one time to mythical bullfighter Luis Miguel Dominguín, mother of Miguel Bosé, and grandmother to several artists. Lucia had agreed to meet me when she heard my name, which she actually recognized because earlier that year I'd had a notable article about angels published in one of her favorite magazines. As she told me later, "I read everything I can about angels and I memorize every detail."

It had been a strange piece, coming out just after an incident in February of 1990 when several youths from Paiporta in Valencia had appeared in the media with the story that they had met with actual flesh-and-blood angels who had given them a mysterious two-thousand-page book, filled with apocalyptic prophecies about the future.[2]

In my article, I uncovered the existence of a second

group of similar "receivers," led by an artist, a painter. This is what had caught the actress's attention, as she was developing her idea for a museum of angel paintings.

I was no sooner in the door, receiving a rushed peck on each cheek and an invitation to follow her into the depths of the construction, than she asked me, "So, do you think those kids really saw actual *physical* angels?"

I shrugged, a little intimidated by the question. I was soon to discover that beneath her volcanic persona there was a very kind heart.

"Well . . ." I hesitated. "It's their word against anyone else's. The truth is, I don't know."

"But, *io si credo*—I do believe it!" she blurted out, in that delicious and easy mix of Spanish and Italian.

"So do I!" added a tanned, fortysomething man with receding hair and an intelligent look, who was waiting for us in the site's improvised kitchen.

"Oh, *caro*. This is my friend, Romano Giudicissi. Since you mentioned you were interested in talking about Rudolf Steiner and his theory about the two baby Jesuses, I asked him to join us. I hope you don't mind, he's quite an authority on the subject."

"Of course not," I replied.

"There's nothing strange about believing that a flesh-and-blood angel can appear here among us," Romano said with aplomb as he shook my hand. He smiled and motioned toward a bench for me to sit down.

"In the Bible there's the story about how two angels appeared before Abraham, and sat at his table and ate and were seen by the whole family. Why shouldn't they appear now, if they want to?"

"With any luck, Romano is one, too," teased Lucia. "Here to drink some of my famous coffee!"

"*Certo!*" he replied, smiling broadly.

The three of us spent a good while discussing this idea: Can the invisible become physical and take on a body? The question intrigued me. From what I'd read since meeting Fovel, I also knew that this was one of Raphael's most urgent preoccupations. And unlike Leonardo, the *divino* of Urbino had not renounced painting the supernatural. In fact, he believed that it should be painted with the same physicality and realism with which you would paint anything else in the material world.

Which is exactly why the Master of the Prado had cited St. Thomas Aquinas as one of his sources of inspiration. As I was on the point of discovering for myself, this great medieval theologian had attempted to come up with scientific and rational explanations for such questions as these. According to him, the invisible can sometimes become visible, tangible, and therefore able to be painted.

"St. Thomas!" exclaimed Romano when he heard me mention his *Summa Theologica*. "Did you know that, at one point, he enthusiastically discussed the ideas of another important theologian—another stubborn Milanese like Lucia here—Pietro Lombardo, who also believed that angels had a physical existence."

"And did St. Thomas argue against this?" I asked.

"Not exactly, Javier," replied Romano. "He did reject the idea that they could have a body *from nature*, as it were. But he believed that if they needed to have one for a particular reason, like for example to appear before Mary to tell her of her conception, then that they had the means to create one."

I was fascinated. "What kind of means?"

"In *Summa Theologica* he says that angels were able to form a body from condensed air. Even from clouds," said Romano.

For some reason the idea sounded familiar to me. Then I remembered why. Raphael had been the first modern painter who began to represent holy, sacred figures, like Jesus in all his majesty, or the Holy Spirit, or even God, without the usual glowing almond shape that medieval painters had traditionally surrounded them with. These aureoles, as they were called, had been used to show the presence of something sacred. For the faithful, they acted like a sort of traffic signal, indicating when a figure or image was of a divine nature. Raphael did away with this, and instead substituted clouds, or glowing skies. Could he have read St. Thomas?

Romano seemed to put a lot of stock in *Summa Theologica*, so I made a note to consult it at the first opportunity. I soon learned that he had been modest in his praise. Conceived by Thomas—or "Doctor Angelicus," as he was known after his death in 1274—over endless nights kneeling before an altar that was lit by a single candle, his great work was a source of infinite surprises. He dedicates a significant number of the over two million words in the work to supernatural questions, suggesting such daring theories as the following, on the occasional corporeality of angels:

So that the air, when it is vapor, has neither figure nor color, nonetheless when it is condensed, can take both form and color, as is clearly shown in the clouds. So do the angels take the forms of physical bodies, formed of the air, condensing these by divine spirit as necessary into the physical forms they wish to take.[3]

"*Veramente*, that's a very poetic notion," said Lucia, serving us a generous and dense *caffè italiano*. "Angels made out of clouds—how enchanting!"

Romano smiled.

"So all those people who say they've seen an angel can at least say they're in the good company of Thomas Aquinas."

"But if we start to think of these biblical figures in such physical terms," I objected, "then don't we end up with a very materialistic reading of the Bible overall?"

"It becomes more balanced," interjected Romano gravely. "It causes us to think that the physical is part of the same whole as the spiritual. Both sides are in a constant and perfect interaction. They're not different places, as they were thought to be by the theological scholars who came before Thomas Aquinas."

Lucia finally moved the coffee pot to one side and sat down with us. "Enough of this *discussione*! It's time for the pasta!"

In her presence, the conversation relaxed, and she recounted her plans for the new museum and the trouble she was having getting her proposal looked at by the local politicians.

"All they want to talk about is voter fraud and the pork industry. Imagine if I threw the *grande segreto* of the two Jesuses at them!"

After our third coffee and our second pastry, we were finally at a point where we could tackle the issue that had brought me there. Romano handed me a small volume that I opened with interest. On the cover, there was a reproduction of the first version of *The Virgin of the Rocks*, beside some other religious paintings I couldn't identify.

"I wrote this," he said modestly.

The book was titled *The Two Baby Jesuses: The Story of a Conspiracy* and had been published by a small, niche press.[4]

"The first thing you should know," he began, "is that the

evidence for there being two child Jesuses comes not only from Rudolf Steiner, but also from the Gospels themselves."

Romano seemed to be quite serious.

"The Book of Matthew tells of a baby born to a couple of newlyweds in which the husband, Joseph, is a descendant of King David. This meant that the baby was a candidate to fulfill a prophecy of the time, that a son of kings, born in Bethlehem in Judaea, would rise to become an immensely powerful king himself. Moreover, it is also Matthew who tells us that King Herod, blind with rage, cooks up a plan to destroy this infant who threatens his lineage, and who plans to use some nomadic wise men to find him."

Another damn prophecy, I thought to myself. But I said nothing and let Romano continue.

"Luke, on the other hand, describes quite a different genealogy, which goes through Nathan, the son of King David, all the way back to Adam and Eve. The Jesus he refers to is from Nazareth, and not the same Jesus that Matthew describes. Luke supports this fact with evidence, citing points of timing deduced from the Roman census. According to this, the two Jesuses were born at least four or five years apart."

Romano then opened his book to a quote of Rudolf Steiner's and handed it to me to read.

At the beginning of our era there lived two men, both named Joseph, one in Bethlehem and the other in Nazareth. Both had wives named Mary. The Mary from Nazareth was pure and virginal, while the Mary from Bethlehem carried with her the full legacy of a painful past. Both of the men named Joseph were descended from David—the one from Bethlehem by way of the royal line of Solomon, and the one from Nazareth by way of the clerical line of David's son Nathan.[5]

Romano smiled. "That's the beginning of the story. Both couples have a son and they both name him Jesus. The royal, or Solomonic, one that Matthew mentions is the one who was found by the Magi. The other, the one descended from Nathan, the priestly or clerical one in the Book of Luke—he is the one adored by shepherds. When we talk about these various stories, which we do mostly from memory, we tend to blend them as if all the evangelists basically told the same stories, whereas in fact that's not the case. The different Gospels sometimes tell different stories, and these often contradict each other."

Once again I began to object. "Yes, but it's difficult to believe that—"

"Hold on, Javier. *Aspetta,*" Lucia broke in. She began to refill my coffee cup. "The best part is coming up."

Romano smiled again. "*Grazie,* Lucia. You see, Steiner is the only person who has managed to give a clear explanation for these contradictions. And he does it using a complex system of thought he developed that he claimed allowed him to get at hidden truths. In his books and conferences he used to refer to a 'spiritual science' as a counterpoint to our traditional science. Under this spiritual form of science, concepts such as the soul, reincarnation, and higher or lower planes of existence, are taken for granted. And it was through this other science, and using decidedly nonmaterial sources, that Steiner somehow managed to reconstruct the life story of those two boys."

"You mean he had some kind of revelation?" I asked, thinking of Amadeo and his raptures.

"Call it what you like, Javier. To experience this spiritual science, you have to actively separate yourself from the physical, material world. This is what Steiner did."

"Was he a medium?"

"No, of course not. Steiner was a philosopher. You know, if he had died at the age of fifty, before he got into the occult, he would now be considered alongside such names as Bergson, or Husserl, or Karl Popper. But his curiosity took him in other directions, which had nothing to do with spiritualism."

"So how did he arrive at these revelations, then?" I asked.

"We can only speculate. Steiner was convinced that behind this material world that we know through our senses there exists a spiritual one. He believed that everyone carried the ability within them to access both worlds. With just a little training, for example, we could learn to take control of that twilight space between waking and sleep, and launch ourselves into the invisible world from there."

"He thought anyone could do that?" I was incredulous.

"Actually, we do this now. When we're reading a book that moves us, we go into an altered mental state, like going into a different world. When a painting or a piece of music reaches into us and really touches us, the same thing happens. It's as if we raise ourselves above the material world and, just for a moment, are part of the sublime. Steiner experimented quite a bit with these altered states of consciousness, and got a lot of information from it."

"Like about the two Jesuses?"

"Exactly. Steiner revealed details in a few of his conferences on how both of the Jesus boys—the Solomonic one and the Nathanic one—ended up living in the same village, and how their fathers actually got to be good friends. "The boy that Matthew describes distinguished himself early and was noticeably gifted, while Luke's counterpart had trouble adapting to life and the world. The first one had normal, mortal siblings; the second was an only child. When the first boy was born, Gabriel appeared to his father in dreams, according to Matthew, whereas the second Jesus was born after Mary saw the archangel in a vision. As you can see, there were a lot of differences between the boys."

My head was spinning. "Wow, okay—let's say I believe all this. How did we end up combining them into one Jesus?"

Romano looked at me gravely. "Something happened."

It sounded ominous.

He sighed. "This is the part that our rational minds have the most difficulty accepting. I'll do my best to describe it."

I nodded, extremely curious, willing him to continue.

"Well, according to Steiner, when the Nathanic—Luke's—Jesus turned twelve, the two families traveled to Jerusalem with the boys for the festival of Passover. Do you remember the story in the Book of Luke, when Jesus is lost in the temple? The Jesus who was lost was the one who found life difficult, and didn't say much. But when they finally found him, three days later, he was transformed, with an erudition and knowledge of the scriptures that was remarkable for someone his age.

"Steiner writes that while in the temple, the souls of the two boys fused together and became one in a spiritual process that lasted three days. It's difficult to explain, to understand. It left the Salomonic—gifted—Jesus debilitated to such an extent that he died shortly afterward, leaving all his knowledge with the other, Nathanic Jesus."

I stared at Romano. "That sounds like science fiction, if you want to know the truth."

"I agree." He nodded. "We're talking about a different kind of logic, you understand. But all four evangelists drop any reference to Jesus from that point in his life until much later, when he reappears in the river Jordan for his baptism, and begins his public life. That's when the Christ that we know emerges—the anointed one, who understands what his mission is and is prepared to die for it."

"And no one figured any of this out before Rudolf Steiner?" I asked, teasingly, recalling what Fovel had told me a few days ago.

"Oh, but of course they did! A number of painters stumbled over this idea unconsciously and even dared to put it into their work. They probably figured it out going down the same path as our philosopher, Steiner. The most famous of these was probably Bergognone,* a painter from the beginning of the sixteenth century who created a fresco depicting what happened to Jesus in the temple. You can see it in Milan, in the Basilica of Sant'Ambrogio, the church of his patron. It really is unique. That is why I have it on the cover of my book, right here."

I looked where he was pointing, and my jaw dropped. I knew that church! I'd run across it by accident while wandering around the streets near the Sforza Castle in Milan during a study trip. I remembered admiring the solid gold altar at the time, and the bronze serpent that would, according to legend, fall from his column as the end of the world approached. I even remembered pondering St. Ambrose's skeleton, displayed in the church's crypt. But I hadn't seen the fresco. Romano explained that it was among the treasures housed in the museum.

The panel is painted in a somewhat primitive style, but it wasn't this archaic quality that struck me. In the image you can see two figures of Jesus as a child! One is seated on a throne and surrounded by church elders. Mary has a protec-

* Literally, "the one from *Bourgogne,* or Burgundy."

95

Ambrogio Bergognone or his school, *Christ among the Doctors* (beginning of the sixteenth century), Basilica of Sant'Ambrogio, Milan.

tive arm around the shoulders of the other, who looks as if he is preparing to leave. How was this possible?

"Well?" Romano was looking at me. "What do you make of that?"

I shrugged, and he went on, with a sureness that was overwhelming.

"As I mentioned, other artists at the time also showed this same idea in their paintings. Steiner suggested that the reason they discovered this secret at about this time was that it had become time to reveal it. There is a magnificent example of this in your Prado Museum. It is a painting by a disciple of Bergognone's who also worked for Leonardo da Vinci. His name was Bernardino Luini. His painting of the Holy Family hangs in the Italian gallery, and was a present to Philip II from the city of Florence. You'll see it; it's quite beautiful. It shows the two boys embracing in front of Mary. She is painted in the style of Leonardo, and is also slightly cross-eyed.* Joseph is calmly leaning on his staff.

"When you get a chance to see this painting, Javier, do not rush. Take your time with it. Try to take in the atmosphere of it. Smell the lily that is flowering. Then, look down at the lower left corner of the painting. Below one of the boys you see the traditional long staff of John the Baptist, topped by a cross Perhaps then, there is no allusion here to a second boy Jesus . . . But what I actually believe, Javier, is that this painting was altered to make it acceptable to Philip II. I believe that the cross was added later, by someone who could not take the idea of a second Jesus."

* The fact that Luini tended to make his Madonnas cross-eyed is all the more notable because of the significance given to that characteristic in the sixteenth century. Vladimir Nabokov, in his 1924 story, "The Venetian," coined the term "Luini-esque eyes" to describe this look.

Bernardino Luini, *The Holy Family* (date?). The Prado Museum, Madrid.

"Added?" Here was another whole angle. It was difficult enough to decipher the paintings as they were, without wondering if they'd been altered.

"Yes, Javier. Many of the owners of these paintings went to some trouble to disguise them by adding items that made it look as if one of the boys was John the Baptist. Nobody wanted trouble with the Inquisition. So they would dress one of the boys in a goat skin or put in a cross like that to cover up the painting's main message. Often they would ask the original artist to make these changes, but if he had died, or refused, they had no problem asking somebody else to do it. The point was to make the paintings seem more orthodox, so that no one would ask uncomfortable questions."

"Can you give me any other examples of paintings that were altered?"

"As many as you like!" replied Romano. "How about Leonardo's *The Virgin of the Rocks*?"

"Are you serious?"

"Absolutely. In the first version—the one in the Louvre—there are two identical babies, but in the second version, which is in the National Gallery in London, one of the babies has the long cross of St. John over his shoulder. The thing is, that cross and the halos—they were not painted by Leonardo. They were added later."

I couldn't believe this. "Who would dare to defile a Leonardo?"

"It's not quite how you think, Javier. You should remember that in those days, the artist was not as important as the painting's message."

Lucia was looking at me, her eyes blazing. "So, Javier. What do you think now?"

I didn't know how to answer. My mind was spinning.

Romano went on. "I believe that the hiding of this truth was actually a large conspiracy."

"But if Steiner was right," I practically whispered, "those Renaissance painters weren't part of it. They did reveal the secret."

"Some did, Javier. Only some."

"Like Raphael," I said.

"Yes," he replied. "Are you familiar with *The Holy Family*, also known as *The Pearl*?"

"Very much."

"Steiner noted that all of Raphael's important paintings except for *The Transfiguration* were paintings of events that happened before John the Baptist's death. And the reason for this, according to him, is that Raphael was . . . *inhabited by* the spirit of the Baptist himself."

"Wait a minute! To believe that, you have to believe in reincarnation."

"True," said Romano mildly. "Tell me, are you also familiar with the *School of Athens*?"

"What—is there a Jesus in that as well?"

"Not one—three."

"Really?"

"And two Raphaels."

That really threw me. I already knew about Raphael's self-portrait concealed among the astrologers, but I had no idea that there was another *divino* of Urbino in the scene. Why would there be two of him?

Romano went on to explain

"This fresco was inspired by Neoplatonic ideas, as I'm sure you know. Raphael wanted to show his contemporaries that science, the ideas of Plato, and the teachings of Christianity could all exist in harmony. So on the right-hand side of the mural he painted the Christian ideas, and on the left-hand side he painted the pagan ones."

"Where is Jesus?" I asked.

"Well, as I said, he appears three times. One—as the intelligent child described in the Book of Matthew, perched on an unfinished column and reading. Two—as the twelve-year-old who was transformed in the temple. This one is on the other side of the same column. And three—as the adult Christ, dressed all in white and standing next to John the Baptist. John is showing him a book but he is not paying attention to it."

I was scribbling all this down as fast as I could so that later I could verify everything in the library. When I was done, I resumed my interrogation.

"What about Raphael?"

"Right between Jesus One and Two. He has his hand on the shoulder of a boy dressed in blue who is also reading from the book on the column. Raphael painted this boy with the face of his first mentor Perugino. By placing himself in

Raphael, *The School of Athens* (detail). From left to right: the Christ Child; Raphael as a child; Perugino; Jesus at twelve years old; and, in front, standing and looking at us, Christ.

that spot, Raphael is telling us that he has known about the secret ever since he began to work in Perugino's studio."[6]

"Interesting," I muttered feebly.

"Not interesting, Javier—" Lucia corrected me sharply, "*affascinante*!"

6

Little Ghosts

"You were with Lucia Bosè and you didn't call me?"

Marina's green eyes gave off angry sparks. We'd met in one of our favorite cafés in Moncloa to see each other one last time before vacation. She was leaving the next day for Pamplona, and I was off to Castellón. Back then in 1990, though it wasn't so long ago, communication was more complicated. Cell phones were a new luxury, and long-distance calls around Spain still cost a fortune. It was better to meet and tell each other everything in person.

Fool that I was, the first thing I did was to tell her the story of my visit to Lucia Bosè in Turégano, not leaving out a single detail. What a mistake! It turned out that she and her father were great fans of the actress, and that Marina would have given her right arm for a chance to meet her. Hurt and furious, she trotted out a long list of things I didn't know about Lucia: how she worked with all the great Italian directors—Antonioni, De Santis, Fellini—and even about her infamous fights with the bullfighter Dominguín, who wouldn't even let her drive alone around Madrid in the fifties.

But if she made me feel guilty for not having thought to bring her on my visit, she also knew how to take advantage of my guilt, placing a small sheaf of paper in front of me.

"What's this?" I asked her.

"While you were off on your travels, I was doing research

in the newspaper archives," she replied, her tone dripping with venom.

"You? What were you looking for?" I wasn't sure I wanted to know.

"For your ghost, of course," she replied triumphantly.

I stared at her, saying nothing.

We used to talk a lot about my interest in the supernatural, and she had made it clear right from the first that she didn't want to know too much about it, that she found it frightening. She considered herself a good Catholic, attended Mass on Sundays, had her Communion, and felt she should keep those kinds of things at arm's length. But now, with all that was going on with me, she was letting her guard down a little. I realized that some of what I'd told her on the outing to El Escorial had continued to gnaw at her, and she'd decided to get some answers for herself.

"You remember how you told me that you thought that the guy who got you started on all this was probably a ghost?"

I gazed out the café window, ignoring the pieces of marzipan that were sitting untouched on the table between us. She continued.

"Remember? How you thought that you were the only one who could see him? How there was no one else around when he was there? How you felt that cold sensation when he touched you? And remember how you told me that he sort of faded away when that group of tourists came in?"

"I told you all that?"

"You sure did! It's true, isn't it?"

"Yes," I replied. "Of course."

"Well then, if you're right, and your strange Master is actually a ghost or spirit of some kind, then it must come from someone who died in the Prado and who is still wandering around there, right?"

Her lack of guile made me grin. She went on.

"And since there can't have been a lot of people who have died in there, I went to the archives to see if I could figure out who it was."

"His name is Luis Fovel. He's a doctor." I reminded her.

"Come on! He lied to you! I couldn't find any Doctor Fovel who died in the Prado. No one by that name has died in Madrid in the last forty years. But," she smiled mysteriously, "I do have a couple of other candidates for you."

I don't know why, but I had no trouble picturing Marina dressed to kill and sitting at one of those nasty wooden desks in the national newspaper archive on Tirso de Molina while a blue-smocked attendant brought her a stack of leather-bound clippings. No one would have stood in her way.

She went on, oblivious to my little imaginings. "The most recent one died in 1961." She rummaged through her stack of papers and extracted one, laying it in front of me. "Here. You see?"

"You can't be serious . . ." I said.

"Would you please read it?" she said crisply.

Marina had given me a copy of a page from the newspaper *ABC*, dated February 26, 1961. The headline read, BURGLARY FOILED AT PRADO.

I picked it up and began reading it in earnest, my curiosity now piqued. According to the story, at about one in the morning on February 25, the museum's caretaker and his wife had been in their bedroom on the grounds when they had heard two loud bangs outside in the street. They rushed out to see what had happened and came upon a seriously injured man with a wire cable tied around his waist. His body was twisted up, and he was having trouble breathing.

It looked as if he had toppled from the façade of the museum onto Calle Ruiz de Alarcón. Apparently, he had fallen from the roof while trying to climb into the building. The article stated that he died just before the ambulance arrived.

"Keep reading," Marina urged. "I also brought copies of the story from *El Caso* and *La Vanguardia.*

The *El Caso* story had more details. "DIED TRYING TO ROB THE PRADO", blared the headline. The paper had done quite a good job of reconstructing the thief's actions. It looked as if his objective had been a skylight over the Italian gallery. The interloper's plan had been to lower himself through the skylight and make his way to the Goya gallery, where he would cut the two *Majas* from their frames, wrap them in brown paper, and make his way back out with them. Unfortunately for him, everything fell apart because of one misstep. The unlucky thief's name was Eduardo Rancaño Peñagaricano, and he had lived in Vallecas for over eighteen years and been a frequent visitor to the Prado. He had no criminal record whatsoever.

"No way," I muttered to myself. "It can't be him; he's too young."

"Are you sure?" asked Marina.

"Absolutely." I declared.

"Too bad they don't have a picture of him," she said. "Then you could have made sure—"

"I don't need to," I interrupted, "I know it's not him, Marina. Doctor Fovel is not a young guy."

She looked at me as if she was actually enjoying herself.

"Okay," she said finally. "I did say that I had another candidate. This one is more educated, and older, and he has an elegance which fits in very well with your doctor. He was a poet named Teodosio Vesteiro Torres. He committed suicide in front of the museum over a hundred years ago."

"I've never heard of him."

"He was part of a well-known circle of friends of the Galician writer Emilia Pardo Bazán, and even published some books himself."

"Are you sure?" I asked.

"Do you want to know what I found or not?" she retorted.

I nodded.

"Teodosio Vesteiro loved art. He was born in Vigo in 1847 and when he was twelve his family sent him to the Tuy seminary in Pontevedra. He must have been pretty smart, because while he was still a student, they put him in charge of the humanities department at his seminary, and that was by order of the bishop of the diocese. Unfortunately, it didn't last. At twenty-four, without yet having attained the priesthood, he left the seminary and made his way to Madrid to earn a living."

"Hmm." Something there didn't fit. "Do you know why he left religious life?"

"It sounds like reason and doctrine collided in his studies. They say that he began to see things in a different light. Who knows? Perhaps there was a girl involved, though I couldn't find anything about that."

"Interesting. What happened afterward?"

"His life in Madrid was no easier than it had been in Pontevedra. He earned a living giving music lessons, and began to write like crazy. The little free time he had he spent in the Prado or in gatherings with other poets. His great accomplishment was a five-volume biographical encyclopedia on famous Galicians, but he also wrote treatises on theology and philosophy, two plays, two books of poems, two books of legends—he even composed a zarzuela, an operetta!"

"What a talent!" I said. "Do you know why he killed himself?"

"No. He didn't leave a note or any kind of explanation.

In fact, he burned a lot of his papers just before his fateful decision. The only reason that we know as much as we do is thanks to some of his friends, who sent letters to the newspapers, blaming the influence Goethe and Rousseau had on Teodosio, as well as the romantic, defeatist atmosphere that prevailed among intellectuals of the time. Did you know that back then, several great thinkers opted for suicide rather than to have to live a mundane, material life? Larra and Nerval were the best known, but there were dozens more."

"Did you say he killed himself in the museum itself?"

"Not *in* the museum—*in front of* the museum, in a part called the Salón del Prado. It was around one in the morning on June 13, 1876, on his twenty-ninth birthday."

"So he was young, too," I mused.

"He shot himself. Listen to how this paper describes it; it's really shocking: 'Teodosio died on his knees, his eyes rolling up in his head, his left hand clutching his heart.'[1] They forgot to add with a revolver in his right hand."

"What a shame."

"I know. It had a big impact on Madrid's Galician community," she continued. "Even a year later they still talked about the death at the Prado. A few of his friends and colleagues—Pardo Bazán, Francisco Añon, Benito Vicetto, and some others—got together and wrote a book of poems in his memory titled *A Wreath in Memory of the Brilliant Galician Writer and Poet, Teodosio Vesteiro Torres.*[2] That caused quite a stir."

"How come?" I asked, intrigued.

"Can't you guess? They were honoring a suicide! In the strict Catholic Spain of those days, anyone who took his own life would be a pariah. They couldn't even be buried in a cemetery. Reading all these articles, Javier, you get a real sense of how many people had a difficult time with Teodosio's death."

I was leafing absentmindedly through her bundle of papers when Marina stopped me.

"Look—there's a photo! I found it in the book of poems."

Even in the photocopy you could see some detail—wide forehead, aquiline nose, neat beard. "That's not him either," I finally replied.

"Are you positive?"

I gave her a stern look, but it was mixed with tenderness. I really didn't want to offend her again. I realized what a great deal of effort she had gone to on my account, and it meant more to me than she could know.

"I am," I began, "for two reasons—one: Fovel looks to be around sixty, and I doubt that I'd confuse him with someone half his age. Second: Even if some of Teodosio's features are similar to Fovel's, those ears are definitely not, nor is the chin."

"Well in that case," she replied, "there's only one way left for us to find out his real identity." Undaunted, Marina took hold of my hand to emphasize what she was about to say. "Ask him!"

I was shocked. "Ask him what? If he's a ghost? If his name is really Teodosio?"

"Fine," she smiled. "If you won't, then take me with you. Since you neglected to take me to meet Lucia Bosè, the least you can do is introduce me to this Master of yours."

I put my other hand on top of hers. "You know, I think you're crazy."

BOTTICELLI, HERETIC PAINTER

It was January 8, 1991, a Tuesday afternoon, and I was stand-ing on Calle Ruiz de Alarcón. For the third time I had come to the museum, and I had come alone. With the holiday, I'd gone almost three weeks without any way of getting in touch with my Prado ghost or of confirming an appointment, and now I was looking for him again.

Our two previous encounters—dramatic, intense, sud-den—had run together in my memory in a strange way. Over the break, what might have been just a good story to liven things up over the dinner table had gradually become something much more, like a personal challenge. In those weeks spent some three hundred miles from Madrid, the events in the Prado had ended up monopolizing my thoughts. Whoever he might actually be, the Master had shot to the top of my list of interesting people I'd met since I moved to Madrid. In just two meetings, he'd told me about things that I wouldn't even have known existed otherwise. I felt as if fate had placed me in the path of the one sage on the planet who could draw aside the veil in art separating the visible and invisible worlds. A Demiurge who, even from a distance, pushed me to understand the deepest meanings in these paintings.

And now, with the perspective I'd gained over the vaca-tion, I felt ready for another lesson from him. I wanted more. I'd been awakened to a new and exciting world, and I wanted to explore it. Standing there facing the entrance to the museum, neither the dry chill of January nor the prick of remorse that I felt seemed too much of a price to pay for the reward that awaited me inside.

The remorse I felt was, of course, about Marina. I had arrived back in Madrid that same morning without telling her that my first stop would be the Prado rather than her building. I had originally intended to bring her along but then decided against it. It hadn't seemed such a good idea. I figured that the Master would not be particularly amused if I showed up with someone else in tow. I also worried that if he were to see me there with a stranger, he might not appear at all, and that was a risk I was not prepared to take.

But I hadn't neglected Marina entirely. This time, I had brought a tape recorder and a couple of ninety-minute cassettes with which, if Fovel was amenable, I would tape the whole session. Perhaps once she heard the Master's solemn and eloquent voice, she'd give up her obsession with famous Prado ghosts.

Maybe I would, too.

As soon as I set foot in the museum I knew this visit would be different. First of all, the place was packed! I had come in through the Goya Alta Entrance, overlooking the ticket windows, and the noise coming from the crowd around the bronze *Fury* statue—which showed an imposing Charles V vanquishing the demon—was overwhelming.

Feeling somewhat put off by the hordes, I found my way to the Italian gallery. If the Master truly had an aversion to crowds, this was not going to be the best time for us to meet.

But I was mistaken.

Crossing the gallery that housed the Tintorettos, Raphaels, and Veroneses, I saw him. He was the lone, still figure standing in the middle of one of the denser waves of tourists that was moving from painting to painting as if they were department store windows during a sale.

Sheathed in his impeccable wool overcoat, he quietly took in the hubbub around him, looking neither curious nor uncomfortable, but rather as if he were standing guard over the room.

I hurried toward him, sidestepping to avoid a drooping Christmas tree being removed by some of the museum staff.

"Good afternoon, Doctor. It's good to see you again." I said.

Fovel acknowledged me with a slight inclination of his head. He didn't seem particularly impressed to see me.

"I thought you didn't like crowds," I added.

The Master waited another couple of seconds before answering, and then, as if emerging from a long nap, he said, "You should know that there are only two kinds of solitude—alone, and in the middle of a crowd."

I couldn't detect any hint of remonstration in his voice, in fact, it was as if we'd just been talking hours before, and had resumed our conversation completely naturally.

"I haven't seen you for a while," he said.

"I was away."

"Well, then I imagine you made good use of the time thinking about what we've discussed. I wouldn't be surprised if you had a few questions for me, no?"

"Yes, I do, Doctor; quite a few. Do you mind if I . . . ?" I showed him the tape recorder.

Fovel looked at it scornfully and waved it away. Chastised, I put it back in my coat pocket without a word. Then I took a run at my question.

"Actually, Doctor, since you mention it, there is one question which I'm not even really sure I should ask you . . ."

"Fortune favors the bold, Javier; go ahead and ask. It will remain between the two of us."

A faint smile flickered over his normally solemn face, barely perceptible, and two dimples appeared faintly on either side of his mouth. His expression struck me as so human and real that for a second I really felt that I could be honest with him.

"Well?" he pressed me. "What's on your mind, my boy?"

"Well," I began, "please don't take this wrong, but, you know so much about this museum; do you know if the Prado has any . . . ghosts?"

I was trying to feel my way carefully. Everything in me was begging just to ask him outright, *Doctor—are you actually a ghost?* or *Your name wouldn't by any chance be Teodosio Vesteiro, would it?* But caution won the day.

"Ghosts?"

"Yes . . ." I hesitated, "someone who—you know—died here before and then, well . . ."

He stared piercingly at me, as if he'd suddenly understood what I was asking.

"I didn't realize you were interested in that kind of thing, Javier."

I nodded weakly, noticing how his previous affability seemed to be evaporating. Suddenly, he spun around and, forcing his way through the throng that surrounded us, he barked, "Follow me!"

I did as he said.

We didn't have far to go. He led me to a corner of a room adjacent to the Italian gallery where we'd met. To my surprise, he seemed completely untroubled by all the tourists and the children running around us in all directions.

My attention was immediately captured by three glorious Renaissance panels in an intricately carved frame directly in front of us. If they had been better lit, I could have mistaken them for real windows looking out into a forest, into a gorgeous, serene world—like a view of a calm sea. I recognized them as Botticelli's panels.

Even if you've only been to the Prado once, you've probably seen them: three striking panels, all of them the same size, depicting a landscape, which at the end of the fifteenth century was a novelty. The scene depicts a hunt, set in a coastal forest of pines beside the Mediterranean, in which a naked woman is fleeing from a horseman.

This is the only work by the painter of *La Primavera* to be housed in the Prado. I knew that it had been acquired by the museum on the eve of the Spanish Civil War, a gift of Francesc Cambó, a conservative Catalan politician and art collector, who had said that "[the paintings] transform my state of mind . . . and give rise to great jubilation in the depths of my soul . . . "[1] Cambó wanted other Spaniards to feel the same thing he did when they viewed the painting. That was how I had learned about them, and why I had stopped in front of them so many times before. I was surprised now to have been led to them this time by the Master's urging.

"Here it is," said Fovel, pointing at the first panel. "This is the only ghost you will see in the Prado."

I must have looked quite confused, because as much as I examined the panels—which I could almost describe from memory anyway—I could see nothing in them that was remotely like a soul in torment.

Fovel realized this. Lowering his voice, he leaned toward me.

"None of the museum guides describes this as a representation of a supernatural appearance, I know," he said. "But that's exactly what it is. Three scenes of terror inspired by one of the tales of *The Decameron* by Boccaccio, written around 1351.

"A ghost story? Like Dickens?"

"Exactly, Javier. And a moral tale much like the ones Dickens would pen five hundred years later. Except that the story that inspired this panel was called "The Inferno of the Cruel Lovers," combining several visions in one story—a curse and a revenge."

I stole a glance at the nearest panel, which was officially titled *The Story of Nastagio degli Onesti*. No hint of either lovers or an inferno. For a moment it occurred to me that Fovel might be trying to divert my attention from the question I'd put to him by engaging me in a new lesson about these intriguing paintings, but that wasn't it. He was quite serious. There were ghosts here.

"That one there is the protagonist—the lad in the gray doublet, with red stockings and yellow boots. He's in all three panels, but in the first one he appears twice, you see?"

I did. "Is he . . . the ghost?" I asked.

"No," he laughed. "It is unusual to see a figure painted twice in the same painting, but it's not usually an indication of something supernatural, but rather, a kind of signal."

"How is that?"

"Whenever you see a figure duplicated in a painting, you can be sure that the painter is trying to tell us something," explained Fovel. "The painting is relating a story. Here, it's almost like a comic book. The figures appear in several frames."

I remembered then what I had learned about the repeated figures in the *School of Athens* frescoes but kept it to myself.

Fovel continued. "The fellow in the gray doublet is called Nastagio. According to Boccaccio, this wealthy youth had

Sandro Botticelli, *The Story of Nastagio degli Onesti* (1483), Panel I.
The Prado Museum, Madrid.

been wooing a young Florentine girl. All we know of her is that she is the daughter of a certain Paolo Traversaro. In a departure from the customs of the time, she has decided to reject the young man. Over on the left side of the first panel here, we can see how the youth, dejected at her refusal, takes to this pine forest near Ravenna intending to kill himself. Look at him closely—he looks desperate, miserable. On the verge of doing something crazy."

I peered at the panel. "What's Botticelli trying to say here, showing the boy holding a branch?"

"Ah, well—here's where our story really begins," answered Fovel. "It's May, which, in the European mind then was the traditional time for visions and apparitions.[2] What happens is that while Nastagio is considering just how he will do away with himself, a horrific scene unfolds in front of him. Suddenly, out of the depths of the forest charges a horseman astride a black steed, brandishing his sword and chasing a redheaded girl who flees before him, terrified for her life.

"Nastagio intervenes, seizing a branch and confronting the horseman and his hounds. His face full of rage, the rider orders him to move aside, shouting, 'Let me fulfill justice divine! I must dispatch without cease the punishment merited by this bad woman . . . Every Friday at this same hour I overtake her . . .'"*

"I don't get it."

"It's very simple. What Nastagio has witnessed is an apparition—ghosts. A scene from the hereafter that repeats itself eternally in that small clearing in the forest. Here—you get a better idea in the second panel. This scene shows the rider, whose name is Guido—dismounting and setting upon

* Literal text extract from Boccaccio's *Decameron*, fifth day, eighth narration.

Sandro Botticelli, *The Story of Nastagio degli Onesti*, Panel II.
The Prado Museum, Madrid.

the woman, whom, according to Boccaccio, he proceeds to disembowel, feeding her heart and entrails to his dogs.

"Guido goes on to tell Nastagio, 'Then right away, by the power and justice of God, she arises as if she had not died, and resumes her miserable flight. The chase resumes again for me and my dogs.'"

"But why?" I asked.

"It's basically very simple, Javier. Both the horseman—Guido—and the woman have been dead for a long time. He also suffered a disappointment at the hands of that naked maiden, and, like Nastagio, came to the forest where he killed himself. Then, a curse befell the pair, and they were damned to this pursuit for all eternity. He was accursed because of his cowardice, and she because 'her cold hard heart would accept neither love nor pity.' Botticelli wanted to bring to life the idea of the eternal circle, in this case with our two phantoms, locked in an endless cycle of pursuit. You see?"

I nodded, moved. "That's a very sad story . . ."

"But not for Nastagio!" smiled Fovel.

I looked at him blankly.

"Having stumbled on this extraordinary drama and feeling very close to the rider's predicament, Nastagio hatched a plan of his own, which we see here, in the third panel of the series. Take a good look; come closer! The plan was as ingenious as it was simple. Nastagio sent an invitation to Paolo Traversaro's entire family for an outdoor banquet to be held there in the forest on the following Friday. As you can see in the painting, everything is beautifully arranged. Then, in the middle of the feast, while everyone was there, at exactly the same hour as before, the phantoms of the maiden, the horseman, and the dogs all burst out, interrupting the party and causing great distress among the guests."

I broke in. "I can see it! Nastagio's beloved and her at-

Sandro Botticelli, *The Story of Nastagio degli Onesti*, Panel III.
The Prado Museum, Madrid.

tendant ladies overturn their table in their fright, while the men stare at the rider, stunned."

"And see Nastagio? He's standing there, unafraid, explaining to the company what is happening. The women take pity on the cursed maiden, and as for Traversaro's proud daughter—the moral of the story is not lost on her. Boccaccio writes, 'This horrific scene had another happy result. So seized by terror were the young women of Ravenna that, from that day forward, they looked more favorably upon the desires of young men.'"

"Tell me." I was now dying to know. "Did Nastagio and Traversaro's daughter end up marrying?"

"See for yourself. On the right of the third panel, you see how this lady takes Nastagio's arm? She is the one who was screaming in the scene before, the one in the red dress—his beloved! Moreover," he added, "there's a fourth panel, which isn't here. It remains in the hands of the family who commissioned this work, in a palace in Venice. That fourth panel depicts a wedding scene, with everyone happily celebrating the daughter's good decision finally to accept Nastagio's proposal."

"Since you mention it," I said to Fovel, "who was the family? Who commissioned the painting, and why?"

"Well, Javier, you may not realize it, but you're looking at a very lavish wedding present from the quattrocento. The panels were part of a *cassone*—a high-class wedding chest. If you look closely at the third panel, you'll notice several shields hanging from the trees, emblazoned with their crests. Identify those crests and you answer your question. The one on the right belonged to the Pucci—a rich and influential family of merchants from Florence. The middle shield is decorated with the crest of the Medici—they ran the city— and the last one, on the right, belongs to the Bini family.

"We know from the old records of the period that in 1483, the wedding of Giannozzo Pucci and Lucrezia Bini took place before Lorenzo de' Medici—'Lorenzo il Magnifico,' as he was known. So you see—this was a warning to the new bride from the great and powerful Pucci family, a reminder intended to keep her loyal and submissive. She would have been confronted with these images for years, adorning the clothes chest in her bedchamber."

I stood there for a moment, absorbing what Fovel had told me about the painting. At the same time, I was admiring his deft maneuvering of the conversation away from my question about the Prado's ghosts, and onto territory where he felt safe—*the painting is relating a story*, he'd said.

His voice broke in on my thoughts, wrapping up the lesson.

"As you can see, Javier, interest in the supernatural goes back a long way."

"That's clear," I agreed.

"But one thing that was very new at the time was the way Botticelli depicted these apparitions. He was thirty-six and had just completed *La Primavera* a year before, influenced once again by the ideas of Marsilio Ficino. He was about to begin his famous *Birth of Venus*. At the peak of his career, knowing by then just how to depict the supernatural, he did so with a sensitivity that would not be seen again until Raphael arrived in the city some years later."

"You know, Doctor, I think it's very interesting how you manage to connect everything together . . ."

"But that's because everything is connected!" he exclaimed.

"The prophecies, too? Can you connect Botticelli to the whole *New Apocalypse* phenomenon?"

Fovel flashed me an ironic grin, and continued. "As any

historian will tell you, just a few years after Botticelli painted these panels, Florence was to become the center of prophecy par excellence."

"Are you certain about that?"

"Absolutely, my boy. In the years after Botticelli painted the *panneaux*, a huge controversy was to develop in Florence the likes of which had never been seen. It hit Botticelli very hard. The source of this apocalyptic outbreak was Girolamo Savonarola, a Dominican who was to become the city's most notorious religious figure. His ardent sermons became famous throughout Italy, railing as they did against corruption in the church and in the political institutions, and more generally against vice, luxury, and Florence's infamous bacchanals. His reputation and following grew to such an extent that both Lorenzo de' Medici and Pope Alexander VI tried numerous times to do away with him without success. Even Michelangelo, having heard him speak, found his voice to be so penetrating, intense, and engrossing that he never got it out of his head for the rest of his life."

"Were his predictions alarming?" I asked Fovel.

"Oh, much worse than that, my boy," he replied gravely. "This 'hound of God,'* repeatedly referred to the church as a 'proud whore,' responsible for betraying Christ's evangelical message. And he made no secret of his wish that Charles VIII of France take all of Italy in order to reclaim his rights over Milan and Naples, ejecting the pope from Rome in the bargain. Savonarola dreamed of a new theocracy based in Florence, and threatened the authorities with all manner of divine punishment if they failed to take steps to consolidate

* In Italian, the Dominicans were called *Domine Cane,* "hounds of God."

religious and political power. In his Convent of San Marco, he would prostrate himself before illuminated panels by Fra Angelico, drinking in the spirit of the biblical prophets, and then emerge, ecstatic, with his own prophecies."

"So he started having visions? And channeling prophecies?"

"He did, and certainly looked the type, with his scrawny frame, wild eyes, and threadbare habit. Along with another of the monks at San Marco—Fra Silvestre d'Andrea Maruffi—he produced countless prophecies about the grim future in store for the city. Maruffi was a sleepwalker, and could be seen on many a night roaming across the tiles of his cloister roof. Upon waking, he would spout horrific visions that Savonarola would faithfully transcribe. Before long, he, too, developed his own prophetic gift.

"Savonarola also published two treatises, *Dialogus de veritate prophetica* and *Compendium revelationum,* both of which confidently predicted a great change for the church and the imminent beginning of the thousand-year rule of Christ on earth."

I was incredulous. "You mean this Dominican friar, who is from the same order as some of the main inquisitors, comes out with all these predictions bordering on heresy and no one can stop him?"

Fovel nodded.

"In those days, you see, Florence was full of heretics, and tolerated some quite unorthodox ideas, so at first no one paid much attention to him. But that soon changed. Florence's intelligentsia had distanced itself from strict Catholic orthodoxy but was not as dogmatic as the Dominican, and it eventually began attacking him. Marsilio Ficino, Botticelli's teacher, even called Savonarola an emanation of the Antichrist. Imagine!"

"How did Botticelli go from following his teacher to getting mixed up with a hothead like Savonarola?"

"Well, now, that's something of a mystery. No one can say exactly when or why he began to drift away from the Neoplatonists at the Academy, but for whatever reason, the mad monk's sermons began to appeal to him. Botticelli, who had been a close friend of Leonardo and even opened a little tavern with him,[3] turned away from the light into the bleakest darkness. In his famous biographies of the great artists of the time, Vasari described Botticelli as becoming 'an ardent follower of the sect,' and that 'this caused him to abandon his painting, and without any income, his life was plunged into chaos.' "[4]

"How terrible!"

"The worst was to come. Savonarola convinced the painter to destroy all of the work he'd done during his pagan period. He suggested that Botticelli bring everything from his studio and burn it in one of the 'bonfires of the vanities' that Savonarola would organize each week. Perhaps you've heard of these—great pyres with sculptures, furniture, clothes, tools, books, and paintings that the repentant Florentines would give up to avoid the wrath of a God who, according to the Dominican, would level their city otherwise."

"My God . . ."

"It was a disastrous time, so unbefitting of the Renaissance. And don't for a moment think that Savonarola's influence over Botticelli was limited to winning him over to his particular fanatical brand of belief, what he called his *renovatio ecclesiae*—no! When the ever-accommodating Sandro finally began to paint again, it was in line with Savonarola's ideas, following his ideology with astonishing faithfulness."

"How horrible," I breathed.

"Indeed," Fovel replied. "In 1501, with the truculent

cleric now dead, Botticelli threw himself into the creation of a canvas which, for the only time in his career, he signed and dated to ensure that there was no question as to its provenance. This would become what we know today as *The Mystical Nativity*, which is at the National Gallery in London. This painting depicts the birth of Jesus not as an event in the past, but rather as a prophecy that will be accompanied by other signs: Angels will embrace man, and demons will be set upon and vanquished. This was what his Dominican teacher had preached in his Nativity sermon of 1494[5]—that the corrupt Florence of the Medici would fall, as would the pope, that Moors and Turks would be converted to Christianity, and that these events would usher in a new era of prosperity and direct connection to God."

Fovel then reached into his coat pocket and pulled out a folded, double-page reproduction of the painting we were discussing. It looked as if it had been taken from an old magazine. I shook my head, wondering how the hell he happened to have *exactly* that painting in his pocket.

Fovel had carefully unfolded the glossy paper, oblivious to the five or six people around us who were observing his every move. Although the print was in color, I knew instinctively that it couldn't come close to doing justice to the beauty and glory of the original.

Having unfolded and flattened out the print, Fovel went on.

"Botticelli painted this three years after Savonarola, Fra Silvestere Maruffi, and Fra Domenico da Pescia—another of his fervent followers—were hanged and burned in Florence's Piazza della Signoria, having been convicted of heresy. The monk's old followers were now all being sought out and persecuted, and so Botticelli had to be particularly careful to cover up his affiliation."

"If that's true, how can you be certain that there's a link between the *Nativity* and Savonarola's heresies?" I asked him.

Fovel smiled broadly. "Simply by reading the monk's works and knowing exactly where in the painting to look!"

I leaned over to have a closer look at the reproduction.

"For example," began the Master, "in his *Compendium revelationum*, Savonarola dedicates several pages to explaining what he called 'the twelve privileges of the Virgin.' These were a series of short litanies that his followers would chant in their processions through the city. If you observe the scrollwork here carefully, these banners being held aloft by the twelve angels who float over the scene, you'll see that they contain certain inscriptions. We can only make out seven of the original twelve, but all of them are these 'privileges' taken word for word from Savonarola, and in Italian, too, just as he had them: *Sposa di Dio Padre Vera, Sposa di Dio Padre Admiranda, Sacrario Ineffabile . . .*"

"That's it? That's all your proof?"

"Of course not, that's just the beginning. Right next to Botticelli's signature there's another hidden mystery. An inscription, written in a very rudimentary Greek, which says, more or less: 'I, Alessandro, painted this painting at the close of the year 1500, during the time of Italy's great turmoil, in the half time after the time, according to the eleventh chapter of St. John in the second woe of the Apocalypse, during the loosing of the Devil for three years and a half, then shall he be chained in the twelfth chapter and we shall see him [fallen] as in this picture.' "[6]

"What does it mean, Doctor?"

"Clearly, it refers to two actual chapters from the Apocalypse of St. John, the Book of Revelation, wouldn't you say?"

"Yes, eleven and twelve."

"Exactly. Chapter eleven talks about the coming of a

Sandro Botticelli, *The Mystical Nativity* (1501). The National Gallery, London.

great tribulation, and mentions two witnesses—Enoch and Elias, according to St. John—who would prophesy a thousand two hundred and sixty days in the Holy City spouting thunder and fire from their mouths. Both would then be killed, and would ascend to heaven on a cloud.

"Savonarola believed that this text referred to himself and his fellow friar, Fra Domenico da Pescia, and in a curious coincidence, the two men had been prophesying for about three and a half years—approximately 1,260 days—before they were condemned to death, hanged, and burned. And in the same way, they were 'killed' and 'rose to heaven on a cloud' of smoke."

"Not to mention breathing fire," I added, wryly.

"Botticelli used the *Apocalypse* as a code through which he could talk about his teacher. Chapter twelve goes on to describe another period of three and a half years, after which an angel will descend to earth to vanquish Satan and install a thousand-year reign on earth in which true believers and martyrs will reign over the world with Jesus at their head. At the time that Botticelli painted this, he fervently believed that he was living in the period just before Christ's new nativity."

"He really believed that Christ would come back?" I asked, amazed.

"It's not such a strange idea, you know. Many people in Florence were convinced it would happen around the year 1500, and although Savonarola tried to downplay this date in some of his sermons, that only made it spread more rapidly by word of mouth.

"And you know the strangest thing about this? Savonarola expected this moment of renewal to occur in about 1517 at the latest.[7] For his followers, all the waiting and the constant changing of prophesied dates eventually became unbearable. The monk also had to contend with twenty of his former disciples for whom a similar wait was proving too much, and who broke off to found their own small convent, naming a certain Pietro Bernardino as the new Angelic Pope."[8]

"Again the mention of an Angelic Pope!" I interjected.

"Yes, this idea of a reforming pope who would appear almost like an angel was never far from people's minds during this time. In fact, once Savonarola and Botticelli were both dead, guess who was one of the idea's last defenders?"

I smiled at him. "Go ahead, Doctor—surprise me."

Fovel raised his great silvery eyebrows and wrinkled his forehead as if he were about to deliver the coup de grâce to our entire conversation. "You remember the name of the family that commissioned these three panels from Botticelli?"

"You mean the Pucci?"

"Very good. Well, Francesco Pucci, who was the great-grandson of that wedding couple—Nastagio and his betrothed—wrote a treatise titled *De Regno Christi* in which he predicted that before the sixteenth century was over, the Roman Curia would be abolished as a consequence of its record of sins, and that the world would see both *uno nuovo ordine* and *uno supremo pastore*."

"The circle is complete!" I exclaimed. "Well, what happened to this young Pucci?"

"He had a very eventful life. He traveled throughout Europe. In Krakow, he met the famous English wizard and astrologer John Dee, from whom, it is said, he learned to communicate with the angels. He and Dee journeyed together as far as Prague in order to pay their respects to Rudolf II, king of Bohemia and Holy Roman emperor—the 'Alchemist Emperor.' [9] With a life like that, it's hardly a surprise that Pucci ended up thrown into prison. Or that he met Giordano Bruno while there. Sadly, he never saw freedom again. He, too, was condemned as a heretic and burned in 1597, in the same public square in Florence where Bruno would also be burned to death three years later."

"Wow—what a time!" I was overwhelmed.

"And what characters, too."

We were both quiet for a few moments. Our eyes traveled back to the rich triptych of *Nastagio degli Onesti*, as if in that forest by the sea we might find some of the peace that was lost to Botticelli after he altered his faith. I suddenly realized that the lesson was over, and, before the Master could disappear without making plans to meet again, I tried to pin him down.

"So, Doctor, when can we meet again?"

Fovel turned his head from the panels and looked at me as if I wasn't there.

"Meet?" he mumbled, lost.

"Yes. Should I come back this week, or is it better for you—"

He interrupted sharply. "Have you ever had to make an appointment before to see me? Let your need guide you, Javier. Let your thirst for truth bring you the next time. Do you remember what I told you about art being the doorway to other worlds?"

I nodded, puzzled.

"Learn to open those doors for yourself and you'll have no trouble finding me. Now that's enough!"

I wasn't paying attention to this last piece of wisdom; I had something else I wanted to ask him.

"Can I bring someone?"

But he gave no response. As usual, without a word, he turned and left, disappearing among the museum's visitors.

8

———

The Path to Glory

The first contact I had with Marina after Christmas vacation was marred by a bad omen. Instead of waiting for my usual eight-thirty call, she had unexpectedly stopped by the reception desk of my residence hall very early to leave a hastily written note in my mailbox that said, "Javier—Don't know if you're back in Madrid yet, but if you are, please come find me in class. It's urgent!"

Our receptionist, Toni, had seen her leave the note and had noticed—not without a certain amount of curiosity—that the young woman who left it seemed very nervous. Even though I knew Marina's small rounded handwriting well, I asked Toni to describe her, in case somehow the whole thing might be a joke, or some kind of mistake.

"Well, let's see, she was blond and quite thin, with light eyes and about your height."

That was Marina.

Toni was looking at me, concerned. "Javier? Is everything okay?"

To all the students in our building, Toni was like a second mother. She knew everything about us—when we came in, when we went out, who called us, when we were in love or in trouble over our grades. I didn't know what to say, I just looked at her. Then I ran nervously up to my room to grab my notebook and coat, and, without stopping for breakfast, raced up the tree-lined Avenida de Gregorio del Amo to the Department of Pharmacology.

Normally, Marina would have spent the last two hours in her department library, waiting for the start of morning classes. So why did she want me to meet her in class?

I got to the main Pharmacology Department building—an imposing but characterless edifice of brick and concrete—just five minutes before classes were due to start. I found Marina sitting in the back row of her lecture hall with a dazed look on her face. You could tell from one look at her that something bad had happened. She was curled up at a desk without a speck of makeup, wearing a man's turtleneck sweater several sizes too large, her hair pulled up into a hasty ponytail. What really stood out were the dark bags under her eyes announcing that she hadn't slept a wink the night before.

"Thanks for coming, Javier," she said flatly, no hint of a smile. "How was your vacation?"

I said nothing—she didn't give me a chance. She got up.

"Please, let's get out of here."

In one movement, she scooped her things into her big shoulder bag and wrapped her wool coat around her. I followed her out of the building, afraid to hear what was coming. All I wanted was to get outside with her and away from people and to find out what the hell was going on. If things were as serious as they looked, I figured it would be better to get away from campus and find some privacy. So, weighed down by a heavy silence, we started walking up along Avenida Complutense. Finally she spoke.

"I don't know how to say this, Javier . . ." the words tumbled out as if she'd desperately needed to say this to me and had finally mustered the energy. "You've got to stop meeting with that guy!"

I stared at her, completely taken aback.

"Last night . . ." she began, but immediately had to stop to catch her breath. She grabbed my arm and, while she dragged me along, she pulled herself together and continued. "Last night this man showed up at my house. At my front door. My parents were away, which is just as well; it spared them a nasty shock." All of this came out in a rush.

"Wait," I said, "you opened your door to a stranger?"

"Yes, I know, but . . . it's just . . . he showed up at about quarter to nine, perfectly polite, and said he had something important to tell me. He mentioned your name. It wasn't that late, and my sister was in the house, so I let him in. I made him coffee. But it wasn't what he did that was scary; it's what he said!"

I still didn't know what to think. "What did he say?"

"That's the thing, Javier. He wanted to talk about you. He knows you, knows what you're studying. Most of all, he knows about your visits to the Prado. He told me that he's been watching us! He knew all about which papers I got from the newspaper archive, about your meeting with Lucia Bosè—he even told me things he knew about the day we went out to El Escorial to look at that book of prophecies!"

"*The New Apocalypse,*" I added automatically.

"Yes—that one." She kept on walking. "I don't know exactly what you're up to, Javier, but he asked me to persuade you to stop, to drop it; all of it. For your own good."

"Drop all of what? What am I supposed to drop?" I asked her, shaken, my voice shrill.

"Stop seeing that . . . ghost, at the Prado. Or whatever or whoever he is. He said not to trust him. And most of all, he said to stop going around stirring things up that don't concern you. Just stop, stop, stop! You get it?"

"But if I—"

"Javier!" Marina pulled away from me and turned to look straight into my eyes, very grave. "This guy was really serious, I swear. He didn't . . . he didn't actually threaten me, but you have to believe me, he came very close. I could see it in his face; his expression was ominous. He scared me."

"But . . . did he say who he was?" I tried.

"No, he didn't!" she cried. "All he said was that he was some kind of art expert, and that even if we didn't mean to, our questions at El Escorial had put an important investigation in danger."

"Aha!" Suddenly, as if someone had just switched on a light, I thought I understood what all this was about. "He must be the guy who was there at El Escorial before us! The one who also went to look at the Amadeo book! That's how he knows about us!"

Marina's face darkened. "Yeah, Javier, I thought of that, too, but what difference does it make? The bad part is that he went to the trouble of checking us out. He followed us, don't you get it? For whatever reason, the stuff that you're doing bothers him, and his visit the other night was a warning. It was so . . . creepy!"

A nervous smile found its way to my lips. "So that's all he wants? Just for me to forget about Fovel? And not to ask questions about . . . about *art*? Is that it?"

"Damn it, Javier! It's not a joke!"

Marina's lips were trembling as she spoke. "Look, I didn't sleep all night last night because of that guy, see what I look like? I came over to the department as early as I could this morning because at least here I'm surrounded by people and I don't think he'd dare try anything. I even told my sister to get out of the house right away, in case he decides to come back."

I tried a calm tone. "Marina, don't. Don't get so worked

up." Gently, I pulled aside an unruly strand of hair that had
fallen in her face. "He's probably just some idiot, some art
geek with an obsession. He saw your address in the register
at El Escorial, and thought he'd try to intimidate you. That's
all. I really don't think—"

"He's been in my house, Javier. He was standing right in
front of me!"

"Okay, okay." I hesitated. Marina was really scared.
"Maybe if we call the police—"

"And tell them what, Javier? That some . . . *historian*
doesn't want us to look at a book he's interested in? That he
had a cup of coffee at my house and left without doing anything? For God's sake, Javi!"

Marina was breathing heavily and squeezing her fists so
tight that her knuckles showed white. For a long while neither of us spoke. The last thing I wanted to do was make her
angry.

We started walking again, all the way to the edge of the
campus, near the La Coruña road, navigating our way between the frozen puddles. Then the first warm sun of the
winter appeared, and, somewhat mollified, we found ourselves drifting toward the shops of Moncloa. We were missing our first classes of the semester, but that wasn't the main
thing on either of our minds at that moment. I put my arm
around her shoulders for reassurance, and we walked like
that for a spell.

It wasn't until we found ourselves in front of the rather
staid window display of the Fondo de Cultura Económica
bookstore that I dared speak again, thinking that maybe re-
visiting what had happened would make it less frightening.

"What I don't get, Marina, is why you felt so threatened
by him. After all, he was polite, civil, and he did leave,
right? Basically, all that happened is that your 'Mister X'

suggested it would be better if I didn't go and see this other guy who, after all, I don't know very well anyway, right? That's all it is."

It felt like a whole week went by before she finally responded. Her eyes wandered slowly over the books in the window as if it was her mission in life to check every book on display in every store. Finally, wearing the saddest expression I'd ever seen on her, her reflection found mine in the window.

"Joke if you want, Javier, but there's something else," she said, very reluctantly.

"What do you mean?"

"He talked for a long time about death. Just him, like a monologue. I don't know why, but he seemed obsessed with it."

"You said he never threatened you!"

"He didn't!" she cut me off. "He was talking about death in the abstract, as an idea. He kept saying something about how it was of great virtue to prepare for a good death. Oh, yes—he also said that we had to learn to 'go unburdened.' To go without luggage, like the ancients, that kind of thing. It was really strange. And really spooky . . ."

I saw that recalling the visit was actually shaking her up, so I took a chance and hugged her close, hoping that would calm her down. It was the first time our bodies had touched like that, and the feeling was powerful—we were swept up in it and stayed close like that for some time. It was impossible to say how long, I wished it would never end. I reached up and gently buried my hand in her hair. "Don't worry. It's over now."

"He just kept on talking about death. So weird!" she repeated, oblivious to my gesture, as if she just couldn't let go of the memory.

"Why would he say all that?"

"I don't know, Javier!" The embrace evaporated and she slid out of my arms before I knew what was happening. "The one thing he was very clear about was that you should keep away from your so-called Master of the Prado. He's exposing you to theories that are wrong, false, to ideas that are full of traps. He scared me, Javier. He really scared me!"

Her eyes filled now with tears.

"This is crazy," I said softly, with all the calm I could muster. "It doesn't mean anything."

"Oh!" she started. "Before he left, he gave me this for you."

She wiped her eyes and, still shaking, rummaged in her purse. Pulling out some pages folded in half, she proceeded to wave them in my face. There seemed to be three or four photocopied sheets with an intricate decorative border. I thought I saw an Egyptian mummy, but dismissed the idea right away.

"What's that?"

"It's a key."

"But to what?"

"He said, 'This is a key to the glory.' He urged you to reflect on this with an open heart, 'putting aside your pernicious beliefs.'"

Fascinated, I took a look at them. They were copies of pages from a very old magazine, *La Ilustración de Madrid,* and on one of them there was actually a picture of a dried blackened cadaver accompanied by an inscription that suddenly made this an extraordinarily rare document: "The Emperor Charles V, copied from life, 1871."

"What are you going to do with it?" asked Marina, lifting her eyes from the macabre picture and watching my sudden interest with a mixture of wariness and fear.

The Emperor Charles V, copied from life, 1871.

"Take his advice, of course!" I smiled now. "Staying away from evil is always a good idea, right?"

"So you'll forget about all this?"

"I can't, Marina." I grabbed her shoulders and spun her away from the bookstore window. "Especially now that it just got so interesting."

Unfortunately, that connection I'd felt a few minutes before had now vanished.

9

TITIAN'S SECRET

I didn't so much read those pages as devour them.

But first I took Marina to her Aunt Esther's and made up some story to persuade her to take Marina and her sister for the night. Though it was late, I desperately wanted to sit down and study my new find. I was doubly impatient—first, I was very interested in the contents of the pages, and second, I suspected that they held the key to some path, some signal that would tell me who this Mister X was who had so unnerved Marina.

At first, I found it hard to concentrate. The idea that someone had been and perhaps still was spying on me bothered me. But as I became engrossed in the pages my paranoia faded. I loved to read old texts. They worked on me the same way paintings did—after a while, they stopped being just a page or a canvas, and instead became a window onto a distant past.

The pages had been taken from an old bimonthly magazine that turned out to be a glorious hodgepodge of material. Edited by the romantic poet Gustavo Adolfo Bécquer—a well-known aficionado of things like ghosts, fairies, and tortured souls—it included everything from the political to the artistic, and much in between. You might see a poem next to a short piece on the current Paris fashions or a story with an Orientalist flavor, followed just as easily by a report on the state of the city construction on Calle Hortaleza. As I would later confirm, the magazine's life was brief; it lasted only three years.

The pages I'd received from Mister X were from the issue dated January 15, 1872, and the first thing that caught my eye was a story reporting that, if it was to be believed, someone had gotten into the tombs in the Pantheon of the Kings at El Escorial, forced open the sarcophagus of Charles V, and determined that his body was mummified and intact, beard and all.

I had never heard anything about the tomb of Spain's great emperor being violated, or about the existence of actual evidence from the time relating to such a macabre event. Why did Mister X think I should see this? Where was he leading me? Or—perhaps more intriguing—was he trying to divert my attention from something else?

There was further, more eloquent text that accompanied the drawing in the form of an open letter from one painter to another. The letter was a kind of dedication from the man who'd sketched the Charles V drawing—Martín Rico, a star pupil at the Academia de Bellas Artes de San Fernando—to the preeminent artist of the day, Mariano Fortuny. The letter was mostly a paean to Fortuny, lavish in its praise, without ever explaining why Rico was recounting the story of his mission to view Charles V's body.

One thing of note was that Fortuny had a close link to the Prado. He had married the daughter of Federico de Madrazo, a painter like himself and director of the museum. Was this where Mister X was pointing me? Or was it toward the gallery of nineteenth-century paintings? Or Madrazo's collection? And to what end?

Just to be sure, I read the document again.

To Señor Don Mariano Fortuny:

Dear Friend—

In the pages of Issue #49 of *La Ilustración de Madrid*, which I have the pleasure of enclosing here, you will see a reproduction of a sketch of mine of the mummy of Emperor Charles V. [. . .] The cadaver is very well preserved, wrapped in a white sheet with a two-inch lace fringe, and is completely covered by a large expanse of red damask. The three centuries that have passed since the emperor was interred have inflicted surprisingly little damage, and no matter what you may have read or heard I can assure you that all in all it is still in almost perfect condition, the sole exception being a few drops of wax on the emperor's chest, allowed to fall no doubt by the trembling hands of those curious souls who have been fortunate enough to view these venerated remains on the few occasions when the casket has been opened. One thing that particularly caught my attention was that the thick, close-trimmed beard is not grizzled and white as so often shown in depictions of our noble prince, but rather a rich dark brown. A golden skullcap covers most of his head, obscuring his hair, and one can discern the outline of bone in the forearms, and on the left side of the neck.

I will not recount the emotion that I felt, the feelings that moved my very spirit upon seeing those still remains of the man who, having filled the world with his greatness, would come to take his leave of this life in the monastery in Yuste, humble and repentant, as I have promised myself not to take up too much of your precious time with this dedicatory letter that already grows too long.

I nonetheless must inform you, and here I beg your further indulgence, that at no time have I ever encountered more difficulties, nor worked with as much trouble and discomfort as I had to in completing this drawing. I was forced throughout to maintain my posture in a perfect *C* shape, and the distance from my face to the model was no more than one foot, and I leave it to your good judgment to imagine the difficulty of drawing in such conditions.

I therefore bring this letter to a close, and trust that you accept this greeting with as much indulgence as I took pleasure in the writing of it.

Your friend,
Martín Rico
Escorial, December 18

Seated there under the cold fluorescent light in the small library of my residence hall, with Volume 51 of the well-loved, black-and-gold *Enciclopedia Universal Ilustrada Europeo-Americana* open to the entry on the letter's author, I began to appreciate the impact of this event on Rico. A notable realist painter of the time, lauded for his mastery of nineteenth-century landscapes, and with a modest exhibit in the Prado itself,[1] he had somehow won access to the tomb of Charles V and had seen with his own eyes the subject of so many portraits by the great Titian himself. It must have been a powerful experience for him. Once in a lifetime. But what did it mean?

Something about the whole Rico story was nagging at me. Marina had said that, right after giving her the material on Rico, Mister X had talked about death in a way that made little sense to her. The more I thought about it, the way she described the whole thing made it sound staged. Like it was an act put on for her—and my—benefit.

One thing I had learned in my studies was that in order to have the brain retain specific information, it helped to associate it with absurd facts or images. For an aspiring journalist intent on reaching his audience, this had been a revelation. For example, they taught us that if we were reporting a dockers' strike, our report would make a much more lasting impression on the viewer if we were suspended from one of the dock cranes, rather than simply standing on the pier. When one upsets the normal, or expected pattern, the human memory is able to retain the smallest details. Was that what Mister X was doing with Marina? Was he trying to make sure that she remembered what he said, and if so, why? What for?

Lacking any other good ideas, I decided to go to work on this hypothesis.

The first thing I did was to isolate the basic ideas contained in Mister X's monologue. There were two. The first was in the somewhat archaic phrase about it being of a great virtue to prepare oneself for a good death; the second, in the expression, "to go unburdened." I wrote these down in my notebook.

Next, guided by these ideas, I combed through the entries in the encyclopedia for Rico, Fortuny, and Bécquer, looking for something that might have a connection or give meaning to these ideas, but found nothing. However, I then pored over the extremely long entry on Emperor Charles V and quickly found something that linked the two phrases. Apparently, this now-mummified emperor had been the first ruler in his time ever to have devoted the last two and a half years of his life to preparing himself for his death—*a great virtue.*

Charles V renounced all his titles and retired to a monastery in the province of Cáceres until his death. Interestingly, he did this *unburdened by luggage*, expressly ordering that he be buried without jewels, baubles, or any other trappings of power.

Encouraged by this little ray of light, I went to track down Santi Jiménez, a graduate student in Geography and History who lived on my floor and who was doing his doctoral thesis on Charles V.

Santi was the envy of all of us. For as long as anyone could remember, he'd always been among the first group of students allowed to choose rooms each semester, and he always picked the same one—a spacious corner suite on the third floor of our building, with its own vestibule, private bathroom, fridge, microwave, and great views of the pool.

The less charitable students attributed his success with girls to a corresponding deployment of funds, rather than to his moon face, thick glasses, or his almost supernatural ability to procure whatever you might need, from a used digital camera to an official Real Madrid warm-up suit. Everyone went to him when they were in a jam. You had to acknowledge his knack with people and his ability to get things done. He was a born fixer, always ready with a greeting, and willing to help you with whatever it might be, even if it was late and you were an unknown freshman, though there would always be some kind of price later.

Now it was my turn to ask him for a favor.

"You want to know if Charles V prepared himself for his death?" he repeated, not understanding. Santi peered at me through his thick lenses, surprised by my request. "You really just want to talk about history? That's all?"

I'd called up to his room from the front desk, and he'd appeared, disheveled, a few minutes later, a half-empty beer in his hand. I apologized for disturbing him, and assured him that my request was purely professional and wouldn't take long. There was nothing else I needed.

"You're in journalism, right?" he asked mischievously, removing his glasses and rubbing his eyes.

"Yeah, but right now I'm interested in the emperor's death."

He smiled. "I can't blame you there."

"So will you tell me?"

"About Charles V? Sure, absolutely, man! He's a fascinating character," he added, as if he were talking about a member of his family. "I'd say he's the only ruler of his era who died knowing what he was doing."

Go ahead, then—tell me all about it," I implored him.

So the future Doctor Jiménez, still surprised by my request, went all out. We found a spot in a corner of the cafeteria by the large window overlooking the entrance to the building. We ordered coffee and donuts, and Santi began to talk.

"When you look at the emperor's last years, one of the first things that jumps out at you is that he abdicated all of his titles and crowns almost three full years before he died. No one had ever done anything like that before. In those days it was always assumed that a monarch or a pope would stay on his throne until the day that God chose to take him. Charles broke the pattern, almost as if he knew that his end was near."

"Did something happen?" I asked.

"Yes, in fact. Not long before he renounced everything, Charles suffered a complete change of personality. He went from being an extroverted ruler who devoted his time to receiving foreign ambassadors, planning military campaigns, and managing the affairs of a family with interests in all the palaces of Europe, to one with a taciturn disposition. His fragile health at the age of fifty-four is often cited as a possible cause. He was plagued by pain from gout and hemorrhoids, and before long it seemed that all he was interested in was atoning for his sins, before it was too late."

"So that's it?" I grumbled. "He abdicated because he was sick?"

"No!" Santi was amused. "That wouldn't have stopped the man whom Erasmus had dubbed the 'New Caesar'! No, what happened was that just before this renunciation of his, he experienced the worst possible thing for someone accustomed only to winning—he lost!"

Santi looked down at the table where our food had just been served, and proceeded to deliver a small history lesson. It was as if just by closing his eyes and inhaling espresso fumes, Santi could access some vast internal historical encyclopedia. I recalled that it was Charles V who had first introduced both coffee and cocoa to Europe from the Americas, and wondered if that had anything to do with it.

According to Santi, sometime around 1554 this stubborn and cultivated warrior who'd always had boundless energy and been admired by his people, began to lose his luster. Some historians blame the disappointment of having failed to realize his plan to lead one last Crusade to the Holy Land, like the ones dreamed of by Columbus and Pope Innocent VIII.[2] Still others attributed it to the declining quality of his life, or even his failures to stop the spread of Martin Luther's new ideas, however actively he tried. Barely a day went by that Charles did not bitterly regret failing to kill Luther when he had had the chance. Whatever the reason, from around the age of fifty he began to give the impression that none of that was important to him any longer. The only thing that now preoccupied him now was how he was going to make his transition to the beyond.

Not long before this, there had been other signs that Charles was abandoning the material world. For example, in the winter of 1548, having consolidated his supremacy over Suleiman the Magnificent as well as Pope Clement VII, who had suffered the Sack of Rome by Charles's troops twenty years earlier, Charles's writings began to betray his fear that the wars he'd waged had corrupted his soul. He was terrified by the idea that his sins might deny him eternal life.

On January 18 of that year, moved to action by his deep Catholic belief, he drew up a proclamation consigning all properties to the future Philip II, whom he addressed saying, "contemplation of my past deeds has brought with it certain pains, which cause me now to appreciate the dangers of life. Now, knowing not what fate might befall me, by the grace of God, I hereby make these resolutions and resolve to take what may come to me . . ."[3]

Santi impressed me greatly with his ability to reel these quotes off from memory. He paused for a moment, then continued, "Looking back with the perspective and hindsight of several centuries," he said, "it's easy to surmise that he was carefully planning his own end."

"But wasn't it irresponsible of him to leave his throne to his son when he was still in full possession of his mental faculties?" I asked Santi.

"Not at all! He had suffered a number of setbacks. In the winter of 1553–54, for example, this Catholic Caesar, who had used the bulk of the wealth brought back from Spain's conquistadores in Mexico and Peru to pay for the wars against the Protestants, lost any hope of delivering Germany back to the Catholic Church. Still smarting from the humiliating defeat at Innsbruck at the hands of a Franco-German alliance, his most loyal duke of Alba managed to lose half of his armies during his failed siege of Metz."

"And that's why he decided to die?" I asked, not wanting to get too deep into the details of specific battles.

Santi rubbed his nose, becoming increasingly disconcerted by my interest. "You'd probably better come up to my room. I have something there that will explain everything."

"What is it?"

"It's something that possesses a unique—even mystical—beauty, which you'd appreciate. It gives a good sense of Charles's state of mind then. He devoted as much attention to the commissioning of this as he did to his own last testament, displaying an effort and persistence that reminds me of the amount of trouble that the Egyptian pharaohs took with the design of their tombs. Remember how they adorned the inside walls with maps of the hereafter which became known as the *Pyramid Texts*?"

I cut him off, intrigued. "What kind of artifact is it?"

"It's a painting."

"Oh, my God!" I cried, "Let's go!"

A few moments later we were standing in his room. When I first looked at the painting I was puzzled, and then my puzzlement gave way to euphoria. I had seen it before! It hung only a few steps away from that spectacular bronze, *Carlos V and the Fury* by Leoni. It's basically the first painting you see when you come into the Prado through the Goya Alta Entrance. I'd seen it dozens of times without ever really stopping to look at it, and now I was wondering how I could have been so dumb.

"It's an amazing Titian," said Santi. "Though you can't really tell, there's not much of his own imagination in it. He painted it according to very specific instructions that he got from the emperor. We know, for example, that Charles took such an interest in Titian's progress with this that he would frequently have his ambassador in Rome visit Titian to make

Titian, *The Glory (The Trinity)* (1551–1554). The Prado Museum, Madrid.

sure that he was still alive and working on the commission. The final result wasn't ready until the end of 1554, and it's easy to see that a great deal of thought and planning went into it. It's too bad there's not more about it in the history books."

I took my time and went over the painting thoroughly; it's an enthralling scene. The sky opens over a mostly empty Castilian field, and we can see the Holy Trinity receiving various prophets, patriarchs, and other well-known figures from sixteenth-century Spain. Since Santi seemed to know all about the painting, I kept quiet, not even mentioning how extraordinary I found it.

Santi continued. "The painting was quite complex, and was conceived in stages. Incredibly, none of Charles's people could tell what he was up to until they saw the finished work, standing by his deathbed. Did you know that Charles ended up organizing his own funeral rites and then proceeded to celebrate them before his death, so that he could preside over them?"

"Are you serious?"

He nodded, and proceeded to show me the text from someone who was actually there, the Jesuit Juan de Mariana, who describes how the emperor, standing with the monks who were singing the funeral service, prayed for his own eternal rest as if he had indeed already departed this life, accompanying them as much with his tears as his voice.[4] According to Santi, Charles threw himself into the funereal psychodrama with such zeal that he ended up lying on the ground and passing himself off as dead.

"This painting was part of the ceremony. Have you figured out what it shows? It's paradise throwing itself open to receive the soul of the late emperor. It's the depiction of a miracle."

My eyes must have revealed my amazement.

"Don't bother looking for another meaning, Javier; I know you. Charles in fact gave very specific instructions to his favorite painter, Tiziano Vecellio, to paint him wrapped up in an immaculate white shroud, his face toward the Holy Trinity he had fought so hard to protect from the Protestants. Charles was very clear about this—he wanted no crowns or regalia. He wanted to see himself alone as he faced death."

Unburdened by luggage, I thought, recalling Martín Rico's spare drawing.

"But of course you know that this isn't the first time that Titian painted the emperor, right?" Santi said, oblivious to my musings. "*Carlos V with a Hound, Carlos V at the Battle of Mühlberg*... Titian was already old when he got this commission, older than the emperor! But he gave his all in order once again to paint the patron who had made him rich and admired throughout Europe, the same man who made him count palatine and a knight of the Golden Spur when he discovered his extraordinary abilities and his erudite conversation. Here—look at this."

Santi pointed to a group of figures on the right-hand side of the painting.

"Here's Charles. See him? You can tell him by his chin and long forehead. Titian painted him with his gaze fixed on Jesus. Behind him you can just make out his son and heir to the throne, the future Philip II. There's his late wife, Isabella of Portugal, and his sister, Mary of Hungary. Some say that this is his mother, Joanna of Castile—'Joanna the Mad.'

"Only Charles and his family are shown wrapped in white sheets. In his regal presence we see a number of other figures, from St. Jerome, holding his Bible, to King David, and including Noah and his ark, as well as Moses with the tablets. All of them from the Old Testament. Guess what the painting is called?"

I shrugged.

"Come on—guess! Say something!" he pressed.

"*The End of the World*?" I tried.

He laughed, shaking his head. "Museums have their own crazy ways of naming paintings. Artists didn't used to choose titles for their works, and if they did, the patrons wouldn't think twice about changing them on a whim. This painting has been called, variously, *The Last Judgment, The Glory, Paradise, The Trinity* . . ."

"Hold on!" I cried. "Did you say *The Glory*?"

I shivered as I recalled Mister X's words to Marina: *This is a key to the glory.*

"Yes," replied Santi. "It's pretty obvious—heavenly glory."

"Right. You don't know if Charles V ever said anything about the painting being a . . . *door*, or *threshold*, do you?"

Santi gave me the look my friends usually shot me whenever I started talking about my "interests." He started leafing through a bunch of papers that he had tucked into a notebook. "There's something else I have to show you. There's this document; where is it? Here we are! This is a text about Charles V's death. In it, a Brother José de Sigüenza mentions Titian's painting. He says that when the 'caesar' exiled himself to the Monastery of Yuste to prepare for his death, one of his first requests was to have Titian's *Glory* sent to him there. Sigüenza made a point of emphasizing the emperor's obsession with the painting. Here, let me read this to you. Shortly before he died . . .

> he called for his jewel guard, and when he was come he called for him to bring to him the portrait of his lady, the empress, upon which he gazed for a time.

He then called for the canvas of the Last Judgment. To this painting he gave more of the room and took a great time in observing it, so much that Mathisio the doctor was come and warned the emperor against such long attention, that it should do him ill to suspend for such a time the soul's force which does directly govern the working of the body. After the passage of some more time the emperor was come again to the doctor, saying, "I feel not well." This was on the last of August, at four in the afternoon.[5]

"There's nothing in there about a door," I objected.

"Why do you think Charles spent so much time looking at himself on the other side? It sounds like Sigüenza's saying that Charles went into a kind of trance looking at his Titian. I know I'm pretty open-minded when it comes to esoteric stuff, but it seems obvious that he was looking for inspiration for the journey he was about to take, and that he thought of this painting as his door to the hereafter. I think even the most skeptical person in his situation would probably make an effort to believe."

10

CHARLES AND THE LANCE OF CHRIST

To believe?

Perhaps Santi's advantage was his certainty. Perhaps reason wasn't enough to really understand a work like *The Glory*—maybe you also needed the certainty of faith to uncover its full meaning.

What if I were to take that risk? What if I were to decide to believe?

It was then, in those first days of 1991, that I came to the conclusion that in life, you had to give yourself over to providence, and it was also then that I decided to live by this idea and to take it to its ultimate conclusions.

I wanted to believe that the master class I'd received from Santi Jiménez—so opportune and at just the right moment—had not been mere coincidence, but rather the most recent step of a plan that had begun the day I first encountered my Master of the Prado. And, as ridiculous as it might sound, I believed that this plan was designed to steer me to the secrets behind certain paintings in the Prado.

What if I were just to give myself over to this plan and let it carry me along? What would be so wrong in following the signs I'd received from so many different and unexpected people, not just in Madrid but also in Turégano and at El Escorial? And if I did let this plan lead me, where would I end up?

With all this pressing on my mind, I found myself standing in front of *The Glory* not twelve hours later.

It was true that everything so far had led me here, to this painting. From the mysterious Mister X, with his article on Charles V and the key to the painting, to Marina mediating, and even to Santi himself. At the same time, I couldn't help turning over in my mind the story of how the most powerful man in the world had surrendered his soul to God.

After our conversation, Santi had lent me two fat biographies of Charles V so that I could get an idea of what the emperor's last transit had been like. From these I learned that it was at about two in the morning on the September 21, 1558—St. Matthew's Day—in a little stone house attached to a convent about a mile outside the tiny village of Cuacos in a region of Cáceres known as La Vera, that the great Spanish caesar took his last breath.

This gaunt and restless man had had plenty of time to put all the affairs of state in order, but nonetheless had not dealt with his own last few possessions. The painting that had so occupied him, his library, his collection of clocks and astrolabes—even the chair that had been specially built to prop up his gout-ridden leg—these were all left forgotten at Yuste.

The Glory lay there, dormant, until at last Charles's son Philip II had it brought back to El Escorial along with his father's preserved remains. It was by this accident of history that both the mummified emperor and Titian's door to the hereafter were admitted at the same time to the illustrious final resting-place of Spain's kings.

I could quite easily picture the grimacing emperor, wracked by the pain in his limbs, his leg propped up on great cushions, transfixed by the image of his own likeness gazing at the Holy Trinity. Surrounded by monks from the

Order of St. Jerome, the most powerful man in the world received the last rites through tears, begging the forgiveness of those present and the mercy of God, all the time recalling St. Augustine's vision of the blessed in heaven, much like in Titian's great canvas.

It was with this bittersweet image in mind, balanced between pain and hope, that I arrived at the Prado.

I fished out my student pass as fast as I could, flashed it at the door, and ran up the stairs to the first-floor gallery, to *The Glory,* which had now acquired a new, sublime magic. The painting was nearly twelve feet tall by eight feet wide, and I realized there was no way Charles could have had it in the little stone house where he died—it was simply too big. What made more sense was to suppose that he had prayed before the canvas at the altar of the monastery church of Yuste, directly above where he was to be first buried next to his wife.

Contemplating the great canvas for some time, I slowly began to realize something else. This painting, which for Charles had been a comfort, a reaffirmation of faith as well as a map to the afterlife, also incorporated within its image the hope that his path as emperor would not end with his death. Somehow, through the intercession of the Virgin and St. John—shown back-to-back on the left of the painting—the sanction of the Trinity, and the continuation of his line, he would continue to exercise his influence over the kingdom.

"Titian and Charles of Hapsburg! How these titans complicate things!"

The exclamation yanked me out of my reverie. It had not come from some random tourist, but had been declared from behind me by someone I knew instantly.

"Doctor Fovel! I . . . I didn't expect to see you today!"

After receiving Mister X's warnings, the one person I had no desire to see had found me in a completely different part of the museum from where we usually met. I took a step backward.

"Oh, no?" Fovel cocked a quizzical eyebrow as he unbuttoned his overcoat. "But I'm always here, remember?"

"Yes. Of course."

"And after all, you've planted yourself in front of one of my favorite paintings. You were bound to find me."

"Really?"

"In fact, seeing you there in front of this painting that, sadly, is usually ignored by the vast majority of visitors, I had in mind to tell you something about the relationship between Charles V and Titian. I'm sure it would interest you."

"I don't really think I'll have the time today, Doctor."

As I tried to excuse myself, I looked around furtively for anyone who might have noticed our meeting. The rather spare room—Gallery 24—was almost empty. It lay on the way to other, bigger rooms, and few people stopped. Today was no exception. Even so, the thought that Mister X might be near and might see us had put my guard up. Fovel noticed.

"What's going on, Javier?"

"It's nothing . . ."

Again I got the eyebrow.

"No, truly; it's nothing," I insisted.

"Are you waiting for someone?"

I shook my head. He smiled, pleased with himself.

"In that case, my boy, I'll just take up a few minutes of your time while I tell you what's behind the first painting in the arcanon of the Prado."

"What is the arcanon?" I asked, mystified.

"Ah!" he responded, a little condescendingly. "You see, that's what I like about you, Javier. Your curiosity is always stronger than your will. Would you let me have those few minutes?"

I let out my breath. "Yes, all right. But what is this 'arcanon'?"

"Well, it's a real pity that so few people know about it. It's really a kind of classification of certain works that the Prado has in its collection. It's a relatively recent notion, from around the beginning of the nineteenth century, when you still had a number of wizards, astrologers, and doctors of occult philosophy scattered about the court. A small group of these spent some time secretly studying the history of these paintings to determine which of them could best serve certain supernatural ends, and which not. They referred to this as the Arcane Canon, or arcanon for short."

"And, Doctor, you're saying that *The Glory* was the number one painting in this . . . arcanon?" I asked.

"Yes." Fovel made a face. "But you know—we should probably revise the list, because in fact, this was by no means the first painting with an occult side to it that Charles V commissioned from Titian. Can I show you the painting that started it all? It's not far."

"Well, all right." I agreed reluctantly. "But I can't be too long . . ."

The two of us walked through the next gallery, passing masterpiece after masterpiece: the twin *Adam and Eve* paintings of Rubens and Titian; Tintoretto's *The Foot Washing*; Veronese's magnetic *Christ among the Doctors in the Temple* . . . Finally Fovel paused in the entranceway to Gallery 12, which held Velázquez's solemn royal portraits. But rather than entering the Prado's sanctum sanctorum, he spun on his heel and we found ourselves facing . . .

"*Carlos V at the Battle of Mühlberg*," announced Fovel solemnly.

Frankly, I was disappointed. I'd seen the painting a thousand times. It was widely credited with launching the fashion for equestrian portraits of kings and queens, and what the average person sees in it is anything but occult. There's nothing particularly mysterious about an enormous, almost square canvas—about eleven feet by nine—showing a resolute-looking Charles V in all his glory, sitting astride a Spanish chestnut horse in full armor.[1] The painting's only purpose was as a piece of propaganda to commemorate a date of great importance to the empire: April 24, 1547, when the caesar's forces crushed the Protestant armies at Mühlberg, near Leipzig.

Everything about the portrait signified strength, dominance, and severity—all superficial attributes. It was just the type of painting that couldn't have interested me less.

"There's a secret in this painting? For God's sake, Doctor," I complained, "this has to be one of the most obvious paintings in the whole place! There can't be anything hidden in *that*!"

Fovel shot me an annoyed look. "Are you quite sure? I can convince you in just one minute."

"One minute, then," I said sternly, darting another fruitless glance around us. We were in a crowded part of the museum, and it was difficult to tell if anyone could be watching us.

Oblivious to my worries, Fovel launched into his lesson. "Like all men of power throughout history, Charles V was superstitious, never mind that he was a staunch Catholic. Did you know, for example, that the emperor had an ongo-

Titian, *Carlos V at the Battle of Mühlberg* (1548). The Prado Museum, Madrid.

ing flirtation with the forbidden sciences, like astrology and alchemy? Or that he went out of his way to protect some of the notable occultists of the time, like Agrippa?*

"And, like all powerful men, Charles used various symbols to bolster himself and to feel less alone at the top. And it's a very short distance from the symbolic to the unorthodox."

"Are you saying that he used . . . talismans?"

"Exactly!"

"Well, it doesn't really surprise me, but I don't see any here."

"You need to look more closely. One of them is quite evident—it's hanging from that red cord around his neck. It's a Golden Fleece, symbol of the Order of the Golden Fleece worn by every ruler in that dynastic line, almost their only emblem of power. It symbolizes the ram's fleece sought by Jason and the Argonauts that ended up in the hands of Hercules, Spain's mythical founder.

"The other symbol here has a more hidden meaning but is nonetheless one of the principal elements of the painting, and carries enormous force—the lance."

"In what way?"

"The one weapon that the emperor is holding has its own name. It symbolizes this royal dynasty's most powerful relic, the *Heilige Lanze,* or Spear of Longinus—the Holy Lance itself. A more likely choice for the emperor would

* The Master is referring to Heinrich Cornelius Agrippa of Nettesheim (1486–1535), cabalist, necromancer, and intellectual, who, in his youth, was in service to both Maximilian I and Charles V. Later in his career he would write an influential treatise describing his conviction that everything in the universe was connected through subtle forces that either attracted or repelled power and wealth. He titled this work *De Occulta Philosophia libri III* (Three Books of Occult Philosophy).

have been a scepter, or perhaps a sword, but Titian opted for a lance. *The* lance."

I shook my head. I knew enough about the Spear of Longinus to be amazed at this revelation. Napoleon had coveted it. Hitler was obsessed with it and actually had it in his possession at the beginning of the Second World War. As far as I knew, since the time of Charlemagne it had been considered the one talisman of power without equal, capable of bestowing on whoever possessed it the power to determine the very destiny of the world.

There was just one thing. The lance that I knew about lived in an armored glass case in Vienna's Hofburg Palace, and consisted of a blade of metal split in two to form a double edge almost two feet long. The blades were fastened on either side of an iron nail. The lance in the painting facing us bore no resemblance to that whatsoever.

Fovel noticed my confusion and, as if he'd read my mind, leaned toward me and said in a low voice, "Obviously Titian painted the Spear of Longinus without ever having seen it. For which we can forgive him. At the time Titian painted this portrait, the lance, being a sacred relic, was safely in Nuremberg. I can assure you that the lance in the portrait is intended to symbolize that mythical spear."

I stood there speechless. Fovel went on.

"Think of the symbolism here, Javier. Charles V is holding in his hands the weapon that pierced Christ's side when he was on the cross! This is a sacred object that has inspired every single Christian monarch in Europe. At the same time, it's not all that surprising to see it in his hands. He would have inherited it when he acceded to the throne of the Holy Roman Empire. It was undoubtedly the dynasty's most precious possession. Are you familiar with its story?"

I nodded. I was aware that the sword got its name from

the soldier who thrust it into Christ's side and caused blood and water to flow from him, as was described by John the Evangelist. [2]

According to what I knew of the story, Longinus returned to Calvary on Good Friday to hasten the deaths of the three condemned men in the traditional way, by breaking their legs. The two thieves who had been crucified with Jesus, Gestas and Dismas, were still writhing in agony, and the soldiers with Longinus broke their legs to speed up death by asphyxiation. But as they approached Jesus, Longinus went ahead of his men and did something extraordinary—he stabbed the point of his spear into the side of the last condemned man—Jesus—to see if he was still alive. There was no response, Jesus's head hung down and his body was completely immobile. That is why they decided not to break his legs, thus fulfilling Isaiah's ancient prophecy that not a single bone of the Messiah's body would be broken.

After that point, the story began to take on numerous magical elements. Some chroniclers claimed that on cleaving that sacred flesh with his weapon, Longinus was cured of a long-time eye ailment and converted. Others said that Longinus was not carrying the usual *pilum** that day, but rather the votive lance of Herod Antipas. As a symbol of power, it had been lent to him to enable him to clear a path through the crowds of Jews surrounding the place of execution. This lance had been forged by the Hebrew prophet, Phineas, who imbued it with supernatural powers, and had been carried by Joshua in the Battle of Jericho, when the city's walls were destroyed, and also by the kings David and

---

* The *pilum* was a lance similar to the javelin, typical of Roman legionaries.

Saul. On touching Jesus's body the lance absorbed even more mystical powers and became invincible.

Whatever its actual provenance, Longinus took the spear back with him to his native village, which some say was Zöbingen, in Germany. From there, through little-known circumstances that even historians seem to have ignored, it ended up in the hands of men like Charlemagne and Frederick Barbarossa.[3] The lance's occult power secured Charlemagne almost half a century of victories in battle and stimulated his clairvoyant abilities, enabling him to find the tomb of the apostle James in Spain. With such a glorious history, the spear was treasured for centuries among the most valued royal objects of the Frankish kings: Charlemagne's sword, an orb of gold dating from the twelfth century, and the crown of Charlemagne, originally made of iron, into which was mounted one of the nails from Christ's crucifixion. These objects would certainly have played a role in Charles V's coronation in Aachen in 1520.

But Titian didn't paint this until 1548," I objected.

"That's right. Which is how we know the artist never set eyes on the actual lance. In all likelihood, once the coronation was over, it was returned to safekeeping in Nuremberg. But it is my considered opinion that Charles gave explicit instructions to Titian to include it in the portrait. And to show him gripping it very firmly, of course."

"Very firmly? Why is that important?"

"Well, according to legend, Charlemagne was returning home from one of his campaigns in Saxony when he was thrown by his horse. A celestial sign—a comet—had startled him. The precious talisman—the lance—fell to the ground, and at that very moment, on a beam in the cathedral at Aachen, the word 'Princeps' was mysteriously erased from the inscription 'Karolus Princeps.' It was a terrible and un-mistakable portent. Charlemagne died soon after.

"Something quite similar happened to Barbarossa years later after he dropped the lance while crossing a river in Tur-key, then the Ottoman Empire. So I imagine that the heir to both of these figures would take care to be shown holding the lance quite firmly, exactly as you see in the portrait."

I frowned. "So the painting was his own idea? The em-peror's?"

Fovel seemed to relish my question. His eyes sparkled, and he took his time answering, enjoying my attention. "We-e-ell, now that's a very interesting question, Javier. In that winter of 1548, Titian was summoned to Augsburg to receive the commission to paint a portrait of Charles. Titian was over seventy, and many people worried for his health, but the fact was that the emperor's state was even worse. He'd defeated the German Protestant armies at Mühlberg, sure, but how much longer could he live?

"We know that Charles tried several times to engage John Dee, the illustrious English magician I mentioned be-fore, as his personal astrologer. Dee was also a renowned ex-pert on talismans, and Charles needed to know how long the stars said he had left on this earth. In those days Dee was traveling from court to court, seeking his fortune, and yet it's generally thought that the two never met, though we can't be sure. Six years later, in London, Dee would cast a horoscope for Charles's son Philip II. Perhaps Dee or one of his admirers—like Juan de Herrera, who would later man-age the building of El Escorial for Philip II—reminded Charles how being shown in a portrait with such a powerful symbol could secure him a longer life."

My mind, once again, was spinning. "Doctor, I'm amazed at how you've managed to connect everything again!"

"The thing is, Javier, it's not me who's doing the connecting. These connections are there to be seen if you can look at history in a particular way."

I stood there for a moment turning Fovel's words over in my head. I'd almost forgotten that I had come here this time because of Mister X, who had warned me of terrible consequences should I continue to seek out these lessons from the man who was standing right beside me!

But why was that? Up until now, everything that Fovel had taught me had been nothing short of fascinating. He was instructing me in a novel way of looking at our past, that paid more attention to the state of mind and beliefs of its protagonists than just to battles and documents, which can be manipulated later. What harm could there be in such a lesson, and why was my attention to this strand of history apparently so irritating to Mister X?

I decided to set aside that disturbing thought as well as I possibly could. Excited by Fovel's latest revelations, I had another question for him. I had resolved to avoid looking at my watch for the rest of the time I was in the museum.

"Tell me, Doctor, do you know of any other paintings that show talismans of power like this one?"

"Of course! There's one that you will really like, which was painted after Charles's death, during the time of Philip II. Believe me, this one is quite an intellectual challenge. Another one. Are you ready to see it?"

11

The Prado's Holy Grail

Fovel and I retraced our steps, passing once again in front of *The Glory,* and continued down the rotunda stairway to the first floor hallway. Our destination, Fovel told me, was a small, vaulted, cream-colored gallery nearby, which housed another of the principal works in the arcanon: Juan de Juanes's version of *The Last Supper.*

"Welcome to the 'Gallery of the Grail'!" Fovel announced as we entered, his voice booming uncharacteristically around the enclosed space, which was at that moment empty.

Fovel positioned me directly in front of the painting by Juanes. It took me a moment to adjust to it, for while it was beautifully detailed, with vivid colors and luminous figures, after the colossal equestrian portrait we had just seen, this one looked almost ridiculously small.

"Take a good look," began Fovel. "Like most of the pieces in this gallery, this was painted for the Church of St. Stephen in Valencia. In fact, it was placed over the tabernacle, where they would store the consecrated bread and wine after Mass. Juanes painted it during the reign of Philip II, and it depicts Jesus surrounded by the twelve apostles as he institutes the sacrament of the Eucharist. Obviously the composition calls to mind Leonardo's enormous *Last Supper,* painted six decades earlier in Milan. Juanes had seen the copy of it that hangs in Valencia Cathedral, though there are some notable differences between the two. In this version, all of the apostles have a halo above their heads inscribed with their name, except for Judas Iscariot. There is bread and wine on the table, and the platter is empty. The sacred host shines in the hands of the Messiah and most important, the Grail sits at the center of the entire composition."

"Why do you say 'most important'?"

"Because, Javier, the chalice that Juanes painted actually exists. It's a cup made of agate, encrusted with gold, emeralds and pearls, which since the Middle Ages has been in Valencia Cathedral, and which many believe to be the actual Holy Grail that Christ used at the Last Supper."

"That's kind of far-fetched," I remarked.

"Don't be too sure," Fovel replied. "Of all the holy grails today in Europe that claim to be the real one—and there are quite a few[1]—this is the only one with a possible ring of authenticity to it."

"You believe in the Holy Grail?" I asked.

"It's not just a question of faith. Some respected archeologists have examined it, and verified at least that it is indeed an opulent stone cup most likely made in a workshop in the Middle East, perhaps Egypt or Palestine, and they can date it back to the first century before Christ.[2] In those days vessels like that were considered extremely valuable, and it's easy to imagine a rich Jew of the time like Joseph of Arimathea having an item like that among his finest possessions."

"Yes, but even assuming that's true, it doesn't mean that this is the exact cup that was used at the Last Supper," I objected. "That's a big leap. And anyway, what's it doing in Valencia? Shouldn't an object like that be in Israel?"

Of course Fovel was ready for me. "Well, Javier, there's an answer to that, and it's quite interesting."

"I'm all ears," I said.

Juan de Juanes, *The Last Supper* (1562). The Prado Museum, Madrid.

"Very well. The chalice that Juanes painted was in Rome for almost three centuries, before it ever arrived in Spain. Of course, to accept that you have to suppose that after the crucifixion, St. Peter took the cup with him back to what was then the capital of the empire, and that once there, it was passed down through the leaders of the Christian faith like a kind of papal chalice. To me, this makes much more sense than the idea that so many medieval French and Saxon writers from the twelfth century would have us believe, that immediately upon the Messiah's death, Joseph of Arimathea took the cup to Britain. That's an absurd notion! Why would someone like him travel to such a remote and unimportant place as the British Isles were in those days? And how is it that there is not one single shred of documentary evidence to support that idea?"

"But still, there were a lot of pretty improbable journeys in the beginnings of Christianity, like the apostle St. James traveling to Spain, for example. Myths like that."

"I am not talking about any myth!" Fovel's voice resounded through the gallery. "It has been established that there was a papal chalice in Rome that was passed down from pope to pope during the first centuries of our age."

"Well then, how did it come to be in Spain?"

"I'll explain. I'm sure you're aware that several of the Roman emperors persecuted Christians quite harshly?"

I nodded.

"Well, between the years 257 and 260, the empire under Valerian launched a new campaign of systematic murder and looting of Christians. They also searched the tombs of sect members for valuables. And here comes the interesting part. At that time, the guardian of the papal chalice was Pope Sixtus II. Before he was beheaded, he entrusted what was probably the church's only treasure to his administrator

174

Lorenzo, a young deacon from Huesca, in Hispania, who couldn't think of a better hiding place for it than with his distant relatives. He sent the cup to its hiding place in the care of some legionaries from the hills around his native village who had been converted to the faith."

"Is there any proof of that?"

The Master's eyes shone. "There is, indeed! In fact, much more proof than for the complete fabrication about the Holy Grail of Arthur and Merlin, which didn't appear until a thousand years later, or that Joseph of Arimathea took it to Britain! There's more, too. Just days after packing the chalice off to Spain, Lorenzo was tortured to death on a red-hot iron grill over a slow fire. This was in the year 258. Eighty years later, on the very spot in Rome where he was buried, Pope Damasus I had the Basilica of St. Lawrence outside the Walls built. In the original fourth-century church there was a fresco showing a cup in a frame with two handles being handed to a kneeling soldier by St. Lawrence. Sadly, the image was destroyed in the allied bombings of Rome during World War II, but the fresco has plenty of historical documentation."

"And that's the same cup as this one?" I asked, pointing to the painting by Juanes. "You're positive?"

"That's not all," replied Fovel, completely ignoring my question. "Today, in that very same tomb of St. Lawrence, or Lorenzo, you can also find the bones of St. Stephen! Now tell me, do you remember which church in Valencia Juanes painted this *Last Supper* for? You can look at the card, but I'm happy to repeat—it was the church of St. Stephen! And these other panels by Juanes all around us here, do you know what they are supposed to represent? The life of St. Stephen! All of these panels, including the *Last Supper*, originally were joined to form one great tableau. This is not coincidence. I believe that Juanes knew all about the relic he was painting and where it came from."

"Okay, hold on," I said. "Let's assume for a moment that he did know all that, and that he painted for this altarpiece all these scenes of St. Stephen and this precious object that his . . . *tombmate* sent to Spain. But we still haven't established how the papal cup got to Valencia."

Fovel didn't hesitate. "That's quite simple to explain. In 712, one year after the Moslem invasion of the Iberian Peninsula, the bishop of Huesca had the relic taken to be hid in various places in the Pyrenees, to ensure that it would not be profaned. Its first hiding place was in a cave in Yebra; later, he had it moved to the monastery at San Pedro de Siresa. Eventually, it was moved again to a place near Santa María de Sasabe. Finally, it was taken to the monastery at San Juan de la Peña, where it remained for two and a half centuries. At each of those stops along the way, a church was built and dedicated to St. Peter, to commemorate the first pope to officiate with the papal chalice.

"Then in 1410, upon the death of Martin, king of Aragon—'Martin the Humane'—as the last Cathars were being slaughtered by the Templars, the cup traveled to Zaragoza and thereafter to Valencia, where it remains to this day. And don't imagine the church itself has any doubts about this—John Paul II actually said Mass using this chalice.[3] None of this is made up, Javier. There are documents verifying every step that this relic has taken though history, something that you cannot say for the Shroud of Turin, for example."

"That brings us back to this painting," I said, "in which Juan de Juanes immortalized the chalice in the sixteenth century."

"But we are still left with an unsolved mystery," added Fovel with one of his mischievous grins. "Long before he

Juan de Juanes, *Christ with the Eucharist* (ca. 1545–1550). The Prado Museum, Madrid. Exposed.

Juan de Juanes, *Christ with the Eucharist* (ca. 1545–1550). The Prado Museum, Madrid. Not exposed.

Juan de Juanes, *Christ with the Eucharist* (ca. 1560–1570). The Fine Arts Museum, Valencia.

Holy Grail (first century BCE). Cathedral, Valencia.

painted *The Last Supper,* Juan de Juanes was already well known for his splendid series of portraits of Christ with the Eucharist. These rich devotional images, which were made on gold leaf, show Jesus holding up the sacrament in his right hand, while his left hand holds the chalice, very much like this one here."

Fovel indicated one of these hanging near us in the gallery. "This was the first one of this series, from about 1545—he would have been only about twenty—and the Grail he paints here is just an ordinary cup."

I took a closer look at it.

"Then, for whatever reason, he painted several more versions in which he replaced the plain cup with the 'real' agate chalice. You get the impression that Juanes was obsessed with this image. It's as if someone had told him that the actual cup used at the last supper was in Valencia, not far from Fuente la Higuera, his home village, and also made him go see the relics of the Holy Face that were so venerated in Alicante and Valencia, and pushed him to keep copying that face compulsively."[4]

"Strange! So you're saying that Juan de Juanes became a kind of self-made expert on relics, especially the Grail?"

"Yes," replied Fovel, "though he didn't become an expert overnight. It took years. There are two of his paintings of Christ in the Museo de Bellas Artes in Valencia, which they refer to as the 'blond one' and the 'dark one' because of their different hair color, and the Grail he paints in these is still rough, as if he'd painted it from memory, or a description. But in the later versions, like the ones celebrated in Valencia Cathedral, which he would have painted between 1570 and 1579, the chalice is beautifully detailed."

"So he had a chance to study it."

"Or he held it in his hands! What we do know for certain

is that Juanes was considered as learned as he was pious. Some believe that he even traveled to Italy to familiarize himself with the magnificent work of Leonardo and Raphael, which he assimilated like few others of the time. It would have been around that time that he decided to change his name from Vicente Juan Masip, which was very close to his father's name, Vicente Masip, who was also a painter. He settled on the more Latinized Juan de Juanes, the name with which he earned his fame."

"Did he leave anything he might have written about the Grail?"

"Not that we know of. I've studied his life as much as the scant documentation allows, and the main thing worth mentioning is that, like Raphael Sanzio, Juanes had an unusual approach to painting."

"In what way?"

"Well, I've just given you a clue," he flashed me a malicious smile. "Some came to call him the 'Second Raphael,' which I don't think was just because of the similarity of their styles. The thing is, before beginning a painting, Juanes would spend days in fasting and prayer, preparing his soul. He would tremble before starting any piece of work that he considered sacred, and on the day that he was to begin a painting, he went to early Mass and took communion. It's little surprise, then, that some critics have said that his work—particularly the paintings of Christ—'are of a beauty so divine that they belie a human provenance.'[5] Or that these paintings 'look as if they had not so much been painted with the hand as with the spirit,'[6] since it could be said that the Lord guided his hand, and the most beauteous of men chose [Juanes] to paint him, much as Alexander chose Apelles of Kos.' "[7]

"What does all that mean?" I asked Fovel.

"That the art looks as if it was inspired by heaven itself. We do know, for example, that often, while he was painting, certain . . . *things* would happen."

"What kind of *things* do you mean?" This was sounding particularly weird.

"Well, there was a lot of talk about what happened while he was painting his majestic *Coronation of the Virgin,* which was also called the *Immaculate Conception*—or *Tota Pulchra*—for the Jesuit church in Valencia. No matter how you look at it, that is not a normal painting."

"Please get to the point, Doctor," I insisted impatiently.

"It's perfectly simple. This enormous painting, almost ten feet high, was commissioned by Father Martin Alberro, a Jesuit from the Basque country who was headed for the seminary of San Pablo in Valencia and who, by the way, was de Juanes's confessor. The Virgin had appeared to Father Alberrro in an ecstasy—a lady shod with the moon, clothed with the Sun, and crowned with stars, like the Virgin of the Apocalypse of St. John, bathed in splendors—and had personally given him instructions on the kind of portrait he was to paint. Alberro in turn passed these instructions on to Juanes. It was an odd request; according to these instructions, the painting was to have neither perspective nor any kind of geometry but was to incorporate in some very visible position the most important mystical names for the Virgin, like *Civitas Dei, Stella Maris, Speculum sine macula,* or *Porta Coeli.*"

"The Door to Heaven," I muttered.

"And in fact, the painting became exactly that."

"What do you mean?"

"The story is that as Juanes was about to finish the work, he had an accident that nearly cost him his life. He had climbed up onto some scaffolding to examine the upper

Juan de Juanes, *The Immaculate Conception* (ca. 1568). Iglesia de la Compañía, Valencia.

part of the painting when it gave way. It was then that the miracle occurred: The Virgin that he had just finished painting extended her arm from the canvas and caught him in the air, setting him gently on the ground."[8]

"That's a great story," I admitted.

"Like all these stories, there's a grain of truth in it. For Juan de Juanes, his paintings were like living beings who could ease the passage through to the spiritual world. They were doors, in other words. And it was probably because they enabled whoever possessed them to transcend the limits of the material world that his works were so admired and copied."

"That's the same thing they used to say about Fra Angelico's work," I noted.

"Exactly. Separated by a century, both of these men believed that their art served a transcendent purpose. And for both of them, their art was often the result of their visions. So it's not entirely irrational to think that they might have sought to have their paintings recreate these types of experiences for their viewers. Interesting, no?"

"It's more than that!" I exclaimed. "It's a revelation!"

For the first time since I'd known him, Fovel actually laughed. "Yes! I couldn't have put it better myself! Truly a revelation!"

12

MISTER X

That afternoon, I left the Prado only an hour before it closed. Somehow I had once again completely lost all sense of time. I'd been in the museum for four hours! In spite of all my precautions, even the fear of encountering the mysterious spy from El Escorial had not been enough to keep me out of the embrace of those galleries.

The winter night had fallen unsparingly over Madrid, turning the rather formal area around the Villanueva Building, the Plaza de Neptuno, and the Ritz into a dizzy whirl of lighted windows and gaunt, glowing streetlights. It was just after seven o'clock by my watch. I would have to hurry if I still wanted to catch Marina at her Aunt Esther's to see how she'd fared there after Mister X's visit.

The fastest way there—barring a taxi—was across Retiro Park, and required walking the entire breadth of Madrid's great urban forest before coming out at Avenida Menéndez Pelayo. Crossing the park meant following the meandering paths that snaked through the trees, but it was early and not too cold, and the idea of the walk appealed to me more than the two changes I'd have to make on the Metro to get to the Ibiza station.

I set off calmly at a good pace, letting myself drift along, my hands stuffed down into the pockets of my parka and my scarf covering my mouth and ears. My head was a whirl of thoughts and feelings, so I took several deep breaths of the cold park air and tried to think where all of this was leading me. I wanted to take advantage of the walk to come to a decision about Marina, and whether or not I should include her in this game anymore, or even continue in it myself. Unfortunately, like a fool, rather than getting down to making practical decisions I avoided them. Instead, I mused over this new way of looking at art that I was learning from the Master, and once again I ignored the human side of my plight.

But the whole situation did have its funny side. Thanks to a total stranger, I'd started to look at some of the paintings in the Prado almost as if they were artifacts from another planet. I now thought of them as tools built by extremely sensitive minds not at all concerned with achieving mere aesthetic pleasure. I'd begun to convince myself that the larger purpose behind these paintings—where their true meaning lay—had always been to keep open certain portals to the "other world." It was as if the art was simply keeping alive its original mystical mission dating back to the cave paintings in northern Spain some forty thousand years before. If Fovel was right, this was a secret that only those painters had known, perhaps along with some of their patrons. And now me.

By that time I was some distance from the museum, standing in the dark on the frozen park grounds, and the idea suddenly seemed little short of ridiculous—Raphael, Titian, and Juan de Juanes opening windows to another world with their paintbrushes! I was astonished that only a few minutes earlier, Fovel had managed to make the whole theory seem convincing, even conclusive.

And why had the Master decided to reveal everything to this particular journalism student? I wasn't an expert in art,

or even the type who sets up an easel in front of an old master's paintings and copies it patiently, painstakingly. I wasn't
part of that world, and I wasn't sure I really belonged to any
world.

"Mr. Sierra?"

I heard a distant panting from some way behind me that
seemed to come from the bottom of the hill leading up to
the statues. It sounded as if someone was trying to catch up
with me.

"Mr. Sierra?" the voice repeated.

My little reverie shattered into a thousand pieces.

"Excuse me, sir, it is you, isn't it? Please wait!"

For some reason the fact that an unknown voice was call-
ing my name from the gloomy depths of Retiro Park was not
as surprising to me as the fact that it called me sir.

"Please, I must speak with you!"

Before I could decide to run, the man reached me,
clouds of breath billowing from his nose and mouth. We
were in front of the statue of Doña Urraca. The man seemed
to have appeared from nowhere, and I cursed myself for not
having taken to my heels, which, frankly, would not have
been difficult—he was dragging one leg slightly when he
walked, and wouldn't have caught me.

"Damn! I knew I'd find you here, Mr. Sierra," he said,
triumphantly, his breathing ragged. And then without waiting for me to reply, he added, "You people always fall!"

"What did you say?" I asked.

"Your type always falls for it! Like flies in honey!" he exclaimed, giving me an unexpected and rather dismissive
clap on the back. "You can't help it!" he said chuckling in a
gloating kind of way. "It's your curiosity—it gets you every
time!"

He seemed to be amusing himself. Because of the dark, I

couldn't get a good look at his face, but I would have sworn that he was grinning from ear to ear. From what I could tell, he had a coarse look to him, with thinning hair and pale skin. There was something about him that seemed familiar, as if I'd seen him before, but taking in his Burberry raincoat, impeccable dark suit, and matching tie, I doubted it. He looked like a respectable type, and apart from some professors and some colleagues at the magazine, I didn't hang out with people who wore ties.

"Excuse me!" he said, smiling. "How rude of me! I haven't introduced myself." He stuck his newspaper under his left arm and extended his right. "My name is Julian de Prada, I'm an inspector."

"Police?" I felt uneasy.

"Something like that. I belong to a unit charged with protecting Spain's historic art and treasures."

I looked at him suspiciously.

"Really? And what was it that you found so funny? Something about flies?"

"Let me explain. We've been trying for years to capture the man that you've been talking to for the past few weeks. He's quite elusive, and only shows himself occasionally. So, without your knowing it, we've been using you as bait to try and catch him." He gave an awkward chuckle.

I was shocked at his reference to Fovel.

"What's he done?" I asked.

"It's more a case of what *hasn't* he done. He used to work for the Royal Palace, many years ago, doing work similar to mine. He inventoried and bought works of art for the collection. Since then, though, he's been freelance, working behind our backs, and collecting a number of works of art. We're not sure how big his collection is or what he plans to do with it. He's always refused to tell us anything.

"Just before Christmas I found out that he'd been in touch with you. First, I saw you together in the museum." He chuckled again. "You looked as if you were having a good time! Then I got confirmation that you were working together when we saw the application from the library at El Escorial for access to *The New Apocalypse*. It's one of the doctor's weaknesses, you know—he's always going on about it."

"So you say you saw me with him?"

"Just before Christmas. Don't bother denying it—you were talking to him in front of *The Pearl*, remember?"

Suddenly it came to me why I'd thought de Prada looked familiar to me. He was the reason the Master had suddenly taken off at our first meeting! He must have been among the group of tourists that appeared suddenly in the galley of Italian art and made Fovel so nervous. But why?

"So it was you who was at the El Escorial library looking at the Amadeo book the week before we went, right?"

De Prada smiled his assent in a flash of white teeth.

"And it was you who went to see Marina yesterday to tell me to stay away from Fovel!"

He nodded.

"I didn't have your address," he replied, "only hers. I had checked the visitors' book at El Escorial and seen it there. I knew your movements in the museum, knew that Fovel's path crossed yours a number of times, but I didn't otherwise know where the hell to find you. Luckily—as I suspected—it was pretty easy to get you to come here." He sounded very pleased with himself.

"Easy?" I didn't like that.

"Oh, yes," he said, pleased as could be. "One of the doctor's weak points is that he always attracts the same type of accomplice. Young. Curious. Malleable." He savored this last word. "After a couple of meetings, he always brings them to

187

The Glory. It never fails!" He clapped his hands together against the cold as more steam escaped from his nose. "What it boils down to is that the old man is fascinated by any painting remotely connected to both death and the *Austrias*," De Prada said, using a term often employed in referring to the Habsburg kings of Spain. "So, once I understood his pattern, all I needed to do was get you interested in that Titian painting so that you'd end up going to look at it on one of your visits, and then wait for the doctor to appear, and— *bang!*"

"*Bang?*" I stared at him.

He laughed quietly. "You don't realize it, but I had everything ready today to grab him. It's a shame he didn't show."

I stood there, stunned.

Then de Prada and I left the statues and made our way toward the edge of the pond, under the bare winter skeletons of the chestnut and walnut trees. At that hour, all the pleasure boats were moored and the only other people on the path that circled the pond were one couple and three people in sweats, jogging.

I turned back to face de Prada, expecting him to continue, to say something that would explain why we had not seen each other in front of *The Glory.*

"It was clever of you to leave the pages about Charles V's mummy with Marina." I said quietly.

"Bah!" he said with a self-satisfied smile. "I could have used anything from that period. Those crazy *Austrias* believed that paintings were alive!"

"You sound as if that bothers you," I remarked.

"Look . . . frankly, it does. I mean, think about it! Charles V dies contemplating *The Glory*, then his son and successor, the great Philip II, creator of El Escorial, dies in his bedchamber surrounded by paintings that he believed were able to sense his pain, as if they were living beings, super-natural beings!"[1]

"You're not the first person to tell me something like that," I told him, remembering the old monk Juan Luis at El Escorial.

"See? Sadly, that kind of madness was pretty widespread back then. It took hold of the people, too—many more of them caught the fever than you'd ever think!"

"Why do you call it a fever?"

"Ideas can be like a virus, Mr. Sierra. That's why I'm here—to prevent another epidemic. Were you aware that soon after Philip II died, both clerics and laypeople all across Spain claimed to have seen the king's soul leave purgatory and enter the kingdom of heaven?"

"Well—" I began.

"Well, they did!" de Prada interrupted me. "Some, like the Carmelite monk Pedro de la Madre de Dios claimed that something similar happened eight days after the king died. Years later there were others, like my namesake, Brother Julian de Alcalá, who claimed that they witnessed two very strange-looking, colored clouds fusing together near Paracuellos del Jarama exactly at the moment that the king ascended to heaven."

"Wow—like UFOs," I remarked drily.

"Don't be clever, young man! Brother Julian's vision was enormously famous. It appears in several texts of the time and was thoroughly documented. It happened at the end of September 1603, and there was so much talk about it that Murillo ended up doing a canvas of it for the Convent of San Francisco in Seville. You wouldn't believe how much it borrows from *The Glory*! There is a column of fire on the ground representing purgatory, and in an opening above, in the sky, the Virgin sits awaiting the monarch. Not only did our kings have these extravagant beliefs that went well beyond their Catholic faith, they also created a whole supernatural artistic style which, believe me, is not a good thing for modern man."

De Prada paused in his harangue to fish out a cigarette from the pocket of his trench coat and light up the middle of Retiro Park. Then I made an attempt to bring our little encounter to a close. Something about his line of argument had struck me as strange. For an inspector in an official role, he seemed to be taking this a little far. Was that really what he was? How could I check? Either way, his mood swings—bitter one minute and grandiose the next—were beginning to make me nervous.

I had to set the stage for my exit, without his getting suspicious. "So, you have a pretty good idea of what Fovel likes, right?"

"Good enough. He's a charlatan from another era. And you're not that different. He's obsessed with this stuff."

I pretended not to hear the insult, but he pressed it.

"Don't take offense now," he said, smiling again. "But the twentieth century's almost over, you know? We've put a man on the moon. We have cable TV now. The Concorde can get us from Paris to New York in less than four hours! What sense is there in going back to things like mystics, or miracles, or the dead reappearing? Who needs a saint who can be in two places at once when physics is on the verge of discovering how to transport particles from one part of the universe to another? Why should you swallow tales of witches flying around on broomsticks when we have drugs that can give you that same sensation?"

"Ahh!" Suddenly I thought I understood what was behind our discussion. "You're saying all this because of my magazine, aren't you? That's why you're trying to convince

Bartolomé Esteban Murillo, *Fray Julián of Alcalá's Vision of the Ascension of the Soul of King Philip II of Spain* (ca. 1645–1648). The Sterling and Francine Clark Art Institute, Williamstown, Massachusetts.

me. You think I'll publish what Fovel has been telling me and it bothers you."

Immediately, de Prada became very serious.

"Look, son, you're still a young man with promise. You still have a chance to give up this foolishness before it's too late. Focus on your career. Get your degree. And keep your nose out of things that don't concern you, or—"

"Or what?" I pressed him, lifting my gaze from the pond and looking right at him.

"Or you'll ruin your future. Listen carefully. The things the doctor is telling you he's told before to lots of other guys like you, and believe me when I tell you that every one of them eventually went crazy."

De Prada's words didn't sound so much like a threat, more like a weird but sincere obsession.

"What I still don't get is why you're so concerned about the kinds of things Doctor Fovel could be telling me. They're very esoteric; they wouldn't interest most people."

"Oh—don't get me wrong." He took a deep drag on his cigarette. "I don't care about what Fovel is saying to you. I care about what you'll repeat. Sooner or later, just like you said, you'll write something about the things he's told you. You'll do it because you think it's interesting, or original, not realizing that if you do that you'll be messing with a system that has been working just fine for hundreds of years! That's what I'm trying to avoid. I'm concerned that the seed of Fovel's ideas will take hold in this real world that has taken so much for us to build. We haven't managed to achieve two hundred years of reason and all the triumphs of science so that you and people like you can come along and get other people interested once again in the invisible and the ineffable. In things that can't be weighed or measured! Can you imagine a Prado filled with people who want to use those paintings to enter some sort of a trance? Do you really want to transform the temple of Spanish culture into a mecca for half the nutcases on the planet? Come on! Grow up, for God's sake!"

I sighed. "That's really not likely to happen, though, is it?"

He was having none of it. "Don't you believe it! You weren't around in the seventies, were you? There was a whole movement then inspired by the book *The Morning of the Magicians,* which later became the New Age movement, and grew through articles in magazines, essays, and programs on TV and radio, and actually managed to seduce a lot of the European intelligentsia. These people wrote about conspiracies, parallel universes, synchronicity, miracles, lost libraries, and remote, forgotten technologies, and tried to rewrite history using these ideas. They reinterpreted the Second World War through an occultist lens, claiming that Hitler and Churchill were engaged in much more than just a military conflict, that this was in fact a mythical battle, involving magicians, astrologers, and mystics of all kinds, just like in the Middle Ages, and that the entire spiritual future of the West was at stake. Imagine! They even claimed that all of these 'disciplines' were the echoes of a prehistoric science that we lost in some great cataclysm and have since misinterpreted. They believed that alchemy contains some deep knowledge of atoms, and that astrology incorporates knowledge of the structure of the universe! They chased one crazy idea after another. And you know what? Those ideas actually took hold in the culture, so much so that, without even knowing it, you're just another product of that lunatic way of thinking, which, thank God, was mostly beaten. Until now."

The turn that the conversation had taken had made me even more suspicious.

"What did you say your job was?" I asked him.

"Inspector of patrimony," he replied.

"You seem more like a priest," I said.

He chuckled quietly to himself. "I get it; you're still young, and of course it suits you to attack anything remotely connected to institutions or authority. You don't have to believe a word of what I've just told you, but you should. Don't be drawn by the dark side, son. Stay away from Fovel . . . or you'll be sorry."

"Is that a threat?"

"Take it however you want."

"Then I'll just take it as your second slipup of the day."

An acid smile unrolled slowly across his face. "What are you talking about?"

"Well," I hesitated, "I wasn't going to say anything, but Fovel, who you say you've been pursuing so diligently, was talking to me this afternoon at the museum. The fact that you missed that says a lot about your abilities."

The tiniest glimmer of bewilderment appeared in his eyes.

"Uh . . . where was this? Where were you?"

"Right in front of *The Glory*, as you thought."

"That's impossible!"

"And you know something else?"

De Prada didn't blink.

"Here's my reply to you and your threat: I'm going to keep on meeting with him, whatever you think it's going to do to your world system. You can't arrest me for that, can you?"

"No, I can't," he replied, his face taking on a sour expression. "But be very careful that you don't become his accomplice, or our next meeting won't be so friendly. That's all I'm going to say."

13

———

THE GARDEN OF EARTHLY DELIGHTS

It took two whole days to rid my mouth of the bitter taste left by my encounter with Julian de Prada. It wasn't until then that I realized what had caused him to approach me: fear. Fear that some dumb, ignorant kid like me would come along and mess up some order of things I hadn't even begun to fathom. In other words, fear that I would use my new journalistic tools—which I had been sharpening through my studies—to reveal something uncomfortable for him.

But fear also spreads easily and is corrosive, eating away at everything it touches, which is what happened to me. Suddenly, I was no longer concerned with myself or my predicament, but was seized by an increasing anxiety about Marina. My encounter with Mister X made me realize that I needed to make a decision and soon. Since I'd involved her in this whole adventure I had spent more time with her than ever before. We were accomplices now, and much better friends, and I sensed that this friendship was on the edge of becoming something more. I felt as if I could almost say that I loved her, and because of this, her safety was becoming an obsession for me. I recalled how Marina had asked me to drop all of this, and suddenly I couldn't get the terror in her voice out of my head.

I wondered what I should do. How could I tell her that her scary visitor had accosted me coming out of the Prado and threatened me as well? Would she agree to let me continue my investigations on my own for a while, keeping her out of it? Wouldn't that dampen our relationship? Damn! If on the one hand I took de Prada's threats seriously and followed his advice, I'd lose Fovel, though I might end up getting to keep Marina. On the other hand, given my pattern, I'd probably keep going. But I'd risk the terrible price of having my heart broken.

Luckily, nothing much out of the ordinary happened during the next forty-eight hours, or at least that's how it seemed to me. I visited Marina twice at her Aunt Esther's house, and finally managed to convince her and her sister that they had nothing to fear. Needless to say, I didn't tell them that I'd actually met Mister X nor that his attention was now firmly focused on me.

I also took advantage of the time to catch up with both my studies and the magazine, as well as to prepare for my next visit to the museum. The calm of those days helped me to reach a decision. In spite of de Prada's threats and Marina's fear, I would keep meeting the Master and try to get to the bottom of things, though I knew I'd be constantly on the lookout for Mister X's shadow. Luckily, I didn't see it, and this absence of his seemed to awaken a strength in me that I didn't realize I had. For the first time I began to realize that I could be the one to have the final word in this story, including what lessons to receive and what paintings to consider.

I resolved, too, that from then on I would record everything that happened, and each revelation. What I was unwilling to see was that de Prada had in effect set my course a second time. Thanks to what he'd told me in Retiro Park, I now wanted to find out everything I could about Philip II. Now it was a need. I had a hunch that this figure—or some of the six hundred or so portraits of him—held the key to just what kind of war I had enlisted in.

And there in the half-light of my desk, in Room C33 of Chaminade Residence Hall, I began to work toward my new goal.

It was not difficult to find a number of accounts of Philip's death, which took place on September 13, 1598, in the royal bedchamber in the Monastery of San Lorenzo at El Escorial. They were all based on the description written by Brother José de Sigüenza, whom I knew from a similar description of his on the last hours of Charles V. Sigüenza was a key figure of his time, keeper of the royal reliquary where the monarchy stored the relics of its saints. He was in effect the first of El Escorial's house historians.

As a result, all of the accounts said much the same thing. At the age of seventy-one, in the waning days of June 1598, with an eye to his failing health—his abdomen and extremities were swollen and he was plagued with pain, gout, and an insatiable thirst—Philip decided to take his leave of the Royal Palace in Madrid and install himself within the enormous palace complex he had built to serve as his tomb. Philip's journey from the palace in Madrid to El Escorial would have been horrific. It took the king and his retinue six whole days to travel a mere thirty-five miles. They journeyed beneath a blazing sun, stopping strategically along the way in houses belonging to the crown, with the most powerful man in the world constantly at the edge of consciousness. The uric acid in his system had reached such levels that it took over not only his feet but also his arms and hands. His entire body felt like raw flesh. The merest brush of his clothing was an agony, he could not walk, and it cost him everything he had simply to remain seated in his coach. The nauseating odors that rose from his many suppurating open sores were harbingers of grim things to come.

As soon as he reached El Escorial, Philip locked himself away in the modest room in the southernmost part of the monastery that he himself had designed. Were it not for the four-poster bed that filled it almost completely, the tiny space would have seemed like a cell to almost anyone else. But not to the king. The room lay in a privileged part of the monastery, directly above the royal mausoleum where he was to be interred, and through a small window opening he had installed on his left, he could see the high altar and follow the Mass without getting up from his bed. A set of double doors opened onto a bright and spacious corridor, adorned by a rustic frieze of Talavera tiles, where one could find his various doctors, confessors, and valets. His meager bedchamber gave onto another equally small room in which he kept his writing desk handy, along with a small library of no more than forty volumes.

On September 1, 1598, less than a month after installing himself in his so-called factory of God, Philip II signed his last official document as monarch and received the last rites. Paralyzed now by pain, wracked by ever-mounting fevers, and unable to speak, he passed his last days on this earth hearing accounts from visitors of the goings-on in his many dominions, or being read the Psalms by his favorite daughter, Isabella Clara Eugenia. The Prudent King, as Philip would come to be known, was preparing himself for death. But, conscious of how close the end was now, the king wanted to avail himself of two further aids.

First, there were his beloved relics. In the reliquary of El Escorial, Philip had amassed no fewer than 7,422 different bones of saints. Along with dozens of blackened finger bones, a foot of St. Lawrence charred from his martyrdom, twelve entire cadavers, and more than forty human skulls, there were strands of hair from Jesus and the Virgin Mary, one of St. James the Apostle, and fragments from the cross and the crown of thorns. Philip summarily ordered that these be placed in turn on his eyes, forehead, mouth, and hands, believing that this would ease his pain and banish any evil. Of this extraordinary collection, Sigüenza wrote, "We are not aware of there being any saint for which we do not have a relic, except for three,"[1] and he justified the extent of the effort as the king's aim to prevent any part of the collection falling into Protestant hands. In this way, the monastery became Christendom's most sacred cemetery.

Philip had one more command. He ordered certain paintings brought to his quarters so that he could pray before them in his final hours.

This last order, of course, rang very familiar to me. This king, who in so many other ways emulated his father, Charles V, wanted like him to have his own *meditatio mortis* before images that he had chosen. In fact, he took his imitation to such a degree that he ordered his father's coffin opened with instructions that careful note be taken of the arrangement of the body, so that he could be interred in the same manner. As de Prada had said, Philip was convinced that his progenitor's spirit and his special death paintings would somehow see him and take pity on him, alleviating his suffering.

Philip no doubt sparked another furor when he requested that one of the strangest items in his collection be brought to his bedside, *The Garden of Earthly Delights*, the masterwork of Hieronymus Bosch, born Jheronimus van Aken. The painting had barely been at El Escorial five years but its irreverent subject matter was already stirring up all manner of comment at court. Where in the Bible could you find this sea of men and women, naked together in a garden full of fruits and great winged creatures and surrendering to the pleasures of the flesh? But of course no one dared oppose one of the monarch's last commands, so without as much as a word from the monks attending him, the imposing work—some seven feet by thirteen—was carried up and installed beside the bed, sparing no effort so that the king could admire it as he prayed before it. So why did Christendom's most powerful man choose to have that particular work beside him while he was dying? The triptych had aroused controversy since it had first been confiscated in the Netherlands from the Protestant prince William of Orange by the duke of Alba and passed through several private hands before ending up at El Escorial. As strange as it was, alien to the Bible in a thousand different details, littered with impossible creatures and packs of terrible demons, Philip—the most Catholic ruler in Europe—would not rest until he possessed it. What was it that the old king knew about that painting?

This question and others I decided to bring to my next encounter at the Prado. I needed to understand the meaning of this image engraved on my mind, of the great Philip II drawing his last breath in the dawn light, fourteen years to the day since the last stone had been laid in the construction of El Escorial, fearful of his demons, and with Bosch's panels hanging nearby in the room or the next door antechamber.

All that remained now was for the Master to heed my silent summons and reveal what lay behind the king's mysterious fascination with Bosch.

It was Friday, January 11, 1991, that I returned to the Prado. My memories from that day remain so sharp as to be almost surreal, even after two decades. I wonder if the vividness and colors of the images I have are simply what happens when you spend that much time exposed to the images in *The Garden of Earthly Delights*.

Whoever reads this, I beg their indulgence—what follows is the result of the impact that a five-hundred year-old painting can have on a young man nursing dreams of understanding the unknowable.

How could I have been so naïve?

As any visitor to the Prado knows, you can find Philip II's *tabla mortuoria* in Gallery 56a, on the first floor, where it has been for almost half a century. The room is rectangular and very warm—heat pours out of ten grilles concealed around the marble baseboard.

In order to avoid running into the wrong person, I had crossed the entire museum quickly with a scarf wrapped around my lower face and my sunglasses on. The heat assaulted me as I entered. I realized that there were a number of small areas that feel quite different from the rest of the museum, perhaps due to the paintings they house, or perhaps due to something else difficult to pinpoint.

As it happened, on that Friday, standing in the middle of the macabre Gallery 56a and clutching my camera bag, I felt something strange. It might not seem like much to the reader, but as I started to remove my outer layer of clothing a weird feeling I had never felt before began to grow in my chest. It didn't last long, but it was as though the heat, the rushing, the many eyes staring at me from the paintings, and my own irrational fear all overloaded my system, and I began to shake from head to toe. I felt dizzy, and put my bag down on the floor Then, after a minute, I started to recover, and as I felt myself stabilizing I became aware suddenly and very clearly—as I did right after I met Mister X—who I was and what I was doing there.

I took all this as a sign. Taking a slow, deep breath, I thought, *I am ready!* This time, my determination was like steel, like fire—a feeling impossible to put into words but very clear to me.

Everything is going to be all right, I said to myself.

As I reoriented myself, I became aware of a strange piece of furniture sitting in the middle of the gallery containing Bosch's paintings. It was unlike anything else in the museum. It was a table, or rather a stand built to hold a painted panel which, as I would learn later, sat in Philip's small study until the day he died.

The guides all refer to the panel as *The Seven Deadly Sins.* It is an unusual circular painting in miniaturist style on poplar wood depicting the temptations of the human soul. What especially catches the eye is that these miniature temptations, or sins, are arranged in a circle contained in a giant, hypnotic eye that looks as if it can see right into your soul.

Cave, cave. Deus videt,* I read, and drawn by the ring of scenes I walked slowly around the table to take them all in.

I'd done something right, after all.

As I orbited slowly around the "eye of God" I had the sense that I was setting something in motion, though I wasn't sure what. A perception? A vision? Or perhaps even the spirit that Juan Rof Carballo wrote about, which is supposed to live in that very table. Carballo was a psychiatrist and art expert, and he wrote about spirits that lived in the Prado. He imagined this one, the great spirit, "mocking the critics for not having lived a better life and for not having navigated the reefs and shoals of meditation, completely unaware of this other way of looking at the world."[2]

I wondered, *Should I open my mind?*

---

* Beware, beware! God sees.

Or continue spinning around this table like a dervish?

Or expand my consciousness by losing myself in these hallucinatory scenes all around me?

But how?

It suddenly hit me with a start that I was lost in my circling of this apocalyptic work—another example of the craziness I found myself in.

Two scrolls in the Bosch table carried Latin inscriptions from Deuteronomy which were quite unambiguous. The first, on one side of the table, said, "They are a nation lacking sense or prudence. If only they were wise, they would understand their end and would prepare for it."[3] Below, the second banner read, "I will hide my face from them, I will see what their end will be."[4]

Uneasy suddenly, I lifted my gaze from the table and realized that everything in that gallery was in some way connected to death. Perhaps this was why this visit felt so different from all my previous ones.

Though most of the paintings in the room were by Bosch—*The Haywain, Cutting the Stone, The Temptation of St. Anthony*—there were another ten masterpieces by foreign painters as well. Brueghel's *The Triumph of Death* and Patinir's *Landscape with St. Jerome* and *Landscape with Charon Crossing the Styx*. And of course, dominating all of these unsettling images is *The Garden of Earthly Delights*, my true objective.

At two o'clock on a Friday afternoon, Madrid was poised to begin its weekend, and the place was deserted. There was no sign of anyone, so feeling a little bolder, I sat down on the floor in front of the famous triptych and waited for Fovel to appear. *He'll show up*, I thought, confidently, *he always does*. I took my Canon from its case, checked it, adjusted the aperture for the gallery light, and held it, ready to shoot. Like a mantra I repeated to myself, *Everything will work out*.

Then I finally gave myself permission to lift my gaze to *The Garden of Earthly Delights.*

The left-hand panel appeared to be the most serene of the three. It occurred to me that if I concentrated on it for a minute it might help calm my nerves. It worked. The painting's colors and the tranquil, nude figures managed to slow my heart and breathing. After a moment, I fixed my eyes on the constellation of details opening up before me.

The painting was a marvel. However many times I focused on one section, I always found something new to capture my attention, even though that first panel was the least busy one. In fact, it appeared to be fairly simple to understand. Compared to the others, it seemed to have hardly any figures in it, though as I looked I realized that this was a kind of optical illusion.

The panel features three main figures in the foreground, but a seemingly endless universe of animals unfolds behind them: elephants, giraffes, porcupines, unicorns, rabbits, and, in the back, a bear climbing a fruit tree.[5] For some obscure reason, in the next panel to the right, the animals—particularly the birds—grow and become gigantic, but here they are small and not the main focus. Clearly the artist wanted us to look at the three figures. So I did.

Only one of the three is clothed. I take this to be God. He is holding a young, naked woman—Eve—by the wrist and presenting her to Adam, who is lying on the ground, presumably because his rib has just been taken out.

Something about it unsettles me.

God, the Great Surgeon, does not look as if he is paying any attention to his two creations, nor as if he has much interest in introducing them. He is looking directly at me. Judging by what is happening, it seems that God is at the

Hieronymus Bosch, *The Garden of Earthly Delights,* or *The Millennial Reign.* Left panel. The Prado Museum, Madrid.

point in Genesis where he says, "It is not good that man should be alone . . ."[6]

Somewhat intimidated by the painting, I picked up my camera and, fiddling with the telephoto lens, managed to shoot some extreme close-ups of those eyes. They are severe, penetrating, and, together with the eyes of the owl that peer from beneath the tree-fountain-what-have-you, they form an unsettling constellation. Being that close to the painting in that deep silence gave me shivers, and I asked myself what could be causing them. Perhaps this particular evocation of paradise was not meant to inspire peace in the viewer.

I took a look around the gallery. The two doorways were empty, silent. There were no visitors in sight. Sitting there cross-legged on the tile floor, I returned to the triptych. I had read somewhere that the first panel on the left represents the creation of man, that perfect time in the Garden of Eden with Adam and Eve together before they committed the terrible error of ingesting the fruit of the tree of knowledge of good and evil, which, it suddenly occurred to me, could have been that strange pink structure in which the mysterious owl was nesting.

So far, that was the easy part of the lesson. I stared at the painting, and it stared back at me. I noticed that by the happenstance of geometry, that same nocturnal bird of prey occupied the exact center point of the panel.

But there was more. As I stared longer, I began to notice that all was not quite right in this paradise. I used the long lens to zoom in on the painting and discovered something disturbing. Emerging from the water by the fountain was a reptile with three heads. I took a picture, and was about to lower the camera and look with my own eyes when I saw another mutant closer to me—this time a three-headed bird. The bird appeared to be fighting with a small unicorn and a fish with a beak. To the right of this, a cross between a bird and a reptile was devouring a toad. And on the other side, a cat prepared to make short work of a mouse it had just caught.

What was all this? Recalling my Bible classes, I wondered—wasn't death banished in the earthly paradise?

"Poor Javier! Without a proper guide, this painting will drive you mad!"

Loud and taunting, the Master's voice reverberated in the gallery. The camera nearly fell from my hands.

"*The Garden of Earthly Delights*—an excellent choice!" Fovel smiled, pleased with the fright he'd just given me. "In fact, it's like a final exam for those who specialize in the arcanon of the Prado."

I couldn't fathom how Luis Fovel had managed to walk across the room without my noticing. Nonetheless, there he was, solid as ever in his leather shoes and wool coat, standing just a step away from my perch on the floor.

"What . . . what kind of exam?" I stammered, still recovering from the surprise.

"It would be full of trick questions, for one thing. There is a great deal of speculation around this work; no one knows anything for certain, not even what it is called. *The Garden* is just its modern name. Others have called it *The Millennial Reign, The Painting of the Arbutus, The Earthly Paradise* . . . It's this very ambiguity that makes it one of the most important works in the arcanon of the Prado.

"For me the work is prophetic. A warning. A portent for our times. But to understand it like that, I'm afraid you need to regard it from a different angle. If you just look at the painting head-on, like the tourists, you'll just end up going down the wrong path."

I could have hugged him right there. After my encounter with Mister X, having Fovel next to me once again, teaching me one of his lessons, gave me a feeling of indescribable joy. He sensed this, and stopped me, hiding behind an icy gaze. He warned me that understanding *The Garden of Earthly Delights* could take a lifetime or more, and that whatever he chose to tell me about it would barely scratch the surface of its great mystery.

"This is not the end of your course of study," he added. "You've barely begun."

So I reined in my enthusiasm and held my questions for a more opportune moment. I put the lens cap back on my camera, got up off the floor, brushed off my pants, and let him guide me over to one end of the painting.

Then he did something that shocked me. He reached his hand out to the heavy gold-and-black frame of the triptych and yanked at it with some force. I heard a soft crunch, and, unable to move, I watched as the left panel—paradise—swung toward us and closed over the center panel like a shutter. Fovel repeated his action on the other side.

"Now that's how one should begin to appreciate this tool," he said.

"It's a tool?"

"You'll see what I mean in a moment. But first, tell me— what do you see?"

Viewing *The Garden of Earthly Delights* with its panels closed like that was a completely new experience. The backs of the panels are meticulously painted but almost devoid of color. The surreal scene is dominated by a huge, grayish transparent sphere containing a large circular island that looks as if it's rising out of the water.

Up above this, at the top-left corner, very small, you can make out an old man wearing a triple crown with a book open in his hands who must be God. He contemplates everything below him. There are two phrases next to him written in Gothic lettering: *Ipse dixit et facta sunt* and *Ipse mandavit et creata sunt.*

"What do they mean?" I asked Fovel, after trying to sound them out them slowly to myself.

"They're from the first chapter of Genesis. This is on the third day of Creation, when God commands that Earth emerge and be separate from the waters, and that it be populated with grasses and trees bearing fruit. They mean, 'He spoke, and it came to be. He commanded, and it was created.'"

"So all this is before human beings appeared?"

"Yes, Javier, in fact, before almost anything had appeared. In Joachimite terms, this corresponds to the Age of the Father."

I was lost. "*Joachimite?* Age of the Father? I don't understand."

"Of course, I forgot—I need to explain all this to you," replied Fovel, more patient than annoyed. "Remember when we talked about Raphael and the battle between Leo X and Cardinal Sauli to become the Angelic Pope who would unite Christianity?"

I nodded. How could I forget? He went on.

"Well, at the time I told you that the first man to prophesy the coming of this almost supernatural pope was a monk from the thirteenth century, a temperamental man from the South of Italy named Joachim of Fiore. That's where 'Joachimite' comes from."

I was working fast to recall our earlier meeting. "I remember you said Joachim of Fiore played a large part in the creation of *The New Apocalypse,* but you didn't say much more than that."

"You have a good memory. That's right, at the time I

didn't tell you about what a huge influence his ideas had in Renaissance Europe because it wasn't an opportune moment, but it is now. Brother Joachim of Fiore was an actual visionary. After visiting Mount Tabor on a pilgrimage to the Holy Land, he started having trances and ecstasies. But he was not only a seer, he was also quite an intellectual, who developed something called *spiritualis intelligentia*—a unique ability to combine reason and faith which made him one of the great thinkers of his time. He was widely respected. He corresponded with three popes, and King Richard the Lionheart traveled to Sicily to hear him speak. His writings were thought of almost as the word of God. In any case, in his writings Joachim announced the imminent arrival of this Angelic Pope who would unite spiritual and earthly power, though what really mattered to him was what came afterward—a millennial reign!"

"What is a 'millennial reign'?" I asked.

"Joachim prophesied a thousand-year era in which Jesus would return to Earth and take control of our destiny. What's interesting about this is that *The Millennial Reign* is the earliest name given to this triptych of Bosch's, and it depicts exactly what this monk believed was going to happen in this world. Thanks to the main religious orders then, Joachim's theories spread across Europe lightning fast, reaching as far as the Netherlands."

"I still can't believe that the educated classes in those days would accept that kind of prophecy," I mused.

"They did so because prophets then were intellectuals themselves. Not like today. Joachim, for example, was a great scholar of the scriptures, and he used that knowledge to classify human history into three distinct ages, or reigns. What you see when the doors of Bosch's triptych are closed like this corresponds to Joachim of Fiore's Age of the Father, the time when God gives form to the world, which Bosch represents in that translucent sphere you see in front of you. The main features of that age are winter, water, and night, all of which are shown there. Now, Javier, open the panel."

I looked at Fovel, uncertain. "Me?"

"Sure, go ahead! Choose a panel and open it up."

I chose the left-hand panel and swung it open gingerly. It weighed more than I would have thought. As it opened, it revealed the scene that had me so captivated earlier. I tried to imagine the dramatic effect that opening the panel would have had on someone from the Renaissance unprepared for the scene behind. To go with no warning from a gray orb to the rich and colorful world behind would have left a number of viewers openmouthed. Once I had the panel all the way open, Fovel declared, "Excellent. You've chosen the path of warning."

I glanced at him quizzically.

"You could have chosen the other, right-hand panel first, and opened it to the scene of hell. If you had done that you would have instead chosen the path of prophecy. The painting gives you a different message depending on which side you open first."

"I still don't understand."

"Let me explain, Javier. Joachim of Fiore, who many experts say was a distant inspiration for this work, had a very particular way of understanding history, and it appears that Bosch shared this view. Joachim believed that you could interpret history two different ways depending on whether you begin with the creation and move toward the birth of Jesus or whether you start with that and move in the direction of his second coming. Joachim saw these two eras as being parallel, lasting the same amount of time, and in effect being mirror images of each other. That's why if you study the first, you can anticipate what is to come in the second. And the first is the path of warning, the one you chose. If you read this triptych from left to right this way, you first see paradise and the creation of man, then you see him multiplying across the land and the subsequent expansion and corruption driven by the sins of the flesh. Then finally—the end. Hell. Punishment for man's excesses."

"What if I'd started from the right instead?"

"In that case, as I told you, you would have chosen the path of prophecy. The first panel, on the right, represents the Reign of the Son, the age we live in today. Take a good look at that inferno. Nature is conspicuous in its absence. The scene is dominated by buildings and things made by man that have all turned against him. This is the world we live in now.

"Then you move to the center panel and you see all that exuberant life, nature, water, fruit, and living beings as what comes next for us. We are being told that humanity will be freed from the burdens of this world and will become a community of greater and greater innocence, less attached to the flesh. More spiritual. On this path, the central panel no longer represents the sins of our species, but can instead be seen as the next, higher evolutionary stage for mankind after hell.

"Now when we look at the last panel on this path, the one on the left, we understand that at the end of days we will return to paradise and stand shoulder to shoulder with Jesus Christ. Have you noticed that the clothed figure on the left-hand panel bears a stronger resemblance to Jesus than to the elderly figure of God on the other panel?"

"Hmmmm . . ." I pondered this. "Is that actually what Joachim believed? That we will share the glory with Jesus at the end of time?"

"Exactly," Fovel confirmed. "He believed that this was our destiny, like it or not, that it was written and unalterable, that at the end of days we would see God and be able to commune with him, and that the church and all its sacraments would become irrelevant."

"That's a dangerous idea," I remarked.

"It is. Very much so. You have to remember that Joachim of Fiore lived three centuries before this work was painted, around the time that the first Inquisitions began, and yet even these could not halt the spread of his prophetic faith. We now know that this belief of his spread quietly all across Europe, winning adherents among everyone who saw the church as being an institution more active in oppression than in spirituality. The man who commissioned this painting from Hieronymus Bosch was in complete agreement, and no doubt wanted to have a tool to help him contemplate the meaning of history and the future of the species."

"You seem very sure about this, Doctor. Why did this necessarily have to have been commissioned? Couldn't Bosch just have painted it for himself?"

"Come now, Javier, don't be so naïve. That's just not how art worked during the Renaissance. I believe I went over this with you when we were talking about Raphael. What's more, have you looked carefully at this triptych? Have you compared it to the other Bosch paintings in the room? It's not only much bigger, but it's also infinitely more populated with figures, more intricate in its detail and much more challenging to interpret. It no doubt took Bosch a very long time to paint, and the materials must have cost a great deal. No one in the fifteenth century painted for pleasure or in their spare time. Painting just wasn't a pastime then. This was definitely a commission."

"Then who commissioned it?" I ask.

"That's the big mystery, Javier. At the height of the Second World War, there was a German scholar named Wilhelm Fraenger who was being pursued by the Nazis. He came up with a theory that, to this day, best accounts for all the various oddities of the painting. According to him, *The Garden of Earthly Delights* was a kind of device used by the faithful of a heretical movement known as the Brethren of the Free Spirit to contemplate their origins and their destiny.[7] In central Europe they were known commonly as Adamites because they believed themselves to be the sons of Adam and as such, to have been created in the image of God and therefore incapable of sinning.

"Fraenger discovered descriptions written by church fathers such as Epiphanius of Salamis[8] and St. Augustine[9] which mentioned the sect among the earliest deviations from the true faith, and described them performing their rituals naked in caves. One description of them said, 'One encounters men and women, naked. They pray naked. They listen to sermons naked. They receive the sacrament naked. For this reason they call their church paradise.' "

I shot a glance at the Bosch, surprised by how well that description fit the images I saw.

"Traces of the Adamites can be found as late as Bosch's time," Fovel continued. "In 1411, a hundred years before this was painted, in Cambrai in the part of France that abuts Flanders, the powerful bishop went after the sect. Wilhelm van Hildernissen, a Carmelite monk from Brussels, and his deputy, Aegidus Cantor, were burned at the stake. It's from those ecclesiastical proceedings that we know that the Adamites performed their rituals in caves and that they resisted authority and were indifferent to Rome. They also believed that the end of days was imminent, and that when it came they would be recognized as the true sons of Adam and be able to roam the earth freely as God had intended."

"Pretty daring for the time." I commented.

"It's true. What's interesting is that they seem to have anticipated the interest in the human body that sprang up among artists of that period. The Adamites spiritualized the erotic. They didn't see nudity as a pathway to lust; on the contrary, they believed that it was possible to have a universal platonic love unmarred by carnal desires. Their ideas were quite advanced for their time."

"Was Bosch one of them?" I asked.

"Fraenger doesn't say. Bosch's biography is murky. We know that he was both the son and grandson of painters, possibly from Aachen, and that he worked ornamenting churches in the area, but we don't know much more than that. Fraenger was able to show that Bosch possessed an unusual level of knowledge about the Adamite sect, which Fraenger concludes could only have come from one of the sect's top leaders. An educated man, and rich enough to finance a work of that magnitude."

"You must have someone in mind!" I pressed him.

"The thing is, there are not many candidates. It's either some merchant who was important then but whom we don't remember, or possibly a member of the family of Orange. More recently, it's been suggested that the triptych was a wedding present from Henry II of Nassau to his wife.[10] Who knows? Perhaps he or some other administrator from the Low Countries was affiliated with the Adamites in some way. But if Fraenger is right and this patron is in the painting then it might not be that long until he's finally identified."

"How do you mean? Do we know what the patron looked like?"

"Exactly what I said, Javier. Following the custom of these

commissioned works, Bosch would have included his patron's face among the many figures he painted. Would you like to know which figure it is?"

I nodded impatiently, and like a child yearning for a candy, I joined the Master in front of *The Garden of Earthly Delights.*

"Right there," Fovel said, pointing. "See?"

In the lower-right corner of the central panel next to a small group of figures, there was a kind of breach in the ground, like a small cave, and leaning out of it was a young man and woman.

"You see that cave?" asked Fovel, moving aside. "As I said, the Adamites would use these as their temples. Take a good look at the man. Two things about him stand out. For one, he is wearing clothes. The only other clothed figure is God

The "Master" of *The Garden of Earthly Delights.* Central panel (detail). The Prado Museum, Madrid.

in the left panel. Also, he is gazing openly and directly at the viewer. Again, just like God. Fraenger believed that this figure is the free spirit who commissioned the painting from Bosch. It's worth pointing out that Bosch placed the figure where painters traditionally sign their paintings, setting him apart from all the other figures and identifying him to the initiated."

"Couldn't it just be a self-portrait?"

"Some people think so, but I doubt it," Fovel said. "He doesn't behave like a painter. He seems more interested in showing us things than in making the painting's case."

"So what is it that he's showing us, Doctor?" I asked, staring at that small corner of the painting.

"Well, according to Fraenger he's showing us the new Eve, who's holding the infamous apple from the Garden of Eden. But there's something else. Take a look behind the young man. Behind him and leaning against his shoulder you can just make out a face, which in this case might very well be Bosch's self-portrait. Here he appears in shadow, meek, his head on his mentor's shoulder."

I stared at that small face. "I'd give anything to have a portrait of Bosch that I could compare this to."

Fovel sighed and arched his eyebrows, in what I took to be resignation before the infinite ignorance of his pupil.

"Sadly, no such thing exists. The earliest portrait we have was painted fifty years after Bosch's death by the Flemish draftsman and poet Domenicus Lampsonius,[11] so it may well not be a reliable likeness. Nonetheless, it was part of a series of twenty-three portraits that Lampsonius did of Dutch artists and showed Bosch already as an old man."

"Is there a resemblance between that and this figure leaning on the free spirit in the *Garden*?" I asked, and right away I saw that for some reason my question had discomfited the Master. He stroked his nose and mouth as he tried to find a suitable response. He began slowly.

"Well . . . it could be that Fraenger confused the two figures in the painting. Or maybe it was Lampsonius. In any case, there is one detail that those figures and the Lampsonius portrait have in common. It's just a small thing, but . . ."

"What is it, Doctor?"

"You can't really tell in the portrait, but in the triptych, the two men look directly at the viewer and pose with the nascent Eve, who appears to be passing through an open glass doorway. The men seem to be signaling both the woman and the doorway, as if these were the whole point of the entire composition."

"The device!" I exclaimed.

A mysterious expression appeared on the doctor's face. "Exactly. You have to think of this painting as a doorway, a portal that will transport you to a transcendent state, or reality. The drowsy, reclining woman represents the key with which we open the doorway. As I said, Fraenger believed that this painting was to be used as a kind of meditation tool with which the members and followers of the Free Spirit would have access to the sect's most important teachings, and to very personal mystical visions in which they set great store. However, my own impression is that the door and the pensive woman together form a sort of hieroglyph, or symbol, which explains what the triptych is to be used for and how to use it. Shall I read you what Fraenger said about this?"

"Of course!"

Fovel went through his pockets and extracted a small book with a dark, well-worn binding on which I could just make out the name of this German thinker who had evidently made a great impression on the Master. He opened the book up to a place he'd marked and began to read.

Domenicus Lampsonius, *Hieronymus Bosch* (1572). Engraving.

To begin their own particular spiritual journey, the Free Spirit disciples would sit facing the panel and begin to meditate. When they reached the moment of maximum concentration, they would be lifted gently from this everyday world into a spiritual realm that they would discover little by little, and which, over time, would reveal to them truths of greater and greater significance. The only way to understand and enter into the panel was to concentrate on it unceasingly. Thus the viewer would become a cocreator of it, an independent interpreter of the solemn and enigmatic symbols in front of them. The painting was never static, but always alive and constantly animated by the living flow of transformation, the organic becoming, the ongoing revelation of life, all of this being in concert with the painting's evolutionist intellectual structure.[12]

Fovel finished and waited for the words to sink in. I didn't need long.

"Does that mean," I searched for the right words, "that you know how to open the portal? Can you enter the painting? Use the tool?"

"I'm afraid not." Fovel said. "Not even Fraenger managed to do that. After the Allied bombers bombed Berlin and destroyed his apartment and his notes, he spent years trying unsuccessfully to enter the portal and cross over. The one useful hint to emerge from his attempts and research was that the voyage would begin with the viewer's gaze fixed upon the fountain of life in the left-hand panel, in the opening containing the owl. From there, one would be transported. Believe it or not, I have tried. In the process, you come to realize just how many of these owls there are scattered about the painting, like multiple keys to the same door, and while I have no problem understanding their significance, getting them to work is another matter."

"Really? What do you think that significance is?"

"Well, these are creatures that can see in the dark, Javier. Since the earliest of times owls, have stood for the ideal of knowledge and for that which can penetrate the invisible. Only owls can move precisely through the darkness, and to the eyes of the ancients this meant that they could also navigate the territory of death. Of the hereafter. They are psychopomps, guides of souls to the afterlife."

"So this is another painting that acts like a medium." I observed.

"In a sense, yes. It's up to us to determine what particular medium the artist is suggesting to get to the other side, to God. Is it simple meditation? Drugs? Perhaps *Claviceps purpurea*—ergot fungus—which in the Low Countries was often used in drinks. Fraenger is not very clear on this point, but I'd wager that by the time this triptych got into the hands of Philip II, in the late 1500s, he and his trusted inner circle would already have known all about the work's visionary power."

"How can you be so sure?"

Hieronymus Bosch, Owls in *The Garden of Earthly Delights* (details). Panels I and II. The Prado Museum, Madrid.

The Master smiled. "It's no secret that Philip was a man of contradictory convictions. On the one hand, he was bound to defend the Catholic faith to the end, to prosecute the Inquisition throughout his territories, and to keep Protestants and other heretics at bay. But then on the other hand, he financed the alchemical experiments of his architect, Juan de Herrera, he was an avid collector of secret, magical, and astrologic texts, and kept no fewer than six unicorn horns in his own personal treasure chest.[13] He was a man in whom orthodoxy and heterodoxy, faith and paganism, walked hand in hand. I'd bet that he had heard about the visionary properties of the painting and made sure that he had it near him at the end."

"But wasn't that controversial?" I objected. "Didn't anybody question the king's interest in such a strange painting, or cast doubts on Bosch, in the most Catholic court in the world?"

"They certainly did!" replied Fovel. "Bosch was called every name in the book. 'Painter of devils' was one of the kindest. Most of those who actually saw his paintings couldn't explain the king's fascination with them. Perhaps fortunately, Bosch was not a prolific painter—there are no more than forty of his paintings all told. But Philip became his biggest collector. He had no fewer than twenty-six of those forty paintings in his possession when he died, most of which he had hung in El Escorial. It could be that Father Sigüenza was mostly able to convince critics that the works were satirical, that they were an invitation to good Christians to contemplate the perversions that lurked around every corner and a warning lest they fall prey to these. What's remarkable is that this explanation was almost universally accepted, and didn't start to fall apart until well into the next century."

My mind was still on what Fovel had said earlier. "Doctor, getting back to the king—why do you think he wanted to have this strange painting at his bedside?"

Fovel gave me a particularly impish look, adjusting his coat and tugging on his lapels. He half turned, his back to the Bosch, and fixed his gaze on me.

"What about you? Can't you think of a reason?"

14

THE SECRET FAMILY OF BRUEGHEL THE ELDER

Before the afternoon slipped away entirely, Fovel led me to another corner of Gallery 56a. Incredibly, not a single soul had crossed our path while we spoke. It was almost five in the afternoon and we were still completely alone. Out of caution, I said nothing, and neither did Fovel. It didn't occur to me then that we had experienced the same thing once before, when we had appeared to be the only two people in a museum that receives more than two million visitors a year.[1] If I had just thought at the time to calculate the odds of experiencing two events like that within a month of each other, I'd have been aware of the magnitude of what was happening. However, dense as I was, it would be a while before I connected the two experiences.

"You mustn't go without seeing this," Fovel said, oblivious to the knot that was forming in my stomach for no reason I could think of. The painting that he led me to would do nothing to improve my state.

To our left, on an exquisitely painted panel approximately five feet in length, an army of skeletons looked set to engage in combat with a handful of humans who were fighting for their lives.

Fovel had chosen a truly extraordinary work.

Death's forces had taken their positions and would give no quarter. One of their carts, overflowing with skulls, crossed the main square. An ominous war machine advanced, flames leaping from it, driven by a sinister hooded figure. Nearby, skeletons brandishing swords slaughtered men and women pitilessly, while others busied themselves hanging the condemned, or slitting their throats with knives, or hurling them into the river, where their naked bodies swelled like balloons.

Speechless at this horrific sight, I turned my attention to a kind of fortified enclosure that gave onto the sea. It was filled to bursting with the walking dead, all exultant and happy, and beyond those walls nothing in the surrounding picture allowed even the smallest room for hope. The rearguard positions were painfully denuded and ruined, clumps of putrefying remains lay everywhere, and smoke rose from the wreckage of various ships and coastal embattlements, adding emphatically to the sense that this was the end. Worst of all, on the horizon you could just make out new skeletal battalions breaking through, marching implacably toward the ruins of civilization. It dawned on me that no one would survive the onslaught of the armies of the dead.

The Triumph of Death is absolutely devastating. Pieter Brueghel the Elder painted it in 1562, long before anyone had even conceived of a zombie apocalypse. It would be just over two hundred years before Goya—that genius of unease—appeared, though Brueghel more than holds his own against him. Both artists were products—you might say victims—of their time.

In Flanders, Brueghel lived through six consecutive Habsburg-Valois Wars and then saw firsthand the horrors of the plague, which decimated the population—rich, religious, children, and poor alike. He was about thirty-five when he started working on this nightmare of his, which, ironically, would prove prophetic for him—he would not

live to see forty. His own brushes having predicted his end, he succumbed to the plague, leaving us the orphans of his talents.

I think I know why Fovel chose this landscape to look at next. Both Brueghel's painting and *The Garden of Earthly Delights* inspire reflection in the viewer. The two paintings are also complementary, in a way. While Bosch's vision is inspired by the first book of the Bible and on a simple level describes the origin of our species, Brueghel's serves as its culmination. Deriving from the final book of the scriptures, St. John's Apocalypse, it shows us an extreme version of Bosch's hell. What were already grotesque horrors in the *Garden* show their true face in Brueghel, revealing themselves in all their base depravity.

Lost in thought, I realized suddenly that *The Triumph of Death* could be seen as a more advanced instance of the *Totentanz*, the Dance of Death, a popular artistic theme in the Central Europe of Brueghel's time. Just as I was about to mention this to Fovel, he introduced something new.

"I'd like to describe an enigma to you, Javier," he said solemnly. "Are you ready?"

His words yanked me out of my thoughts, and I looked at him a little discombobulated.

"What kind of enigma?" I asked.

"It has to do with something we haven't yet talked about, called the 'art of memory.' It's a kind of practice that I trust you will benefit from greatly whenever you're in a museum looking at paintings."

"Go ahead," I said, now intrigued.

"The first thing you should know is that until the arrival of printing, in the Renaissance, this kind of practice, or art, was reserved for the privileged—intellectuals, the nobility, and artists—and so very few people have heard of it. With the advent of moveable type and the spread of printing, it was left behind, and with it the ability that we once had to read through images."

"How do you read through images?" I asked, somewhat skeptical.

"I'm talking literally about reading via images. Not interpreting them, as we have been doing, deciphering the meaning of a symbol or gesture, such as seeing a cross upon a tower and knowing that there is a church there. This art of memory was invented by the Greeks in Homer's time as a way to record large quantities of text that they couldn't inscribe in stone. It turns out to be the greatest mnemonic tool ever invented by man, a practice that has survived for hundreds of years and has been used to record everything from scientific knowledge to literary texts. Generally speaking, it involves associating images, landscapes—even statues and buildings—with pieces of knowledge, which can then later be decoded and understood by any member of the elite who knows the code."

"You're saying this has been used for over two thousand years?"

"That's right. Possibly even longer. We can't know how it is that these Greek thinkers discovered the human brain's ability to retain mountains of information, or this method of storing and recalling it by associating pieces of information with geometric, architectural, artistic, or other common distinctive images. That is how the method is described in ancient texts like *Rhetorica ad Herennium,* which is thought to have been written by Cicero himself. If, for example, one has been trained to link a body of medical facts with a particular building or statue or even painting, then all one has to do is to recall that structure and the stored facts can be easily retrieved. Do you understand?"

"I think so."

The Master continued.

"Then it won't surprise you that once this method was perfected, it became a well-guarded secret that passed from civilization to civilization, especially since it allowed messages and complex bodies of knowledge to be transmitted in secret, completely hidden from the uninitiated."

"Let me see if I have this right." I said. "If, for example, I connect some mathematical formula to one of the skeletons in this painting, then anytime in the future that I see or recall that skeleton, I'll remember the formula, no matter how much time has passed? And then also if I divulge the details of this link to someone else, it will work for them as well?"

"Yes, that's more or less how it works," Fovel agreed calmly. "You should also know that the last people to use this method lived during the time that Brueghel painted *The Triumph of Death*. As I said before, once printing came along, the art of memory lost a great deal of its usefulness. No one needed to store great quantities of information with images anymore, nor write with them, except . . ."

"Except?"

"Except that a code still needed to be used to store and protect certain knowledge that only a few were privy to."

"Like who?"

"Well . . . I can think of a few. The alchemists, for example. Have you ever seen their texts? *Mutus Liber*, for example—*The Silent Book*? This is an alchemical manual—a textbook—without words! Just images, full of encrypted information that can be decoded by a select few. Alchemy has always aroused greed, and so practitioners of that 'sacred art' created a whole universe of pictures and exotic symbols with which to keep their secrets safe. Of course, these images appeared incomprehensible to the uninitiated—a lion devouring the sun, a phoenix rising from ashes, a three-headed dragon, or a creature that is half man and half woman—but in fact these held the complex chemical formulas, instructions, quantities, elements that were needed to create the magical compounds."

"I suppose they must have kept these things secret because of the Inquisition," I said. "Though, what do I know? Brueghel wasn't an alchemist, too, wasn't he?"

Fovel seemed amused and answered swiftly.

"Come now, Javier; what painter isn't? Don't you realize that every great painter must mix his own colors and create his own textures and tones? These are among the things that differentiate one master from another. And wouldn't you agree that that is very similar to what we suppose alchemists do?

"But then Brueghel did betray a certain familiarity with the art and its pitfalls, as he showed in one of his most popular engravings. It shows a man in his laboratory having spent every last penny on his pursuit of the legendary philosopher's stone while a lunatic stirs the fire and his wife has nothing to feed his children."

"That's not very strong evidence, Doctor."

"No," replied Fovel, "but there's more. For example, I recall a letter written by Brueghel's eldest son, Jan, in 1609 to Cardinal Federico Borromeo, in which he complains that the Holy Roman emperor Rudolf II's craze for collecting his father's paintings has left him without any himself. And if there was one thing that Rudolf II was known for, it was for his patronage of the occult arts. Everyone called him the 'Alchemist Emperor,' so that should give you an idea of why he had such a passion for Brueghel's work."

"Was Brueghel the only one he felt that way about?"

"Not at all. Bosch, too. What I haven't yet told you is that

Pieter Brueghel the Elder, *The Alchemist* (1558). Engraving. Kupferstichkabinett, Berlin.

Rudolf was Philip II's nephew. And it was the king of Spain, a collector in his own right of Bosch and Brueghel, who educated him between the ages of eight and eighteen at El Escorial."

"Hmm . . . I suppose you'll say that anecdotes like this prove that Brueghel, the secret alchemist, was well versed in the art of memory, right?"

Fovel nodded. "It's obvious. But it wasn't just alchemists who used the art of memory. Members of other unorthodox cults also mastered the art so that they could disguise their ideas using Catholic imagery. Not unlike *The Triumph of Death*."

"What was it that Brueghel was trying to hide here?"

"The same thing as Bosch!" Fovel replied emphatically.

"Wait—you mean he was an Adamite as well? A member of the Brethren of the Free Spirit?"

"More or less," Fovel said. "There are historians who think that like Bosch, Brueghel the Elder was a member of a secret millennial cult that believed in and was preparing itself for the imminent end of the world.[2] He tipped his hand when he painted *The Triumph of Death*."

"But Brueghel painted plenty of other paintings with different themes!" I objected. "Paintings full of vitality, showing the customs of life in his village. The celebrations, the nights of drinking . . ."

"Very true," said Fovel, gesturing with his big hands. "But all of those he painted for money. Believe me, this one was different; this was not just any commission. And just like *The Garden of Earthly Delights*, there's not a definitive piece of evidence to tell us who commissioned it. Nor why in 1562 Brueghel painted another two paintings the same size in the same tones and with the same apocalyptic themes: *Dulle Griet*, which is also known as *Greta the Mad* or *Mad Meg*, and

The Fall of the Rebel Angels. Some people believe that the three works were ordered together, but it's impossible to be sure. However, what I am sure about is that *The Triumph of Death* was critical for Brueghel. For him, it was unlike any other. Unique."

"In what way?"

"In the only biography of Brueghel from his time, published as early as 1603, Karel van Mander[3] claims that Brueghel always considered *The Triumph of Death* his magnum opus. Moreover, it became so famous in its time that Brueghel's sons made copy after copy of it, even well beyond the paterfamilias's own death, and that was not the case with any of the other paintings you mentioned."

"Touché, Doctor," I said. "But I still don't see where this is leading."

"Open your ears, son! What I've been saying is that *The Triumph of Death* was not just any painting. There's a very celebrated art historian, Charles de Tolnay, who is also one of the world-renowned experts on Flemish art, and back in the 1930s, he put forth the theory that Brueghel was part of an obscure Christian sect.[4] Based more on his excellent instincts than on any hard evidence, he labeled Brueghel a 'religious libertine' and left the door open for further investigation."

"What was the final conclusion?" I asked, intrigued.

Fovel took a deep breath. "Well . . . Brueghel appears to have been very well connected, with friends in the highest intellectual circles of the time. After a long educational journey through much of France and Italy—typical for painters of his era—Brueghel befriended the cartographer Abraham Ortelius, a disciple of the brilliant Mercator and author of the very first world atlas, printed in 1570. He also visited the humanist Justus Lipsius, who had his portrait painted by both Rubens and Van Dyck. And he knew Andreas Masius, the noted orientalist; Christophe Plantin, the most important printer of his era; and even Philip II's personal librarian, that most erudite priest, Benito Arias Montano. At the time, Montano was in Antwerp overseeing Plantin's production of the famed *Biblia Regia*—the polyglot bible. Montano had spent years in the Low Countries directing this enormous project that had so captivated Philip. During this time he also traveled across much of Europe, infusing a number of select painters with his unorthodox ideas."

"Did they all know each other?"

"They did," the Master acknowledged, "thanks to their discreet involvement in the *Familia Caritatis*—or Family of Love—sect, whose existence we can confirm. The sect was founded in about 1540 by Hendrik Niclaes, a respectable Dutch merchant, and it left its mark on the central European elites of their day."

"What did this group believe in?"

"Well, first of all the Familists, as their enemies labeled them, believed that the end of the world was imminent. They accepted that only Jesus Christ could save them but they were suspicious of the church, which they considered corrupt. Their principal idea was the belief that at the beginning of time humans had been one with God, but that this had ended when Adam ate of the forbidden fruit. However, Niclaes believed that even this fall had not dimmed our divine brilliance, and he preached to whoever would listen that we all have within us the potential to talk directly to the Eternal Father. He wrote fifty-one books expounding this idea and detailing various instructions, methods, and ideas for confronting what he referred to as 'the Last Era.' He signed all his books with the initials 'H. N.' "

"Hendrik Niclaes," I added.

"Perhaps; perhaps not," cautioned Fovel. "If Niclaes was hiding behind those initials it was to protect himself from persecution by the Inquisition's holy office, and with good reason. He claimed that his writings were the 'last call' for Christians, Muslims, Jews, and followers of all other religions to come together as a single faith, with him as its messiah. When that happened, we would recall that we were all sons of Adam, created in the image of God."

I frowned. "Now you're going to tell me that this Niclaes of yours had something to do with Bosch's Adamites, right?"

The Master's face lit up. "The ultimate aim of Niclaes's faith was man's return to paradise. The Familists wanted us to return to our original state as sons of Adam so that we could be once again face-to-face with God. They promoted the appearance of a *Homo Novus*—H.N. And among other things, this would involve the return to the naked state that we saw in *The Garden of Earthly Delights*. As you see—none of these ideas are terribly different from the basic credo of the Brethren of the Free Spirit."[5]

"But are you sure that Brueghel was also a . . . Familist?"

"Quite sure. He also illustrated one of Niclaes's treatises, *Terra Pacis*, in which, through allegory, he narrates his journey from the 'Land of Ignorance' to that of 'Spiritual Peace.' In fact, it's worth noting that Brueghel's most cherished themes, the ones that appear repeatedly in his work—death, judgment, sin, eternity, and the rejection of religious bonds—were, without a doubt, also Niclaes's favorite themes."

The Master paused. It was clear to me how seriously he took all this. He went on to explain to me in solemn tones how this Hendrick Niclaes would have had a great deal in common with the prophets we had talked about when we were viewing the paintings by Raphael and Titian, and especially that Niclaes's ideas derived from the same source as those of Joachim of Fiore or Savonarola—trances. And even though Niclaes had experienced his first trances when he was nine years old, it would be another thirty years before he decided to form his own bastion of the faithful. Thanks to his elevated position both socially and economically, Niclaes was able to befriend intellectual and other influential people and to convince them that he was a kind of messianic minister, sent to this world to continue Christ's work. Like Joachim of Fiore and Savonarola, Niclaes had an answer ready for every question and an interpretation for every event or situation of the time. He had followers in Paris and most of all in London, where his books—under the name Henry Nicholis—remained in print more than a hundred years after his death."

After hearing all this, I ventured, "But how did Niclaes influence *The Triumph of Death*, if you don't mind me asking?"

"Hah!" Fovel gave a little laugh, seeming to realize how much he had gotten off track. "Right! Well, if you're familiar with the Familist credo, this painting takes on a rather special meaning. If we accept that *The Triumph of Death* was Brueghel's favorite work, and that he was active in Niclaes's sect, then we would expect the painting to tell the apocalyptic, end-of-the-world story much as Brueghel would have heard it from the sect leader's mouth. In other words, how one era was ending and another beginning."

"But all I see in that work is the end . . ." I objected.

"That is indeed what it seems!" the doctor agreed.

"So then . . ." my voice trailed off.

"Brueghel is tricking the uninitiated, non-cult viewer with a vision totally lacking in hope. Armies of cadavers are marching on the planet's last city to devastate it. There's no room for even the wish for a better life. Have you realized what the skeletons' overriding intent is?"

I looked back at the painting trying to make sense of the chaos that stretched out before me.

"Their intent?"

"Yes, Javier. It looks as if the skeletons' goal is to push all the mortals into that enormous container on the right-hand side of the scene. That's a very direct metaphor for the gates of hell. It's a representation of a portal to the beyond, with the difference that unlike *The Garden of Earthly Delights*, which Philip II sought so ardently and which led to heaven, here we see only confusion and horror waiting for us on the other side."

"I . . . I'm not sure I understand," I muttered.

Fovel shrugged, and prepared to explain more fully.

"You know," he began, "I tried for years to resolve the apparent contradiction in this work, until I realized that the artist had to be very careful not to leave clues about his faith. Niclaes was persecuted by the Inquisition, and his writings were on the *Index Librorum Prohibitorum*—the *List of Forbidden Books*. It was no joke. But if Brueghel was part of a secret faith that hid and protected the existence of a higher kind of life, how could he then paint something like *The Triumph of Death*? Why did he consider it his favorite? The whole thing didn't make sense. The answer had to be that there was some thing hidden there that I hadn't seen—some puzzle, or hidden image. Whatever it might be."

"And did you find it?" I asked.

"Yes! Tell me, have you ever heard of the *Alphabet of Death*?"

Unprepared for this, I stared, gaping at him.

Fovel clicked his tongue disdainfully and walked over to peer at one area of the Brueghel.

"Pay attention, now. A few years before Brueghel painted this, Hans Holbein the Younger—a notable painter and a

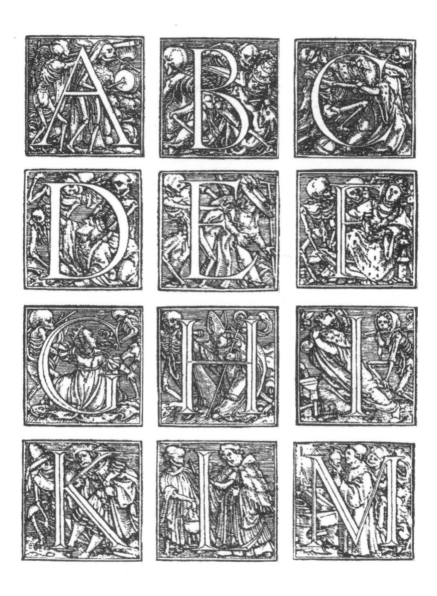

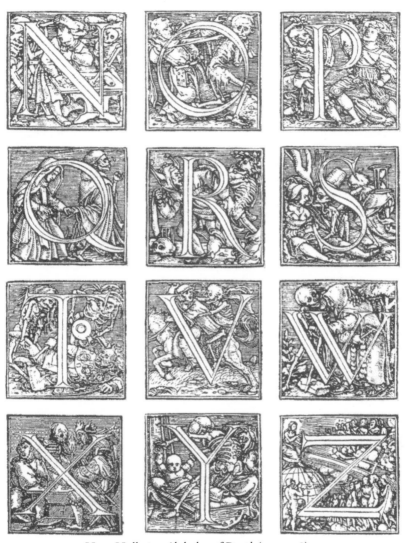

Hans Holbein, *Alphabet of Death* (ca. 1538).

friend of Erasmus who was highly regarded by the circle of intellectuals around Niclaes—created a kind of alphabet of twenty-four capital letters, each about one inch square, adorned with skeletons. As part of this alphabet Holbein had created something seemingly terrible—each of the letters was surrounded by 'soldiers of death,' very similar to the skeletons that Brueghel would paint not long after.They gave the impression of being creatures devoid of souls, who liked to hunt mortals in order to carry them off to their graves.

"Holbein's *A*, for example, is intertwined with two musically inclined skeletons who appear to be playing the eternal Dance of Death. This is followed by skeletons pursuing babies and young damsels, and others chasing their victims on horseback, until it all culminates in the *Z*, in which Christ oversees the Last Judgment."

"Ah!" I cried, "A whole alphabet!"

"Much more than that, Javier, from what I have gathered." Fovel let that last hint just hang there.

"What do you mean, Doctor?"

"It wasn't that Brueghel was inspired by Holbein—Brueghel deliberately used specific images of Holbein's in his painting. It's almost as if he actually traced them! And he thoroughly employed that old idea from the art of memory that you can write using images. Now do you understand?"

But all I could do was look at him quizzically, much to his irritation.

"For God's sake, Javier! By taking images from Holbein's typography and putting them in his painting, Brueghel was surreptitiously inserting letters into the work. He wrote a message using Holbein's skeletons! Using the art of memory! Let me show you."

From the same pocket in his coat where he'd previously extracted the book on Bosch, Fovel removed a sheet of paper with Holbein's alphabet on it. He unfolded it and handed it to me, inviting me to examine it more closely.

"Now, take a good look at the letter *A*. Can you make out the two skeletons? One playing the drums and the other the trumpet? They are walking across a landscape that is strewn with skulls, almost to the exclusion of everything else. Now, turn your attention to the painting. Where do you see a scene like that?"

I rubbed my eyes and focused on *The Triumph of Death*. It took me a little over a minute to locate the small groups of skeletons on the horizon, where I thought I would find what the Master had referred to. But I was wrong.

Nothing in the background remotely resembled a musical skeleton. There were only lancers, defilers of tombs, executioners, and two bell ringers. But when I switched my attention to the foreground, in the lower-right corner of the painting I came across a skeleton playing his lute next to a pair of lovers, consorting, oblivious to the death all around them. Another skeletal figure more in keeping with Holbein's style sat atop the container of hell banging maniacally

Letter *A* of Holbein's alphabet and detail of *The Triumph of Death*.

on two drums. Below him, the skull-littered ground evoked Holbein's alphabet.

"Is that it?" I asked, hesitantly.

"Excellent!" cried Fovel. "Now just imagine that that image represents the letter *A*. Hold that thought right there, hovering near the door to hell, and see if you can find more scenes in the painting that correspond to letters in Holbein's alphabet. What else do you see?"

Paper in hand, feeling like I was playing a rather strange version of *Where's Waldo?*, I began to scour the Brueghel with all my senses at the ready. It took ages for me to find links between the painting and the alphabet, and the ones I did find were tenuous, or incomplete. From time to time I drew a circle in the air above the painting with my finger when I thought I had something, and glanced at the Master out of the corner of my eye to see if I was right. He shook his head each time until, on my fourth or fifth attempt, my finger hovered over a figure near the geometric center of the composition—a fierce skeleton astride an emaciated nag wielding a gigantic scythe.

"That's it," murmured Fovel. "The horseman. Have you seen that he's also there in the letter *V?*"

I glanced at the paper, frowning, not entirely sure.

"Brueghel's horse bore only one spectral rider, but his fierce expression, sparse hair blowing, macabre horizontal grimace, and the stance of his nag left little doubt that the two images were connected."

Fovel was encouraging. "There! Now you have another letter. Keep going!"

Suddenly I realized it had become an addictive game. As my brain worked to familiarize myself with the various deathly figures that populate Holbein's alphabet, I tried to locate them in Brueghel's composition.

Letter *V* of Holbein's alphabet and detail of *The Triumph of Death*.

I found the soldier battling Death himself, who could be the embodiment of the letter *P*. The cardinal fallen prey to the sword from the letter *E*, which appears almost unchanged in the painting.

For some reason, Fovel urged me to redouble my efforts among the mass of figures in the area around the doors of the great container of hell. "The key to what we're seeking has to be there," he whispered in my ear. "Of all of them, this is the most important area of the entire painting, for it is here that we find the last living mortals on earth."

So I did as he asked and after a few minutes, I unearthed two more connections.

One was a figure who has his head covered and his face up to the sky, pleading for mercy.

The Master linked him to the letter *I*.

The other letter, which took me much longer to find, came via a skeleton emptying an extravagant metallic water container, which Fovel showed me to be the *T* from Holbein's alphabet.

"So, now, what do we have?" said Fovel in satisfaction.

"Four letters," I replied, "*A, V, I, T*."

Letters *I* and *T* of Holbein's alphabet and details of *The Triumph of Death*.

"What do you get from that?"

I strained my memory for any trace of my high school Latin and offered a couple of lame suggestions that just made Fovel laugh.

"No, Javier, no. It has nothing to do with birds or even grandfathers. Think! You've uncovered four letters that encircle the last living human beings, people who are being driven into hell, devoid of all hope. What if Brueghel was hiding the very secret of his faith in these four letters? And what if, right at the point of the greatest desolation in the entire composition, the point with which the viewer—any viewer—would most identify, what if it was exactly there that our Brueghel was shouting out the very remedy?"

I stared at Fovel, astonished. He had suddenly turned and locked his eyes onto mine and his gaze was burning. I sensed his lips barely quivering, as if what he was about to say was extremely important. "Javier," he began, "if you play with these letters and reorder them with the horse going first, then the imploring man and the skeleton with the water container, and finally the musicians, you'll have what I'm trying to tell you."

"V-I-T-A," I spelled out "*Vita*—life!"

"And what can you tell me about the way the letters are placed? *Vita*—life—comes down from the sky to earth, from above to the ground, and then returns once again, rising again. Just like this game of letters. Isn't it a beautiful lesson? The perfect prophecy? After the pain and terror of death, waiting, hidden—is more life!"

I stood there unable to speak, not even knowing what to think. Mute and perplexed, unable to make sense of the Master's conclusions or properly accept the lesson in occult art that I'd just been given. And Fovel, aware that he had completely saturated my senses, clapped me on the back in a kind of commiseration.

"You're young still," he said, seemingly exhausted by the whole effort. "Death does not yet concern you. But when, in some years, it captures your attention, then you'll want to know more about this."

"Are there more paintings with messages written like this?"

"There are, Javier. All around us."

15

———

El Greco's "Other Humanity"

I don't think I ever felt as much doubt in my times at the Prado as I did that afternoon. My instinct urged me to remember every detail that I'd learned about the paintings we'd just discussed, but my head felt ready to explode, so the effort was useless.

Dragged along by an increasingly harried Doctor Fovel, in no time at all I found myself whisked from the Bosch gallery to the gallery upstairs that housed the works of El Greco. At first, I wasn't sure where he was taking me, but when I saw him quicken his pace down the corridor leading to the collection of Doménikos Theotokópoulos's exaggeratedly elongated figures, a strange unease came over me. If this was where we were headed, the progression of my learning was going to take a profound leap, unless Fovel had uncovered some subtle connection that linked Flemish painters to this exotic Greek who had settled in Toledo and had always been known for following his own path.

Our destination turned out to be not one gallery but three rooms in a row in the Eastern Wing of the museum. As we approached the doors of this sanctuary, just a stone's throw from Velázquez's *Maids of Honor* and *The Triumph of Bacchus,* I noticed that the Master hesitated, cautiously looking in both directions before entering, without a word.

Fovel stopped in front of El Greco's brooding *Pentecost,*

247

and, as if unsure about whether to warn me about what lay ahead, muttered another "Ready?" that just unsettled me more.

I nodded uneasily.

"Javier, I'm afraid that the painting that illustrates what I'm about to tell you is not here, but hangs in the monastery at El Escorial. You really should go and see it."

"Is it an El Greco?" I asked naïvely, noticing his *Resurrection* visible at the end of the galleries.

"It is indeed. But it's not just any El Greco, Javier. It's a painting that many critics think proves that this genius among geniuses admired and imitated the contemplative paintings of Bosch and Brueghel, like the ones I've just shown you.

"But, Doctor, you've never paid much attention to the critics," I pointed out.

"That's true," he agreed. "However, the painting I want to talk about is for me primarily proof of something much more important. Something which, if we didn't have it, would leave us with an incomplete and mistaken understanding of the works that surround us here, and above all, the piece of evidence that shows that Doménikos Theotokópoulos—known in Philip's court as El Greco—was no less than a distinguished member of the apocalyptic fraternity of the *Familia Caritatis*. Another artist for whom paintings served principally as repositories of a revolutionary credo that prophesied the arrival of a new humanity and of direct communication with the invisible. Let's not forget— El Greco was a mystic before he was ever a painter."

"Which painting do you mean, Doctor?" I asked, my curiosity now stimulated by this revelation.

"In El Escorial everyone calls it *The Dream of Philip II*. Unlike the Bosch paintings, it hangs in the original location

El Greco, *The Dream of Philip II*, or *The Adoration of the Name of Jesus, An Allegory of the Holy League,* and *The Glory* (ca. 1577). Monastery of El Escorial, Madrid.

chosen for it by Philip the Prudent. But don't judge it on the basis of that name. You and I have already discussed what happens with the titles of these paintings—hardly any of them are chosen by the original artists!"

"I like paintings with many names," I said. Thanks to my time with Fovel, I'd learned that the more names a painting had, the more mysteries it was likely to hold.

"Well, this one takes the cake," said Fovel. "It's called everything from *The Adoration of the Name of Jesus*, because in the top half of the painting you can see the anagram IHS, to *An Allegory of the Holy League*, because the bottom half includes portraits of Philip's principal allies in the fight against the Ottomans at the Battle of Lepanto: Pope Pius V, the Doge of Venice, and John of Austria. However, I don't find any of these titles quite adequate. My own favorite, which you'll understand right away, is the one the monks of El Escorial gave to the painting upon first seeing it—El Greco's *Glory*."

"You mean like Titian's?"

He smiled broadly. "Exactly. And it's important that you understand why."

Fovel then proceeded to lay out a fascinating story. Even though the painting wasn't signed and there was no document or contract from the time that could verify when it was painted, many art experts believed that it was done right after El Greco arrived in Madrid in 1577. In fact, according to the Master, it was the first painting he did in Spain.

Doménikos had had a mixed reception in Italy, where he'd immersed himself in the work of the Venetians, Titian, Tintoretto, and Correggio, and had also been influenced by the later work of the great Michelangelo. But upon reaching his thirtieth year, he began to set his sights higher.

"It was at this point in his life," Fovel declared theatrically, "that Fate decided to smile upon him."

While no one can say how it happened, Fovel seemed sure that while in Rome, El Greco had crossed paths with a rather dejected Benito Arias Montano who, as if placed there by Fate, became El Greco's mentor. The man who was to become El Escorial's librarian had come to the Eternal City to try to convince the papal authorities to approve the *Biblia Regia* project. Montano was already a distinguished member of *Familia Caritatis,* and winning the Vatican's approval was as vital to him as it was to his fellow initiates, who were involved with the printer Christophe Plantin. Getting it would advance their aim of a *unio Cristiana,* the fusion of all churches, which would also put them closer to Hendrik Niclaes's ultimate secret aim of presenting himself as the Messiah of the new humanity.

But something went wrong. In Spain, professors at the University of Salamanca were suspicious of some of the translations and of the fact that Montano cited the Talmud as a respectable source. These suspicions reached the Holy See, and the pope ultimately frustrated the plan.

It was then that Montano and El Greco met, most likely through the circle they both frequented that existed around Doménikos's patron, Cardinal Alessandro Farnese. El Greco had befriended the Cardinal's librarian, Fulvio Orsini, and he was probably the one who introduced him to Montano. Things proceeded from there. Seeing El Greco's work, the Spaniard persuaded him to come to Madrid to work on the ambitious decoration of the monastery at El Escorial. This was during Philip II's obsession with the artistic side of his great project, and they needed all the help they could get. Sometime between late 1576 and early 1577, newly arrived in Spain and keen to win the king's favor, El Greco painted *The Glory.*

The Master continued his lesson. "It's not hard to imagine Doménikos wandering through the monastery taking in all of the king's favorite paintings, with no one to talk to in Greek save for Montano. There were a few Bosch works in the royal chambers, as well as Brueghel's *Triumph of Death*, and I'm sure that as a notable Familist, Montano would have shown El Greco how to interpret it and asked him to paint a version of his own."

"So that's how El Greco came to be part of the court?" I asked.

"Yes, son; more or less. The *Glory* of El Greco certainly didn't go unnoticed. But according to Brother Sigüenza, the monastery's historian, the king didn't like it. Or to be more precise, it 'failed to please his Majesty.' Even though it made use of some of his Majesty's most beloved symbols: a great apparition directly above the king's head, implying heavenly witness; a clear division of the just from the sinners; even a great, one-eyed monster that devours the souls of the sinful, all very much in the style of the Flemish painters."

"And not just them," I interjected.

Fovel raised one eyebrow. "What do you mean?" he asked.

There was moment of discomfort as I tried to gauge the wisdom of introducing something pretty far outside Fovel's syllabus. Finally, I decided to risk it.

"I'm referring to the ancient Egyptians, Doctor."

His face took on a puzzled expression.

"I'm very interested in ancient Egypt and, as it happens I'm also quite familiar with the painting you mean; it's one of El Greco's most famous. I think there's a parallel here. The idea of a monster devouring sinners behind the king's back appears in the pharaohs' religious texts several times going back at least three thousand years!"

Fovel rewarded me with an attentive look. He didn't

contradict or hush me; on the contrary, he looked interested in what I was saying. After all those times being his student and learning from him, seeing his look of surprise felt to me like a small triumph. Since I had never mentioned it, he couldn't have known that I had this passionate interest in the ancient culture of the pyramids.[1]

I grinned at him. "Don't make that face, Doctor! In the Egyptian *Book of the Dead,* which is over thirty-five hundred years old, there's a scene with a monster just like El Greco's. They would use scrolls of parchment that they placed underneath the head of the cadaver as a kind of map to the hereafter. No two of these were exactly the same, and yet—guess what? One scene that was repeated without fail in all of these texts for the dead was that of the diabolical monster!"

Fovel stroked his beard thoughtfully. "Now that you mention it, El Greco's monster may not have its origins in the Bible . . ."

"It doesn't. But there's another connection with our sixteenth-century painting that comes to mind. El Greco's painting deals with the idea of a final judgment of the dead. The Egyptians 'invented' the whole notion of a tribunal of souls long before the Jews or Christian ever began to mention it. Their pictures place the monster in the middle of the trials that the pharaohs faced on their journey from the earthly to the eternal life. It would serve as witness while Anubis, the god with the head of a jackal, would place the soul of the pharaoh on a scale to determine whether or not it held sin. If it did, Ammit, the devourer of souls, would open her enormous gullet wide and gobble up the pharaoh, denying him eternal life. There was nothing the Egyptians feared more than Ammit."

Fovel seemed captivated by my lesson, and pressed me for details.

"How is it that between the Egyptians and El Greco no one has painted this Ammit?" he asked.

"Actually that's not entirely true," I replied. "The builders of the great Gothic cathedrals included the weighing-of-the-soul scene in many of their façades. They would put the saved souls on one side of the scale, and the condemned souls on the other. In fact, if you recall El Greco's *Glory*, the blessed are to the left of the monster, entering a sort of divine doorway. So the only real difference between the Egyptians and the builders of the cathedrals is that the builders substituted an angel for Anubis."

Fovel smiled. "Excellent! I'm delighted that you're able to connect two disparate visual elements and wonder about their origins."

"You know, Doctor, every time I come across these traces of Egyptian icons in western culture, I wonder how these transcendental symbols get transmitted from civilization to civilization, from religion to religion, across thousands of years!"

"That is indeed a great mystery," agreed Fovel, without taking his eyes off *The Annunciation*, which we were now facing. "That drive to trace the various sources of art reminds me of discussions about which traditions could be the sources for both the Brethren of the Free Spirit and the Familists. I participated in a number of them, and came to my own conclusions."

"Were you able to find a common source for both of those heretical movements?"

"Think about the *Familia Caritatis*, which had such an impact on Montano and, then later, El Greco," said Fovel, tapping his temple with his forefinger. "Its members felt part of a minority faith that believed it had surpassed all other religions. In contrast to Christians or Jews, for example, they preached a direct relationship to God. They believed that the Creator dwells in each of us, so that there is no need to appeal to the divine to invoke his presence. What's interesting is that we find all that two hundred years earlier, in the Cathar faith, and even before that among the Gnostics, in the earliest days of Christianity.

"We now know that the Familists that Brueghel associated with were one of the last glimmers of Catharism in history.[2] In fact, the Familists called themselves the Family of Love, since the Cathars had previously named themselves the Church of Love, in opposition to Rome. Notice that, in Spanish, amor—'love'—is Roma backward."

I jumped in. "So the Cathars are the source? The most persecuted heretics of the entire Middle Ages?"

"The Good Men, yes, the Bons Hommes," he replied. "All massacred in the South of France in 1244 by troops loyal to the pope. Their ideas and beliefs had spread throughout much of Europe: that nature was the product of dark forces, that the corporeal, material world was no more than a prison for the soul. They also believed that there was not just one creator—God—but also an evil Demiurge, arguing that a tangible universe so fragile and corrupt could not be the product of one single, perfect, and supreme maker. They had many followers. They also agitated tirelessly for the translation of the Bible from Latin into the vernacular languages, a mission that would not bear fruit until the first polyglot Bibles of Cardinal Cisneros and Montano.

"But, Javier, what earned them the worst persecution ever seen of Christians by Christians—and which helped launch the infamous Inquisition with all of its terrible practices—was their belief that we all carry within us in our mortal bodies a part of the divine spirit which allows us to communicate with God. Directly. Without the need for intermediaries. Needless to say, that meant the church. It is this that inspires all those paintings of mystics, kings, and biblical characters who behold in the distance the intangible, pure world. The one created by the good God."

Dubiously, I asked, "Is this simply your opinion, Doctor, or have you researched it?"

Fovel smiled. "I've studied this, Javier, of course. Sadly, these issues are not widely known about, as you might imagine. There aren't many universities where you can study these things. I remember one particular essay that was quite controversial by Lynda Harris, a professor of art at London University. She proposed the idea that the Adamites who commissioned *The Garden of Earthly Delights* were descended from Cathar survivors.[3] According to her, the art from the time before the Cathar massacre in 1244 provided their one hope for escaping the darkness of the material world they felt trapped in. For them, meditating before the right painting would remind them of that part of reality that couldn't be touched or measured. And that we all possess a spiritual dimension that we can cultivate in order to attain what the Greeks called *Theoretikos*: the ability to see the transcendent world."

"Do you think El Greco believed in this ?" I asked him, glancing at the paintings all around us.

"Whether he did or didn't is itself the subject of some sharp debate among specialists. What seems indisputable is that his work overall radiates the sort of supernatural quality much favored by the Familists. Some of his most important biographers, like Paul Lefort or Manuel Cossío, both quite oblivious to Familist doctrine, have no trouble accepting that El Greco sought a mystical union with God through his art. I myself am convinced that some of these masterpieces of his come directly from visions he had."

"So you're saying El Greco was a mystic."

Fovel smiled ironically. "He's really the only one who could tell you that, Javier. But it's only fair to warn you that the true mystic keeps his visions to himself. So if he was, he took care to keep it quiet. However, we do know without doubt that he used the work of other mediums and visionaries to help him create his greatest works."

"Like who, Doctor?" I asked.

"Would you like a name?" he asked, archly.

"Of course!"

"Very well. How about Alonso de Orozco?"

I shrugged. For a moment I thought Fovel was going to make one of his great leaps, connecting El Greco with St. Teresa of Ávila, for example.

"You don't know who he was?"

I shook my head regretfully.

"Don't worry," he said, glossing over my ignorance, "hardly anyone remembers him nowadays. But believe me, he was one of the most popular religious figures of the sixteenth century. An Augustinian as well. He was so popular that when he died, he was proposed as a possible patron saint of Madrid, to replace St. Isidore."

"Was he a saint?"

"Beatified,"[4] Fovel corrected me. "He was preacher to both Charles V and Philip II, and the confessor and friend of Gaspar de Quiroga, the all-powerful archbishop of Toledo."

"How did he know El Greco?" I asked.

"Well, he was responsible for commissioning a number of pieces from El Greco for the altarpiece of the Seminary of the Incarnation in Madrid."

"Where's that located?"

"It was originally built near the Royal Palace, but the

French destroyed it during the Peninsular War, El Greco's pieces were scattered, and we lost the original plan for their positions on the altar. They built the senate building on the site afterward. But the point is that, when Alonso de Orozco commissioned the altarpiece work from El Greco, he was already well known around Madrid for his ecstasies and supernatural visions."

"Let me guess—another prophet!"

"Well, more of a theologian, though his life seemed to lend itself to the mystical. According to Orozco, while his mother was pregnant with him, a voice—'very soft, like a woman's voice'[5]—spoke to her in her dreams and told her not only that she would have a boy, but also that she should name him Alonso.

"Years later, when he was already prior of the Augustinian monastery in Seville, a similar thing happened to him. The Virgin appeared to him in the middle of a dream, and gave him an explicit order. 'Write!' she said. So of course Orozco obeyed, and wrote dutifully to the end of his days, publishing thirty-five books and establishing friendships with such notable writers of the day as Lope de Vega and Quevedo, thereby creating that narrowest of paths between faith and reason."

"What do you mean, Doctor?"

"Simply that he was a respected man as well as an intellectual, and word quickly spread that his sermons performed miracles, and could cure illness and even raise the dead. However, as far as we know, there were only two occasions when he showed any gift for clairvoyance. The first was on the night that the invincible Armada was sunk in the English Channel, during which Blessed Alonso passed the time praying and sighing, 'Oh, Lord! That Channel!' The second event occurred some time before his death, when he predicted that he would surrender his soul to God on September 19, 1591, at midday, which in fact he did."

"Knowing that, it doesn't surprise me that El Greco would want to paint his visions." I noted.

"Actually, Javier, it was María of Aragon, who was then a lady-in-waiting to Philip II's last wife, who persuaded El Greco to do the paintings, not Orozco. She was an enthusiastic supporter of Orozco, who died five years before the painter began his work. Orozco and María had founded the seminary together, but the plan for the work was based on his visions."

"Does that mean that she was the one who directed El Greco?"

"Exactly. Two of the paintings from that lost altarpiece are here in this gallery, *The Annunciation* and *The Crucifixion*. Take a good look, Javier. They're the same size, and there almost certainly were two other smaller panels that went with them—*The Adoration of the Shepherds* and *The Baptism of Christ*, which, sadly, are not in the Prado. What all four of these panels have in common is the presence of angels, which is not a small detail, since Orozco believed that priests should try to emulate angels. After all, it was for them that the seminary altarpiece was intended, not for whatever faithful happened to be in attendance. Based on this, neither *The Resurrection* nor *Pentecost* were thought to be part of María of Aragon's altarpiece, since neither contained angels."

"But that's what it says on this card," I said referring to the museum's description ascribing the two works to the altarpiece.

"It makes no difference what that says," Fovel retorted. "I happen to agree with the historian Dr. Richard Mann,[6] who recently made public his thesis that, hidden behind the seminary paintings is a mystical program designed to work closely with Alonso de Orozco's visions.

"Take another close look at *The Annunciation*. You see how El Greco has removed any physical reference to the room in which we see Mary? Alonso de Orozco wrote a fair amount about this event, and is quite clear that at the moment when the Archangel Gabriel planted the divine seed in Mary, all the furniture in the room faded away, and at that instant, Gabriel crossed his arms over his chest, enchanted by Mary's meekness. That is what we're being shown here!"

I turned to look at the painting. I had to take a few steps back in order to get the full splendor of the work, and even at that distance, it was unsettling to see such a young-looking Mary delivered to the will of her visitor. There was something hallucinatory about the scene. The colors, the tall columns of cherubim up against a leaden sky, even the way Gabriel's form was twisted—all gave a strong feeling of the unreal, almost as if they were melting before our eyes.

Fovel then began complaining about the Prado's decision to rename this painting from the original *The Incarnation* to *The Annunciation*, claiming, "they're not the same!" He explained the subtle differences between the two. In *The Incarnation*, Mary is already pregnant with the Son of God, while in *The Annunciation*, she is being told that she is going to be pregnant. Thus *The Annunciation* would have come before *The Incarnation*. He said that Orozco was always more interested in the notion of incarnation, feeling that it served better in the meditation upon two critical aspects of priestly life: the vow of chastity and transubstantiation, which is the literal conversion of the Host into the body and blood of Christ during Mass, in the same way that the Word takes form in the Virgin's womb.

Fovel went on. "It would have been more usual for El

El Greco, *The Incarnation* (ca. 1597–1600). The Prado Museum, Madrid.

Greco to have painted this *Incarnation*—because after all that is what this painting is about—showing Gabriel's arm extended toward Mary, as in so many other representations of this moment. Moreover, that is how he appears in an *Annunciation* of El Greco's which is in another gallery here.[7] But Orozco was clear in his writings that this pose of pulling back in surprise corresponds to the moment when Mary becomes a mother. And Doménikos captures it exactly."

My mind started to whirl. How many Annunciations had I seen where the angel had his arms crossed? There was one almost directly beneath our feet, on the floor below, perhaps the most famous one in the museum—Fra Angelico's *Annunciation*. If the Master was right, Alonso de Orozco would certainly have changed the title to *The Incarnation*, since both the Virgin and the Angel in the painting have their arms crossed over their chests.

"Excuse me for being devil's advocate for a second," I said, "but is that all? Is that the entire basis for the link? The whole Orozco–El Greco connection is built on crossed arms?"

"Not at all!" cried Fovel, in protest. "There's another very Orozco-esque detail that shines a light on the question of what the source was for these images. Look between Mary and Gabriel. You see what that is? It's the burning bush that spoke to Moses during the Exodus[8] and which reappeared in Mary's room at the moment of the Incarnation, according to Orozco. Nowhere else in the whole history of art is the bush depicted next to Mary. It's very affecting to see it here."

"What about *The Crucifixion*?" I asked him, turning to look at the powerful nocturnal depiction of the execution of our Lord. "Does this one also bear the mark of one of Orozco's visions?"

El Greco, *The Crucifixion* (ca. 1597–1600). The Prado Museum, Madrid.

"Of course it does! And more people meditated on this painting than any other. I haven't told you about one of Orozco's habitual exercises, which was to spend hours contemplating an old crucifix very much like this one, which eventually went with him to his grave. It was on display for years on the high altar in the Church of San Felipe Neri, in Madrid. One day, while he was in one of his long meditations, the eyes on the crucifix opened and looked at him in a way that he never forgot. Many more visions followed that one, and they inspired him to create a Passion story even more real and more detailed than those of the Evangelists."

"That sounds pretty daring. If Orozco was really a good church man, it seems strange that he would let himself get carried away by his visions to the extent of commissioning these paintings . . ."

"Let me remind you that he wasn't the one who commissioned the paintings, but rather his mentor, María of Aragon, and her principal obsession was to make sure that his tomb, which lay beneath the seminary's high altar, be adorned in a manner befitting his station and promoting his ultimate beatification."

"It still seems risky to diverge from the Gospels during the time of the Inquisition."

"They were subtle deviations, Javier, which not too many people noticed," Fovel clarified. "Let's submit the painting to two tests. The first has to do with how Jesus's feet were nailed to the cross. All of El Greco's paintings show the left foot nailed over the right foot—except for this one. And that's actually how it appears in most depictions of the crucifixion by other artists. But in his writings, Orozco tells us that the Romans instead placed his right foot over his left, which according to him caused greater pain. He also went on to include another detail. When the Romans suspended

Jesus on the cross, they made sure to stretch his body as much as possible to prevent his being able to arch his back and take in air, again in this way magnifying his agony and distress. Look at the powerful torrent of blood and water pouring out of the wound in his side. Orozco also wrote extensively on this. He believed that just one drop of that liquid would be enough to redeem us of our sins, which is why we see an angel collecting it, representing the good priest, remember? El Greco studied all these details meticulously and incorporated them into his painting."

This far into our discussion, I had just one question left to put to Fovel. I was clear about what connected Doménikos Theotokópoulos to Montano's sect, and his predilection for mystical questions explained his willingness to paint Orozco's visions. While they were more orthodox and less prophetic that those of Savonarola, they, too, were the result of revelations. The same invisible source, in fact, that fed Hendrik Niclaes, Joachim of Fiore, and Amadeo of Portugal. But what I wanted to know was, why did El Greco paint these scenes the way he did? What drove him to give his figures that extraordinary texture, so exaggerated and so . . . impressionistic?

Fovel's response to my question threatened to be one of his strangest yet. He steered clear of modern theories that suggested that El Greco might have suffered some kind of visual impairment, or episodes of madness; and he dismissed as stupid the ideas of Ricardo Jorge, who in 1912 called this room in the Prado a "rogue's gallery," with "nothing left out: horrific faces, imbecilic figures, the headless and the swollen-headed."[9]

Then he proceeded to tell me about an old friend of his, the historian Elías Tormo y Monzo, who, years before, had come across a possible answer to my question.

"You may not like this," Fovel warned, "but it's the essential key to everything I've been showing you. In a series of conferences in the Madrid Athenaeum, Tormo y Monzo said the following:

> I would go as far as to place El Greco in the company of the very few painters who have created beings quite different from the humans that we are . . . The product of El Greco's palette are not men like us, nor titans like the Sybils and Prophets of the Sistine Chapel, nor sorcerers in a world of seduction, as painted by Correggio. They are animated by the potent breath of life, not to say life itself; I would say even that they are alive.[10]

This left me so bewildered that I didn't dare reply. For the second time in our acquaintance, Fovel was referring to the inhabitants of paintings as living beings. Did he really believe that?

I did not have the courage then to ask him about the famous El Greco masterpiece entitled *The Burial of the Count of Orgaz*, which hangs in the Church of Santo Tomé in Toledo. We would most likely have talked about whether the twenty-one figures who present themselves to the deceased represented the major arcana cards of the Tarot, and he would surely have pointed out which of them was El Greco's mentor, Benito Arias Montano. We might even have debated whether or not the painting embodied some kind of desire for reincarnation, as some critics have recently suggested.[11] Or if the two keys in St. Peter's hands were to open the doors of the material and spiritual worlds, those eternal opposites of the Cathars. But there just wasn't time between my reticence and his sudden and familiar urge to disappear, which he did, unexpectedly, saying something that left me wondering.

"I should go, Javier. My time is drawing to a close. Good-bye."

What could he have meant by that?

16

———

CHECKMATE TO THE MASTER

I returned to the Chaminade Residence Hall at around nine-thirty that night, feeling more preoccupied than usual. Toni's lively eyes caught mine as soon as she saw me passing in front of the window of her receptionist's booth. She called out to me and stopped me in my tracks.

"What the heck have you got yourself mixed up in, Javi? I've been trying to find you all day!" she complained, waving a small wad of paper at me. "Everyone's looking for you! This one guy has called five times! He's been leaving messages since three!"

She handed me what turned out to be a bunch of phone message sheets. "He says it's very urgent," she insisted. "And that you should call as soon as you can. So do it, okay?"

"Okay, okay," I said, taking the notes reluctantly.

"And don't be so hard on Marina, okay, Javi?"

Seeing Toni's huge smile as she said this made me blush.

"What? D-did she call?"

"Twice," she nodded. "But you should still call that guy first. It sounds more important."

At first, I couldn't figure out who it was who had called. There was an unfamiliar name and number, written out repeatedly in the unmistakable scrawls of both Toni and the receptionist from the previous shift.

"Toni, who's Juan Luis Castresana?"

"Oh, right . . . " Toni lifted her gaze from the small black-and-white TV she had in her cubicle, which had the news on. "He said something about El Escorial. That you would know who he was."

"El Escorial?" Immediately I had it. Padre Juan Luis! Of course! The librarian!

Without even thanking Toni, I raced to the pay phone in the corner and dialed the number she'd written down. I pushed my last coin into the slot and waited. It picked up after one ring, and a flat voice informed me that I had reached the student residence at the Augustinian fathers of San Lorenzo de El Escorial. I gave her Juan Luis's name.

"Father Castresana? One moment please, I'll put you through." And so, after a few more clicks and pauses, his unmistakable voice thundered in my ear.

"Javier! Thank God you called."

"Hello, Father. Has something happened?" I asked him as tactfully as I could. His voice sounded agitated. "Are you all right? I just got your messages."

"Fine, fine . . ." he replied somewhat irritably. "It's not easy to get hold of you."

"I've been out all day." I told him. "I just got back now from the Prado. I'm sorry I didn't get your messages earlier—"

He interrupted me, "No need to apologize. It doesn't matter. Listen—I called you because this morning I discovered something very serious. Something that, one way or another, concerns you."

For a moment I was unsure what to say.

"Javier," he continued, and I heard him swallow. "Do you remember what you asked me to look for in the library?"

"Umm," I hesitated.

"I've come across something very strange, Javier, and I mean really very strange. I don't want to discuss it over the telephone. I'll be waiting for you here at exactly nine o'clock tomorrow morning, in front of the monastery's main entrance. You know where that is, next to the student residence. All right?"

"Bu . . . but . . ." I tried to protest.

"Make sure you're there. It's important." And he hung up.

Heart racing, the very next thing I did was to return Marina's calls. She had never left me two messages like that before, so I knew it must be something important.

"Javier! Thank God you called," she said as soon as she heard my voice. She sounded just as scared as she had on the day that I'd met her at her lecture hall, though there was also something else—a certain tone, a certain tension— that was new.

"What is it, Marina?"

"It's what I told you," she burst out. "You have to stop!" She sounded even more nervous than I was. "Don't you get it? You have to quit! Forget all about your Prado Master!"

I was stunned; I didn't know what to say.

"Listen," she went on. "My parents got back from their trip last night and when they heard about that guy's visit they were really mad!"

"Wait a minute," I stopped her, amazed. "You told them about that?"

"Aunt Esther mentioned that we'd been sleeping at her house because of how scared we were, and then my sister told them everything today at lunch. They can't believe we let this dangerous lunatic into their house, Javi, and they say that it's all your fault!"

"It doesn't matter, Marina," I said. "The important thing is whether you—"

"I've had it, Javier. I'm finished."

"What . . . what are you saying, Marina?"

"I liked coming along with you, Javier, seeing El Escorial, and being with you while you did your . . . investigating, or whatever. But it's not fun anymore, not at all. Now it seems really dangerous."

I didn't know how to reply. There was something about the last thing she'd said that I must have missed.

"Marina," I stammered, "I don't understand."

"Wait a minute," she said. "Here's my dad."

She put down the receiver for a moment as a wave of heat washed over my face. Her dad?

"Javier Sierra?" The voice sounded ominous, with the stern tone of a teacher giving an exam. "I'm Thomas Sanchez, Marina's father."

"How are you, sir?"

"I want you to listen carefully to what I'm about to say to you," he went on severely, not giving me a chance to say anything. "Marina and her sister, Sonia, were put in a very dangerous situation. I don't know if you understand exactly what happened. This man came into our house, taking advantage of the fact that we were away. He sat at our family's kitchen table! He threatened the girls, and he could have hurt them!"

"But—"

"I'm not done!" He was checking himself, trying not to yell at me. "You've exposed not just Marina but our whole family to danger. We don't know if he'll come back or even if he's watching us or the girls right now. We're seriously considering whether we should file a complaint against you with the police."

"The police? Against me?"

"As an accessory."

I went pale.

"Sir, I—"

"Listen to me, Javier; I'm only going to say this once. You are not to go near Marina. Ever. If you so much as call her, or if I get even a hint that you've tried to see her or involve her in whatever it is you're up to, I swear . . . I will press charges, you understand me? I will not quit until your life is ruined!"

"Papa!" I heard Marina cry out in the background amid some commotion. I waited a few more seconds, expecting one of them to say something else, but the line went dead. I stayed like that for a while, motionless, with the phone against my ear. My blood felt cold in my veins as I waited for someone to explain to me what had just happened. No one did.

As it turned out, that was the last I would hear of Marina for a long, long time.

The next morning, Saturday, at eight-fifty, with the remains of the last snow still on the cobblestone path leading to the El Escorial monastery, I turned and walked up to the main entrance. What else could I do? I had decided only days before just to let events carry me along and let fate—or whatever else it might be—determine my path. This seemed like a perfect opportunity to test my new faith. Was I wrong? Was it a good idea to experiment like this? Unfortunately, I couldn't be sure. I was alone, I hadn't eaten, and I was in the worst funk. Between the early morning and the news on the car radio, I had no appetite. All around me the world was falling into chaos.

The UN Secretary General, Javier Pérez de Cuellar, was meeting that very day with Saddam Hussein's envoy to demand that Iraq withdraw its troops from Kuwait. The Americans were beating the war drums, and as if that wasn't enough, our prime minister Felipe Gonzalez had just ordered Spanish troops to prepare to support an eventual allied invasion of Iraq.

And in the middle of this collective madness a young journalism student being buffeted in all directions, some Master who had appeared from God knows where, a father aggressively guarding his daughter's safety, a sinister kind of art policeman, and now an old Augustinian from the El Escorial library who had something urgent to tell me. It was all far too strange. I felt like I was in a whirlpool that was threatening to overwhelm me. However, there wasn't much I could do about it. Whatever path I was on, there was no going back.

I rubbed my eyes with my gloved hands and tried to concentrate on what had brought me here. I was happy not to be entirely alone. An intermittent flow of people—caretakers, security guards, staff, and even the odd early morning tourist—were all trying earnestly to negotiate the icy paving stones and get to the main door in one piece. I decided to follow their example and pick my way carefully to the rendezvous point I'd arranged with Father Juan Luis.

At that hour, the place was particularly imposing. Its bearing, its solemnity, the silence broken only by the echo of visitors' footsteps and the overall impression of gravity and perfection conveyed by the majesty of those great walls, all announced that this was not just any other monument. Nor was it. Those vast façades that Philip II had built hid 2,673 windows, 88 fountains, 540 frescoes, 1,600 paintings, and more than 45,000 books. Those numbers, burned into my memory over numerous tours, made my head swim. El Escorial had always held a fascination for me, and I had visited it whenever I could. I was familiar with its legends, and I could well imagine it hiding any number of answers to the arcanon of the Prado.

But what did Father Juan Luis want to tell me? And why not over the phone? Had he uncovered some new clue to *The New Apocalypse*? Another angelic prophecy, perhaps?

I had no inkling of the dramatic turn that events were about to take.

At exactly nine o'clock, as precise as a Swiss watch, Father Juan Luis appeared in the doorway of the Alfonso XII residence. He was impossible to miss. Stooped, his black robes fastened at the front and without a coat, he made his way slowly down long side of the building toward the main entrance, not even pausing to glance around him. If he was really on his way to meet me at the main door, he was doing a good job of hiding it.

I headed in his direction and intercepted him partway.

"Good morning, Father," I began, reaching for his arm. "Is this a good time to—?"

Feeling my touch on his bony shoulder, he jumped. "What the devil!" he exclaimed. "You gave me a fright!"

"Just like the one you gave me last night," I replied with a smile.

He understood immediately, or so it seemed. No one observing us at that moment would have suspected that our meeting had not been accidental.

"Fair enough, fair enough . . ." He gave me a quick wink before lowering his voice and saying, "I'm very glad you're here. Are you alone?"

"Marina wasn't able to make it," I lied. "I hope that's okay."

He opened his hands as if to say "What can you do?" and then shot a glance around him with a wariness that reminded me of the Master. Why was it that everyone I spoke to ended up feeling as if they were being watched?

Turning back to me, he whispered, "I think it's better if we first talk out here, all right?"

I nodded, somewhat rattled.

"Excellent. Now, when we go into the library and I show you what I've found, keep quiet; don't say a word. Don't ask any questions. I won't talk either, understand? If they were to hear us, I'd be locked up as crazy, and you . . . well, I have no idea what they would do to you."

"Are you sure you want to talk out here, though? With this cold? You don't even have a scarf."

"Let's walk!" he replied.

Then the monk took my arm so that he wouldn't slip, and together we began to traverse the fifty or so yards between us and the monastery entrance. Neither my shivering nor my attempts to speed up did any good. Oblivious to my discomfort, Father Juan Luis began to talk in a voice so slow and halting that I had to incline my head toward his to hear what he was saying.

"—that I should have noticed sooner," he finished.

"Noticed what, Father?" I interrupted, lost.

"The dates, Javier! The dates!" he scolded. "When you asked me to check who had shown an interest in *The New Apocalypse* before your visit, remember? I checked the register and noticed something interesting in our records."

Hearing the name of that prophetic work once again, I leaned even closer.

"At first I didn't think it was anything. I assumed that it was just a mistake. But then this week I finally had a chance to go back to it and I got a big surprise!"

"What happened?" I asked him.

The monk sighed. "All right, now, Javier, listen carefully. The register for access to the Blessed Amadeo text couldn't be clearer. In the whole of last year, no one—absolutely no one—requested access to the book, until you and that other investigator who was there just before you."

"Julian de Prada," I interjected.

His eyebrows shot up in surprise. "Yes, exactly. I didn't realize that you knew him."

"I don't, much. Marina and I met him in Madrid after we talked to you. But please, go on."

"Well, here comes the strangest part, Javier. It intrigued me that a book like that—beautifully bound, with glorious calligraphy—had so few requests to view it, so I went back through the register to see: 1989, 1988, 1987, and nothing! It's incredible! No one seems to have cared a whit about *The New Apocalypse* for a long time. And then I was really disturbed when I decided to check the archives going all the way back to the 1970s, and again—nothing! Not even an internal request."

"So there's nothing for twenty years and then two in a row?"

"Very suspicious, don't you think?"

"Very," I agreed.

"You have to realize that each year this library receives many unusual requests. With the kind of archive we have here, unique in many respects, we get scholars from all corners of the world. One of the most frequent requests that we get, for example, is for the *Enchiridion* that belonged to Pope Leo III, and that he presented to Charlemagne as a gift. From then until his death, it granted him happiness, protection, and many military victories, as it was said to have magical properties. Charles V, his son Philip, and other distant descendants of theirs all sent experts across Europe to track down this extraordinary talisman in parchment. If they ever found it, they did not bring it back here. We also get asked for the signed works of St. Teresa, Alfonso X's *Canticles of Holy Mary,* and the *Beatus of Liébana.*

"Now, *The New Apocalypse* is properly listed in our catalog and part of a notable collection. For there not to have been a single request for it in twenty years, and then to have two requests in one week—that just seems too strange." Father Juan Luis shook his head slowly.

"Although," I said, trying to make a case for why this might have happened, "with all the books that you have here, there must be many that remain untouched for centuries!"

"No, no," objected Father Juan Luis, "that's not what's so odd here. The strangest thing is that the last person before you to request the book did so back in the spring of 1970, and you know what his name was?"

I frowned and shook my head. How could I know?

"Julian de Prada!"

"It can't be!" I breathed.

"It's all down in the register. There's no question about it. Between the months of April and June of 1970, two men requested Amadeo's *The New Apocalypse* three times—Julian de Prada and another man called Luis Fovel. The microfiche is the proof."

"Luis Fovel?" I could barely get the words out. For a moment there seemed to be a great distance between us, and I felt the blood drain from my face. "Are you sure?"

"Yes. Do you know him as well?"

I nodded, feeling apprehensive.

"How long ago is it since you've seen him?"

The question surprised me. "I saw him just yesterday, Father. Why?"

I noticed a strange expression cross the monk's face, and only when I felt his fingers digging into my arm did I realize that it was anxiety.

He cleared his throat. "Tell me . . . is he very old?"

I pursed my lips and said, "Well, no more than you, Father." At which he moaned, seemingly more disturbed still.

"Just what I feared . . ."

"What is it, Father?"

The old librarian took a couple of steps toward the door of the chapel—just enough to get out of the shadows and place himself in the one spot blessed by the rays of the morning sun. After a moment, he spoke. "Yesterday morning, I went back through the library register one more time, and I found something that alarmed me greatly. This is why I called you. You see, between 1952 and 1970 there were no requests at all to see the Beato's book. But I did find one in 1952, in October, signed by Luis Fovel."

"In 1952? That's forty years ago."

The old monk looked at me, swallowed, and nodded. "But that's not the end. I went to one of the technical kids who are transferring all our old records onto digital, and asked him to search the old archives for any instances of the names Luis Fovel or Julian de Prada. He found something that . . . well, I don't know what to make of it!"

"What did he find?"

"Well," he turned his face toward the sun and forced a nervous laugh. "The computer trail for Julian de Prada goes cold, but not for Fovel. There are several records for him: in 1949, 1934 . . ." He took a shaky breath. "1918 and 1902. We don't have any records before that, unfortunately."

"It must be a joke, don't you think, Father?" I objected, very perplexed. "It can't be that—"

He cut in. "That's what I thought, too, young man! Or I thought that they might be related, you know—a grandfather, father and son, all with the same name, coming here through the years, all interested in the same kind of things. Why not? Things like that happen. But there was a problem . . ."

"What kind of problem?" My voice had gone flat.

"Yesterday I finally dug up the entry that Fovel signed in 1902. It's in the oldest register we have. Luckily it's all on microfiche. And I compared his signature from that with the signature from 1970 . . ." He was actually shaking.

"What, Father?" I asked, gently.

"It's the same person. Lord above, Javier, I'm not a handwriting expert but I would be willing to swear that it's the same signature! Do you realize what that means?"

I took in a huge lungful of cold air. If what the old librarian was saying was true, a man named Luis Fovel had requested a forbidden text from the El Escorial library on and off over the course of almost seventy years. And if it really was the same Fovel that I knew, who looked to be in his sixties, then the Master of the Prado would have to be something like a hundred and ten or a hundred and twenty years old!

"It's impossible," I protested, with all the conviction I could muster. "It has to be a mistake, Father. There just must be an explanation somewhere!"

"None that I can see."

"Could I see the signatures?"

"Yes, I think you should have a look at them."

Ten minutes later, the man who knew the monastery library better than anyone alive was leading me to his small desk to show me his discoveries. Very little had changed since my last visit. It was still the refuge of some wise man or scholar from another time, straight out of the past, without a single computer or other trace of technology, right in the middle of a corridor otherwise filled with people much younger. We all greeted each other, Father Juan Luis grunting a reply.

He pointed at something, and I then noticed the one new addition to the setting. Resting on a small side table was an enormous metal contraption shaped something like a bell, topped with a series of wheels and levers. Seeing my surprise, the monk muttered, "That's the new 'Teepee.' A relic from the Cold War. The Americans who sold it to us in the seventies said it reminded them of something from the trading posts of the Wild West. Officially, it's a Recordak MPE-1, the most reliable microfilm reader you can get."

Whereupon this monk, who I'd thought to be one of the least technologically-minded people I'd met, proceeded to thread a spool of microfilm expertly through the slots on top, then adjust the tension bars, and flip a switch that lit up the interior of the device. He motioned me to sit before an opening on one side of the reader that held a screen, and as he rummaged in a drawer for his glasses, he ordered, "Now concentrate, young man!"

But as the first image appeared on the smooth surface of the Teepee's screen, I felt a small pang of disappointment. In front of me was an unremarkable-looking copy of a sheet from a ledger, yellowed with time, its type and letterhead faded, bearing a date just before the Spanish Civil War, with the heading, "Library of the Royal Monastery of San Lorenzo del Escorial. Reading Room—Books Borrowed."

"Now, memorize that signature there," the monk instructed me, pointing to the bottom of the page. We went through the same exercise three more times, and he pointed out signatures on several other sheets, dating from the beginning of the century to the later years of the Franco era. By the time he had finished his little demonstration, my original disappointment had turned to a kind of vertigo.

"Well?" he said quietly, bringing his finger up to his lips at the same time to remind me of the need to keep my reactions discreet.

As quietly as I could, I said, "You were right, Father. I see the problem." I wanted to curse or yell, but I contained myself. If those documents were authentic, which I didn't doubt for a second, then Father Castresana had made a sensational discovery. It was strikingly obvious that we were looking at a series of library requests separated by over seventy years and all bearing the identical signature. There was no room for error—each "Fovel" was enormous, clear, beginning with a large, stylized uppercase *F* and ending with the tail of the final *l* seeming to crack like a whip beside the last name. All exactly the same.

How was this possible?

I spent a while going back over each signature again, comparing them, changing the microfilm spools myself. As I confirmed each one, I dared do no more than just incline my head slightly so that our neighbors would be none the wiser about what we were up to. When I was done, far from easing my doubts, my initial feelings of surprise and astonishment had given way to more doubt—and to fear.

With a brusque "Very well," Father Juan Luis brought the Teepee session to a close, replacing the rolls of microfilm in their boxes and leaving them stacked casually next to the machine. He turned to me. "Why don't we go down to the basilica? I think in the house of God we should be able to relax a little more, and talk." I nodded.

Father Juan Luis and I found a discreet spot on a bench in the back of the great church of the El Escorial monastery, and were there for the better part of two hours. At first, our whispered discussion wandered as we tried to understand what on earth all this could mean. We posited various mistakes, jokes, and plots, none of which led anywhere. It was all very frustrating, and after a long time talking the one thing we could agree on was that each of us, as if guided by fate, had stumbled upon something that was far greater than us. Something beyond logic.

It was then, as we were both deciding just how much more to reveal to the other, that, almost without meaning to, I took the first step. I badly needed to confide in someone, and so I talked—I talked and I talked until I had told him everything. It was the closest thing to a confession that I ever remember having made.

I told him all that I knew about Fovel. I went patiently and meticulously through everything I have written here in these pages, as well as some of the Master's explanations about the influence of *The New Apocalypse* on Spanish and Italian artists. Most of all, I made sure to emphasize Fovel's last lesson, where he talked about Bosch, Brueghel, El Greco, the Adamites, and Niclaes's *Familia Caritatis*.

I even told him, with some hesitation and at the risk of sounding far-fetched, that according to Fovel, one of the principal members of those sects was El Escorial's first librarian, Benito Arias Montano.

"Does that name mean anything to you?" I asked him.

The old Augustinian seemed completely unmoved. For him, none of what I'd told him really helped to explain the unbelievable sequence of requests for *The New Apocalypse* that had come from Fovel, and to a lesser extent, Julian de Prada. Realizing he was essentially at a dead end, the old monk was silent for a while. When he finally spoke again, it was to ask me for my personal interpretation of the whole affair. "And don't tell me that you think it's ghosts!" he warned. "Ghosts don't borrow books from libraries!"

I couldn't do his question justice. As it was, I didn't know what to say to him. And just as it seemed that the road had ended for this young apprentice journalist, the old man pulled an ace from his sleeve.

"There's one thing that we have not yet talked about,"

he said, crossing his hands in his lap and gazing up fixedly at the imposing altarpiece that presided over the basilica.

"What is it?" I sighed wearily. I had spilled everything to this man and wasn't sure I had the strength to handle one more thing.

"Do you remember when I told you I had searched our digital archives for all of Luis Fovel's library requests?"

I lifted my eyes to his worn face, waiting for him to go on.

"Well, when I went through all of his and de Prada's entries, I saw that it wasn't just *The New Apocalypse* that they were requesting. There were other books, too. And always the same ones each time."

I blinked, rocked by this new revelation.

"It's quite a varied group of books," he continued, anticipating the obvious question. "From Matías Haco Sumbergense's *Prognosticon*, which contains Philip's astrological chart and some predictions for his reign, to works on alchemy, books on natural magic, notebooks of Arias Montano's, and texts from earlier eras, like the seventeenth and eighteenth centuries. Judging from the list of requests, it seems as if the two of them were on the trail of something. Circling around the same set of themes. Not only that—I'm fairly sure that both of them got involved in some kind of race, and I have a feeling I know what kind."

"Really?"

"You've been honest with me, and now it's my turn," he said.

I felt a wave of relief. "I have all these papers set aside up in my office," he continued. "Without exception, they all have one thing in common. They were all requested within a short time of each other. First Fovel, then de Prada, and so on, always alternating, beginning and ending with *The New Apocalypse*. When I first went through them I thought I had stumbled upon a pair of alchemy nuts on the hunt for the philosopher's stone who might have managed to distill an elixir for extending life."

"And you don't think so now?" I asked.

"No, that's not it. Their interest in alchemy is a given, but to judge by the texts they've requested, it seems like they're also trying to cultivate certain metaphysical visions to use in their experiments. It came to me when I saw that their requests included the work of our own 'Doctor Illuminatus,' Ramon Llull, the great physician and alchemist from the thirteenth century. Llull started with those kinds of visions in developing his formulas and recorded all of it in his writings, which are only to be found within these walls here. My guess is that, like him, Fovel and de Prada have been trying to discover their own formula for transiting through the portal between this world and the next, and you know what? I think Fovel has done it, and that de Prada is stalking him trying to learn the secret so that he can get that access, that key."

I tried to take this all in, too tired to offer any argument. When I could muster the energy to reply, I said, "But, Father, what role do the paintings play in this race? Why do you think they're so important?"

"Oh, *The New Apocalypse* explains all that, Javier. And I went through this with you when we first met. Amadeo wrote that in times of great trouble, certain paintings would be able to perform miracles, and could act as doorways between this world and the next. And if the old hermetic texts are to be believed, whoever manages to get hold of the alchemical masterwork will not only possess the elixir of life, but will also enjoy the power of invisibility, how to communicate with the other world, and will never stay long in the same place."

"But . . ." I began. He went on unheeding.

"Whether or not we believe in these kinds of things makes absolutely no difference. What matters is that they do."

"Okay, Father," I said. "But that still leaves another question unanswered. If Fovel really is in possession of a secret like that, then why has he been spending the last few weeks giving me these lectures in the Prado and showing me all these special paintings? Why me? Why would he risk his anonymity?"

The monk shifted on the wooden bench and rubbed his forehead. Then his face lit up.

"To understand that, I have to appeal to the 'Rosicrucian factor'!"

I made a face, uncomprehending. He began to explain.

"The Rosicrucians were a society of initiates that emerged in the seventeenth century and that attracted intellectuals and liberal thinkers of all stripes. Today they are mostly thought to be extinct, and anyone claiming to be one now is usually given the same consideration as Neotemplars or Neo-Cathars, which is to say none. But interestingly, in the beginning, their members used to claim that the brotherhood had been started by a group of teachers or 'mysterious supermen,' led by a certain Christian Rosenkreutz. Rosenkreutz was said to have achieved an extraordinarily long life for his time, though not the kind of immortality that the Taoists speak of, or the Himalayan yogis or classical heroes of the Holy Grail, or that magical imam from twelfth-century Iraq who the Shiites believe will reappear to do battle with the Antichrist. No, Rosenkreutz—or whatever his real name was—lived for over a hundred years and carefully guarded the supreme medicine or 'total science' that allowed him to break all the known biological barriers. Apparently, once he reached the age of one hundred, he devoted himself to training disciples who would pass on the formula for extending life from generation to generation. They are the real Rosicrucians, and Fovel and de Prada are very likely two of them. Alchemy aficionados always refer to these people as 'invisibles,' and one of their main objectives is supposed to be to foment a social and scientific revolution in the West that will allow the acceptance of the long-life elixir without causing chaos."

"Do you really believe . . . ?"

But Father Juan Luis was not done.

"What's strange is that these kinds of teachers seem to emerge every hundred years or so, sow their intellectual seed in a handful of chosen followers in the hope that they will help advance the development of the world, and then disappear until the next historical cycle. If you go back and track these appearances, you can see their influence among the first Christian Gnostics, the Arian heretics, the Cathars, and the Family of Love. So why wouldn't we think that your Fovel, who knows so much about these ancient sects, could be one of these mysterious teachers, back from the shadows to recruit more custodians for his secret?"

"I don't know . . ."

"I'm an old man, Javier. I've read a great deal about this in the books of this sacred building, and it seems obvious to me what's going on. One of these secret teachers has chosen you to be the custodian of his teachings. Or at least you're a candidate. Like a good guide, he is not showing you everything at once, but instead teaching you how to look, providing you with the tools and then letting you decode the messages left by other unknown supermen—in this case painters. Once he thinks you've mastered this sufficiently, he will disappear—probably for quite a while—and leave you to complete your training at your own pace. Then at some point he will reappear and reveal your role and obligation, letting you know that you are part of a long chain of transmission for this secret knowledge.

"This is how these people have done this for centuries. They always disappear just before their pupils discover who they really are. They look like regular people, but they occasionally make predictions, they know what others say about them, they disappear without any notice, and as I've told you, they never stay long in the same place."

"But that's absurd," I objected, while at the same time recognizing many of those things in Fovel. "Why would someone like that choose me, Father? I'm no art expert, I don't really know the Prado well, or its world. If Fovel is what you're insinuating, then he's made a mistake in picking me."

The old man shook his head. "Come, Javier. How many times have you two met? Three? Four?"

"Five."

"In that case we have no time to lose, believe me!" he said, his eyes suddenly burning with impatience. "These teachers appear only occasionally. If we really want to confirm his identity, you need to go find him as soon as you can, look him in the face, and demand that he reveal who he is and whom or what he serves. He will tell you if you corner him."

I was suddenly anxious. "How am I supposed to do that?"

"Tell him you found this."

Father Castresana took a folded piece of discolored but exquisitely fine paper from under his habit and handed it to me.

"What is it?" I asked him.

"A puzzle. A clue written in Fovel's own hand."

I unfolded the paper carefully. In the same neat hand-writing that I'd seen on the microfiche in the Teepee, it had been written on a sheet of Bible paper that smelled musty.

"How . . . how did you get this?" I asked.

"Fovel and de Prada used the books in our library as mailboxes to pass messages to each other. That's why their requests always specified only a small number of volumes, or even a single book. For whatever reason, this one message never got to its intended recipient, and lay forgotten in the pages of a treatise on astrology. I came across it this morning quite by accident as I was going back over all the books they'd requested, page by page."

I looked at the sheet of paper without knowing what to say.

He smiled. "It's quite a piece of luck."

"Is there any more?"

"Not for the moment. Why do you think I had all the books that they consulted sent up to my office? That piece of paper was in a book that Fovel requested in 1970 and that de Prada never got to. It seems to me like a warning, as if your Master meant to stop his rival in his tracks, at the same time challenging him to learn his identity."

Then Father Juan Luis leaned forward. Seizing my shoulders, and with excitement in his voice, he added, "When he sees that you have this message and that you've managed to interrupt his game, you'll be in a position to ask him what we need to know."

"You really think he'll tell me?"

"Of course! Read this when you're calm and you'll be convinced as well. I'm sure that when you confront him with this and show him that you're about to uncover his true na-ture, he will be honest with you. At that point, he'll want to give you his version of things."

"You're a real optimist, Father."

"Not optimistic, Javier, just thorough. This is what I would do in your place. Do you realize that no outsider for centuries has gotten as close as you to the secret of the Rosicrucians!"

Epilogue

———

The Last Puzzle?

These are the last few lines of my Prado diary, much to my regret.

After the visit to El Escorial and my talk with Father Juan Luis, there was barely enough time for me to get back to the Prado and confront Fovel with the monk's piece of paper. Could Fovel, my "ghost," be a Rosicrucian? An immortal? Or would he have some explanation that even an imagination as active as mine could not have anticipated? I was just one step away from solving the great puzzle of my Prado Master, or so I thought.

As it happened, by the time I found myself back in those galleries, I had learned the text by heart. It consisted of a handful of simple but ambiguous verses which, through several readings, and without my meaning to, had turned themselves into a song that I now could not get out of my head, and I repeated it silently like a spell that could somehow be used against the man in the black coat.

All in vain.

To my despair, that Sunday, January 13, Luis Fovel did not appear in the Prado's galleries, and so I was unable to present him with my gift. Nor did he appear the next Tuesday. Or Thursday, when I went back for a third time. Despondent, I spent Friday wandering from gallery to gallery until closing time, but still no Fovel. After all my waiting, I found myself imploring the heavens to let either Fovel or even de Prada find me once more, as they had before, so that I could have the chance to ask them at least one last question.

But nothing happened.

During those frustrating days, I kept in touch only with Father Juan Luis, who continued to encourage me not to give up.

"Something's happened," I complained. "It's never taken him so long to appear!"

"Never mind; he'll come. Keep at it! Find him!"

But it turned out the old monk was wrong, too.

I spent the rest of the month going to the museum each day. I went after class, bringing each day's assignments and working on them, sitting on a bench in Gallery A and keeping a lookout from the corner of my eye for whoever should pass by in a black coat. It was a complete waste of time.

Finally, on Thursday, the last day of the month, when I called El Escorial to give an account of my predictably fruitless week, a stranger's voice answered, bringing my *Alice in Wonderland* existence to an abrupt end. It was as if the floor had just disappeared from under my feet, taking with it everything that had happened in the last two months.

"I'm afraid Father Castresana passed away early this morning," said the voice, sounding genuinely sorry. "Were you a student of his?"

I hung up without saying anything.

I had never felt so helpless. Seemingly overnight, I had lost not only my Master of the Prado but also the one person to whom I'd divulged the whole of my own story of these events. And the pain I felt over the death of the good Father Castresana lodged itself in my soul like an enormous splinter.

In the midst of all this, and to add to my sense of solitude, Marina and I had spoken no more about the matter; in fact, we hadn't seen each other again. Her father had gotten his way, ending our relationship practically before it had begun. After a while I heard that she had started seeing a guy who was four years older, and I . . . The truth is that, sad and disoriented, I tended to my other needs and devoted myself to my studies and to my assignments for the magazine.

For a while, I tried to overcome the periodic waves of anger I felt over the whole business. Thinking back to how it had all started, and recalling the phrase, *when the student is ready, the teacher appears,* I'd become enraged, frustrated at not knowing how I could have been chosen like that only to be discarded so soon after and left to my fate. At the core of it all, I couldn't accept the fact that Fovel had simply disappeared without giving me the chance to see him one last time.

In this way, little by little, worn away by the steady erosion of time's passing, Luis Fovel and the text of his little puzzle lost themselves in the oblivion of my notebooks. Only God knows why I now suddenly felt the need to retrieve them and share them with whoever has managed to make it to these last pages. Twenty years later I'm still no wiser as to why all of this should have happened to me, only this time, having put it all in writing for the world to see, I hold out the faint hope that someone out there will finally figure out the meaning of the puzzle that Father Juan Luis entrusted to me at El Escorial the last time I saw him. Who can say? Perhaps this patient reader will manage to find the mysterious Master and put to him the question that I could not.

If that should happen, please let me know.

For now, all I have to prove to myself that this was not merely a dream are these lines, left forgotten for so long in the pages of an old book in the library of El Escorial:

Do not pursue me
Though I hold the key
You seek my name
Unable to see

All of these paintings
I've kept from the start
Know that my source
Lies in their art

Against all your efforts
With tooth and with nail
I will keep rending
That terrible veil

Giordano, Titian, Goya
Velázquez, Bosch, and Brueghel
They all went in pursuit
Of that desire universal

Square up to death
In fate put your trust
With eyes opened you know
I will do what I must

NOTES

Epigraph

1. Synod of Arras, chap. 14 in *Sacrorum Nova et Amplissima Collectio,* ed. by J. D. Mansi, Paris and Leipzig, 1901. Cited by Alberto Manguel, *Leer imágenes,* Alianza, Madrid, 2000, p. 151.
2. Cited by David Freedberg, *Apolo, David, santa Cecilia: música y pintura en algunas obras de Poussin en el Prado,* en VV.AA., *Historias inmortales,* Galaxia Gutenberg/Círculo de Lectores, Barcelona, 2002, p. 240.
3. Juan Rof Carballo, *Los duendes del Prado,* Espasa-Calpe, Madrid, 1990, p. 80.
4. Ramón Gaya, *El sentimiento de la pintura,* Arión, Madrid, 1960, p. 167.

Chapter 1: The Master

1. Luke I:5–25.
2. Doctor Fovel is referring to the painting *The Visitation* (ca. 1517) by Giulio Romano and Giovanni Francesco Penni, based on a drawing by Raphael.
3. Luke 1:39–45.
4. St. Teresa said something similar: "This vision, though imaginary, I never saw with my corporeal eyes, nor with any others but the eyes of my soul." *The Life of St. Teresa of Jesus,* 28:5.
5. Read the chapter by Josephine Jungic, "Prophesies of the Angelic Pastor in Sebastiano del Piombo's *Portrait of Cardinal Bandinello Sauli and Three Companions,*" in Marjorie Reeves (ed.),

Prophetic Rome in the High Renaissance Period, Oxford University Press, Oxford, 1992.

6. This was suggested by a former director of the Prado, Diego Angulo, in response to other unconfirmed theories identifying the subject as Juan de Silva, Marqués of Montemayor and Chief Justice of Toledo.

7. "Prophesies of the Angelic Pastor."

Chapter 2: Deciphering Raphael

1. Édouard Schuré, *Les prophètes de la Renaissance*, Perrin, Paris, 1920, p. 181 (a Spanish version exists: *Leonardo da Vinci y los profetas del Renacimiento*, Abraxas, Barcelona, 2007, p. 162).

2. I devoted an entire chapter of my book, *La Ruta Prohibida* (Planeta, Barcelona, 2007, p. 285) to the amazing story of the multiple versions of *The Virgin of the Rocks*.

3. Giorgio Vasari, *Las vidas de los más excelentes arquitectos, pintores y escultores italianos desde Cimabue a nuestros tiempos* (*Lives of the Most Excellent Painters, Sculptors, and Architects*), Cátedra, Madrid, 2002, p. 524.

4. Ibid., p. 525.

5. Benjamin Blech and Roy Doliner, *Los secretos de la Capilla Sixtina*, Aguilar, Madrid, 2010, p. 52.

6. Not everyone agrees with this identification. Some have thought it to be Archimedes or Pythagoras.

Chapter 3: *The New Apocalypse*

1. This peculiar idea has been emphasized by some experts on Amadeo and his era, and more recently by Martijn van Beek, *The Apocalypse of Juan Ricci de Guevara. Literary and iconographical artistry as mystico-theological argument for Mary's Immaculate Conception*, in *Immaculatae Conceptionis Conclusio* (1663), in the *Anuario del Departamento de Historia y Teoría del Arte de la Universidad Autónoma de Madrid* 22 (2010), p. 220.

2. Contract dated April 25, 1483, and made out by the notary Anto-

nio de Capitani. This was the first document to confirm Leonardo's arrival in Milan.

3. From 1454 to 1457.
4. Without explicitly citing John, *Pseudomateo*, chap. XVIII mentions the episode of the cave where the Holy Family stayed on the way to Egypt.
5. BNE, ms. 8936, f. 3r.

Chapter 4: Making the Invisible Visible

1. Pier Carpi, *Las profecías del papa Juan XXIII*, Martínez Roca, Barcelona, 1977, p. 55.
2. Ibid., p. 104.
3. Ibid., p. 127.
4. This is how Christian Jacq described it years later, in *El Iniciado*, Martínez Roca, Barcelona, 1998, p. 15.
5. Moreover, Christian tradition also refers to Thomas as *Dídimo*, which in Greek also means "twin."
6. In his *Estudios sobre iconología* (Alianza, Madrid, 1972), the erudite Erwin Panofsky defined Florence's Platonic Academy as, "A select group of men united by friendship, a shared liking for ingenuity and human culture, a near-religious veneration for Plato and the greatest admiration for the generous and kind sage, Marsilio Ficino." I cannot think of a better description for the place where the seed of the Renaissance was originally planted.
7. Marsilio Ficino, *On the Platonic Nature. Instructions and function of the Philosopher*, in *Meditations on the Soul*, Inner Traditions International, Rochester, VT, 1996, p. 88.
8. See my novel *Las puertas templarias (The Templar Gates)* (Martínez Roca, Barcelona, 2000) for a full treatment of this idea in fictional form.
9. Manuel Ríos Mazcarelle, *Savonarola: una tragedia del Renacimiento*, Merino, Madrid, 2000, p. 132.
10. Marsilio Ficino, *In Platonis Alcibiadem Epitome*, bibl. 90, p. 133: *Est autem homo anima rationalis, mentis particeps, corpore utens*.
11. Marsilio Ficino, *Theologia Platonica*, III, 2, bibl. 90, p. 119.

Chapter 5: The Two Baby Jesuses

1. I ended up publishing an article based on those notes entitled "Prophesies and War," in the magazine *Más Allá de la Ciencia,* in a March 1991 issue devoted to the Gulf War, pp. 30–35.
2. "Paiporta: los ángeles y el Libro de las dos mil páginas," in *Más Allá de la Ciencia* magazine, 14 (April 1990), pp. 76–83. I also used part of his story in a book that I wrote years later with Jesus Callejo, *La España extraña,* DeBolsillo, Barcelona, 2007, pp. 239–42.
3. Thomas Aquinas, *Suma Teológica,* part 1, question 51, objection 3.
4. Romano Giudicissi and Maribel García Polo, *Los dos niños Jesús: historia de una conspiración,* Muñoz Moya y Montraveta, Cerdanyola del Vallès, 1987.
5. Ibid., p. 25.
6. This idea fully developed in Giorgio I. Spadaro's *The Esoteric Meaning in Raphael's Paintings,* Lindisfarne Books, Great Barrington, MA, 2006.

Chapter 6: Little Ghosts

1. Carta de Victorino Novo and G. M. Curros, in *El Heraldo Gallego,* July 18, 1876.
2. VV.AA., *Corona fúnebre a la memoria del inspirado escritor y poeta gallego Teodosio Vesteiro Torres,* El Correo Gallego, Orense, 1877.

Chapter 7: Botticelli, Heretic Painter

1. Francesc Cambó, *Memorias (1876–1936),* Alianza, Madrid, 1987, p. 403.
2. David Cast, *Boccaccio, Botticelli y la historia de Nastagio degli Onesti,* en VV.AA., *Historias inmortales,* Galaxia Gutenberg, Barcelona, 2002, p. 74.
3. This happened around 1478. The tavern was named Sandro and Leonardo's Banner of the Three Frogs. The two artists jointly designed the sign, which is now lost.
4. Giorgio Vasari, *Las vidas,* p. 414.

5. The first person to establish a connection between the sermon—which we know by reference only—and the painting was John Pope Hennessy, in *Sandro Botticelli, the Nativity in the National Gallery*, The Gallery Books, London, 1947, p. 8.

6. In the original:
ΤΑΥΤΗΝ ΓΡΑΦΗΝ ΕΝ ΤΩΙ ΤΕΛΕΙ ΤΟΥ Χ ΣΣΣΣ ΕΤΟΥΣ ΕΝ ΤΑΙΣ ΤΑΡ[ΑΧ]ΑΙΣ ΤΗΣ ΙΤΑΛΙΑΣ Α ΛΕΞΑΝΔΡΟΣ ΕΓΩ ΕΝ ΤΩΙ ΜΕΤΑ ΧΡΟΝΟΝ ΗΜΙΧΡΟΝΩΙ ΕΓΡΑΦΟΝ ΠΑΡΑ ΤΟ ΕΝΔΕΚ/ ΑΤΟΝ ΤΟΥ ΑΓΙΟΥΙΩΑΝΝΟΥΕΝ ΤΩΙ ΑΠΟΚΑΛΥΨΕΩΣ ΒΩΙΟΥΑΙ ΕΝ ΤΗΙ ΑΥΣΕΙ ΤΩΝ Γ ΚΑΙ ΗΜΙΣΥ ΕΤΩΝ ΤΟΥ ΔΙΑΒΟΛΟΥ ΕΠΕΙΤΑ ΔΕΣΜΟ ΘΗΣΕΤΑΙ ΕΝ ΤΩΙ ΙΒΩΙ ΚΑΙ ΒΛΕΥΟΜΕΝ . . . ΝΟΝ ΟΜΟΙΟΝ ΤΗΙ ΠΡΑΦΗΙ ΤΑΥΤΗΙ.

7. This is how it was described in his *Convivio de' segreti della Scriptura Santa*, published around 1508.

8. Marjorie Reeves, *The Influence of Prophecy in the Later Middle Ages*, Oxford University Press, Oxford, 1969, p. 438.

9. John Dee is one of the pivotal historical characters in my novel, *El angel perdido* (*The Lost Angel*) Planeta, Barcelona, 2011. I recommend this book for anyone who wishes to know more about him.

Chapter 9: Titian's Secret

1. His paintings include *Orillas del Azañón* (1858), *Desembocadura del Bidasoa* (1865), *Torre de las Damas* (1871), *Alcalá de Guadaira* (ca. 1890), and his magnificent *Vista de Venecia* (ca. 1900).

2. See my book, *La ruta prohibida y otros enigmas de la Historia*, Planeta, Barcelona, 2007, where I discuss this.

3. Instructions from Charles V to Philip II, Augsburg, January 18, 1548. Cited by Manuel Fernández Álvarez in *Carlos V, el César y el hombre*, Espasa, Madrid, 1999, p. 705.

4. Juan de Mariana, *Historia de España*, vol. VII, bk. 5, Francisco Oliva Impresor, Barcelona, p. 497.

5. Cited by Gabriele Finaldi in *La Gloria de Tiziano*, in VV. AA., *Tiziano y el legado veneciano*, Galaxia Gutenberg, Barcelona, 2005, p. 115.

Chapter 10: Charles and the Lance of Christ

1. The steel and gold armor in which Charles V posed for this painting can be found in the armory of the Royal Palace in Madrid. In comparing the actual armor to the painting, one can see just how faithful Titian was to the original.
2. John 19:34–37. "But one of the soldiers with a spear pierced his side, and forthwith came there out blood and water. And he that saw it bare record, and his record is true: and he knoweth that he saith true, that ye might believe. For these things were done, that the scripture should be fulfilled, A bone of him shall not be broken. And again another scripture saith, They shall look on him whom they pierced."
3. A good summary of these myths can be found in Trevor Ravenscroft's *El pacto satánico*, Robinbook, Barcelona, 1991.

Chapter 11: The Prado's Holy Grail

1. Good examples include the Holy Basin, in Genoa, a hexagonal plate recovered during the First Crusade in Caesarea Maritima, between what are today Haifa and Tel Aviv; a marble glass kept in Troyes Cathedral, in France, which was destroyed during the French Revolution; the chalice of O Cebreiro, on the Way of St. James, which brought about the depiction of the Holy Grail on the shield of Galicia; or the Chalice of Ardagh, a piece of metalwork dating from the eighth century. Others believe that it still lies buried in Rosslyn Chapel, on the outskirts of Edinburgh, or on Oak Island, or in Glastonbury, none of which are very likely historical candidates to be the resting place of this invaluable relic.
2. Antonio Beltrán, *Estudio sobre el Santo Cáliz de la catedral de Valencia*, Instituto Diocesano Valentino Roque Chabás, Valencia, 1984.
3. November 8, 1982. More recently, Pope Benedict XVI did the same, on July 8, 2006.
4. Around twenty different paintings of Christ with the Eucharist

were thought to have been produced by Juanes or his studio over the years. Almost all of them show the Holy Grail either in front of Jesus or in his hands. Aside from the two in the Prado (one of these—depicting the conventional chalice—came from Fuente la Higuera and is thought to be the first one painted by the artist; the other one shows the St. Lawrence grail), there are other notable examples in the Valencia City Hall and Cathedral, in the parish of Sot de Chera (Valencia), the parish of Jávea (Alicante), in the Szépművészeti Múzeum in Budapest, in the Museo Lázaro Galdiano in Madrid, and in the John Ford Collection in London and the Grasses Collection in Barcelona. There are also the Benimarfull (Alicante), Sueca (Valencia), and Segorbe (Castellón) examples, and others in various parishes around the Spanish Levante, though their exact whereabouts are unknown. Many were undoubtedly destroyed during the Spanish Civil War.

5. Antonio Palomino, *El museo pictórico y escala óptica,* vol. 3: *El parnaso español, pintoresco y laureado,* Aguilar, Madrid, 1947, p. 88. The original work, also in three volumes, is from 1715–24.

6. Barón de Alcalahí, *Diccionario biográfico de artistas valencianos,* F. Domenech, Valencia, 1897, p. 173.

7. Marcos Antonio de Orellana, *Biografía pictórica valenciana,* edition prepared by Xavier de Salas, in *Fuentes literarias para la Historia del Arte español,* Madrid, 1930, p. 57.

8. This story, mentioned by the painter Francisco Pacheco, was included by Richard Cumberland in his *Anecdotes of eminent painters in Spain,* vol. 1, J. Walter, London, 1782, p. 149; and before this, also by the Jesuit Father Juan Eusebio Nieremberg in *Firmamento religioso de luzidos astros en algunos claros varones de la Compañía de Iesús* vol. 2, María de Quiñones, Madrid, 1644, p. 553.

Chapter 12: Mister X

1. Some historians have referred to this belief of the king's, albeit in passing. One notable reference is Geoffrey Parker's *Felipe II: la biografía definitiva,* Planeta, Barcelona, 2010, p. 951.

Chapter 13: *The Garden of Earthly Delights*

1. Fray José de Sigüenza, *La fundación del monasterio de El Escorial,* Aguilar, Madrid, 1988, p. 367. The original work is from 1605.
2. Juan Rof Carballo, *op. cit.*, p. 153.
3. "Gens absque consilio est et sine prudentia. Utinam saperent et intelligerent ac novissima providerent." Deuteronomy 32:28–29.
4. "Abscondam faciem meam ab eis et considerabo novissima eorum." Deuteronomy 32:20.
5. I'm not imagining this. In fact, the painting is also known as *The Painting of the Strawberry Tree,* possibly because of this one detail, which would have been unmistakable to the inhabitants of Philip II's Madrid. In 1593, when Philip acquired it and had it sent to El Escorial to add to his collection, it was recorded in the monastery's register of acquisitions, as, "a painting of the variety of the world, called 'of the Strawberry Tree.'" As everyone is aware, since the Battle of Las Navas de Tolosa in 1212, the symbol of the bear and the fruit tree have represented the inhabitants of this part of the Iberian Peninsula. Why this should appear where it does in *The Garden of Earthly Delights* is yet another of the painting's mysteries.
6. Genesis 1:18.
7. Wilhelm Fraenger, *Hieronymus Bosch: Il Regno Milenario,* Abscondita, Milán, 2006, pp. 82–83.
8. Epiphanius of Salamis, *Panarion (Adversus haereses),* LXXII.
9. St. Augustine (Augustine of Hippo), *De haeresibus,* XXXI.
10. This idea was most recently suggested by Hans Belting, in *El jardín de las delicias,* Abada, Madrid, 2012, p. 71ff.
11. Domenicus Lampsonius, *Pictorum aliquot celebrium Germaniae inferiores effigies,* Hieronymus Cock, Amberes, 1572.
12. Wilhelm Fraenger, *Hieronymus Bosch,* p. 84.
13. Manuel Fernández Álvarez, *Felipe II,* Espasa, Madrid, 2010, p. 505. According to the inventories, the horns were sold in 1603.

Chapter 14: The Secret Family of Brueghel the Elder

1. According to the *Boletín del Museo del Prado* (vol. 11, no. 29, p. 117), in 1990 this museum in Madrid had a record 2,529,995 visitors.

2. H. Stein-Schneider, *Pieter Brueghel. Peintre hérétique. Illustrateur du message familiste*, en *Gazette des Beaux-Arts*, #57 (1986), pp. 71–74.

3. A more recent edition exists: Karel van Mander, *Het Schilderboek*, Wereldbibliotheek, Amsterdam, 1995.

4. Charles de Tolnay, *Pierre Brueghel l'ancien*, 2 vols., Nouvelle Société d'Éditions, Brussels, 1935.

5. Alastair Hamilton, *The Family of Love,* James & Clark, Cambridge, 1981, p. 37.

Chapter 15: El Greco's "Other Humanity"

1. A complete summary of this myth can be found in my book, *En busca de la Edad de Oro*, Plaza & Janés, Barcelona, 2006, p.50ff.

2. H. Stein-Schneider, "Une secte néo-cathare du 16e siècle et leur peintre Pieter Brueghel l'Ancien," in *Cahiers d'Études Cathares*, vol. 36, 105 (1985), pp. 3–44.

3. Lynda Harris, *The Secret Heresy of Hyeronimus Bosch*, Floris Books, Edinburgh, 1995.

4. Years after this conversation, on May 19, 2002, John Paul II canonized Alonso de Orozco, and added him to the Calendar of Saints.

5. Alonso de Orozco, *Confesiones del beato Alonso de Orozco del Orden de Ermitaños de N. P. San Agustín*, bk. 1, chap. 6, Imprenta de Amigos del País, Manila, 1882, p. 14.

6. Richard G. Mann, *El Greco and his Patrons: Three Major Projects*, Cambridge University Press, Cambridge, 1989. A Spanish translation also exists: *El Greco y sus patronos*, Akal, Madrid, 1994.

7. The Master is referring to a small painting by El Greco of approximately 8 by 10 inches from about 1570, which shows the Archangel Gabriel extending his arm toward Mary as he announces to her that she is to become a mother.

8. Exodus 3:2–5.

9. Ricardo Jorge, "Nova contribução biografica, crítica e médica no estudo do pintor Doménico Theotocopuli," *Revista da Universidade de Coimbra* 1, no. 4 (1912).

10. Elías Tormo y Monzo, speeches from the Madrid Athenaeum, April 7, 21, and 28, 1900. Included in José Álvarez Lopera, *De Ceán a Cossío: la fortuna crítica del Greco en el siglo xix*, Fundación Universitaria Española, Madrid, 1987, vol. 2, pp. 489–90.

11. Juan Sánchez Gallego, *Esoterismo en la pintura de El Greco: el entierro del Conde de Orgaz*, Rosa Libros, Seville, 2006.

———